Kissed
by the Wave

Kissed
by the Wave

A Forbidden Realm Novel

SERENA GILLEY

FOREVER
YOURS

New York Boston

Forever Yours
Hachette Book Group
237 Park Avenue
New York, NY 10017
hachettebookgroup.com
twitter.com/foreverromance

First published as an ebook and as a print on demand: August 2014

Forever Yours is an imprint of Grand Central Publishing.
The Forever Yours name and logo are trademarks of Hachette Book Group, Inc.

The publisher is not responsible for websites (or their content) that are not owned by the publisher.

The Hachette Speakers Bureau provides a wide range of authors for speaking events. To find out more, go to www.hachettespeakersbureau.com or call (866) 376-6591.

ISBN: 978-1-4555-8447-5 (ebook edition)
ISBN: 978-1-4555-8457-4 (print on demand edition)

To M.K., who knows all the crazy details behind the inspiration for this story. Thanks for daring me to write it. You're the best friend a girl could ever wish for.

Acknowledgments

I'd like to acknowledge all the hard work of my wonderful, tireless agent, Cori Deyoe, and my brilliant editor, Megha Parekh. You ladies are magical, and I thank you so much for sharing my vision and helping me sparkle.

Kissed
by the Wave

Chapter One

Aliya flipped her fins and let the cool water of the lake glide over her. The moonlight glittered like tiny stars in the lapping waves. Her pale hair fanned around her, then fell slick against her naked skin as she pushed up through the surface, scanning the skyline and finding the large, familiar shape.

A boat—a very specific boat. *He* was here again. She knew he would be. After all, she was a mermaid; her mind sensed things like that. When this human was near, she could feel his presence. Her people generally did not reach their minds out to touch the humans who came onto the lake, but something about this man was different. Aliya had felt his thoughts, the burning pain and aching emptiness deep inside him, and it had triggered something inside her. She'd yearned to know more.

For nearly two cycles of the moon now she'd watched him, tracked his movements in the evenings when he would leave the safety of the human shore and venture into her world on his big, gleaming boat. Every time, she'd felt his suffering. She could not explain why this man's emotions should touch her in such a way, but she had come to expect it. He was here now and she had to get closer.

Yes, she could feel him more strongly now. Strange, it was almost as if this human—this man—were reaching out for her, trying to touch her in some way…but of course he could not be. Everyone knew humans did not possess powers like that. She must be imagining it.

To make sure she was not, she stilled herself and opened her mind to let his emotion flood her. Yes, she could feel the familiar ache she always sensed from him, knew the emptiness that filled him. He did touch her, but he clearly had no awareness of it. And his touch reached more than just her mind. Her body felt something, too.

The velvety scales of her lower body tingled…the satin skin of her arms and her breasts pricked with sensation. She went rigid, floating helplessly as her body responded to sensations she could never put into words. They were energizing, delicious…and forbidden. Whatever she felt from this human, whatever he did to her, it was not something she ought to encourage.

She liked it, though. She wanted more. The Great Code of all creatures in the Forbidden Realm dictated she avoid any sort of interaction like this. It was bad enough that she'd come so near this same human on numerous occasions, but to let his mind and emotions touch her in such a way…she knew it was wrong. Still, it drew her like a moth to an inferno.

She was near his vessel now. The crystal surface of the water changed and distorted her view, but she could see him. He was tall and broad, standing alone to gaze out over the water. His shirtless form was solid against the night sky and moonlight glowed off his bronze skin. She broke through the thin surface of the water. He would see her.

The Veil could not protect her tonight, not while the man was so empty and so very lost. Usually she made sure when she needed to approach humans that they were occupied, busy with their mundane concerns that kept the Veil firmly over their eyes. If they caught sight of her they shrugged it off as a shadow, a fish, or a shift in the current. All her life she'd been careful that way; she knew her place.

But tonight… the feelings were too strong. The man needed her and she needed him. She needed to learn what it was that drew her to him, that made her feel hot and shivery all at the same time. She needed to let him see through the Veil and recognize her for what she was.

Her movement caught his attention. Her heart pounded as she felt the cool air on her skin, the damp weight of her pale hair lying against her neck. Unfiltered moonlight glittered off the wet droplets at her eyelashes. She blinked, determined to see clearly when finally his eyes met hers.

And they did. He saw her at last and she gazed steadily at him. It was too dark to know the color of his eyes, but she did not need her telepathy to read the astonishment in them.

"Where in the world did you come from?" he asked.

She was suddenly afraid. No human had ever spoken to her before! Instinct told her to get away from this place as quickly as possible. Humans brought danger and destruction; she was in peril right now. Why was she not filled with panic?

Another instinct—something deeper, ancient, and unfamiliar—told her to stay. She would obey that one. She would remain where she was, allowing the human to gaze at her. And somehow she would find a way to answer in a language he might know. If only she could find her tongue.

"Are you stranded here?" he asked when she made no reply. "Do you need help?"

His astonishment was turning to concern. She liked how that

felt, the warmth it conveyed and the tremors of care he sent out around him. He needed to be reassured, though, so he did not worry in vain. Despite how pleasant it was to feel those emotions directed toward her, it was not fair to leave him in such uncertainty.

But her reply was interrupted before it even left her lips. The human was not alone. It appeared he had a companion with him, a partner. A human female moved into view, sliding up beside him as he stood at the railing.

Aliya's mind was only vaguely aware of her. The woman transmitted very minimal vibrations of sensation and emotion. It was obvious enough what she wanted, though. She paid no mind to the water or the mermaid just below her. Instead, her attention was fully on the man as she ran her hands over his body and murmured into his ear.

Aliya could feel the man's reaction, visceral and immediate. His eyes left her and he blinked, as if rousing himself from sleep. The woman ran her fingers through his wind-tousled hair and he turned to her. The cold emptiness washed over Aliya once again.

"Who are you talking to?" the woman cooed at the man.

He hesitated before answering. "No one. I thought I saw… no, nothing. We're all alone."

The woman murmured some more and the man pulled her tight up against himself. He did not look back over the lake. His pain resonated in the waters around Aliya even as he led the woman out of view, inside the boat's body. It was not difficult to guess what would happen next. Aliya knew the man's pattern.

He came out to the lake to escape whatever it was that plagued him. He brought females with him, women he seemed to know little about and cared little for. He distracted himself with the women, playing at games of human passions that both fascinated and confused Aliya. As the man's emptiness attracted her, the inevitable passion drew her to stay.

Just as she did now. She pushed up next to the boat, touching its smooth polished side and waiting for the sensations from inside the boat to travel out to her. Yes, as expected, there they were. The man and his woman were beginning the strange dance of coupling that humans engaged in.

Aliya shut her eyes, letting vibration surround her, reaching her mind up to connect with the man. She could feel what he felt, the building sense of longing and burning desire. She was rocked by the waves even as the humans rocked up above her.

Slowly she became aware of something else…someone else. Someone was coming! She could feel the magic coming closer. She pulled away from the boat and blinked up into the sky. There, she was just in time to notice the small, nonhuman form that glittered above. A fairy, her pink glow reflecting off the sides of the craft and her tiny wings humming, was hovering.

"Come to visit the human again?" the little creature asked. "Not that I blame you. He is pretty interesting, this one."

Aliya tried to calm her beating heart and hide her nervous tail flicking. She splashed a few droplets of water up toward her friend.

"Raea! You're looking especially sparkly tonight."

"You seem to be glowing a bit yourself. Anything unusual going on?"

"No, of course not. I'm simply patrolling these waters and thought I'd make sure things were going well with this vessel."

The fairy buzzed up to peer in through one of the circular windows on the boat. "Oh, things seem to be going very well for the humans, I'd say."

Aliya shook out her hair and hoped her color was fading back to normal. She hoped the glow Raea mentioned was gone, too, although parts of her still felt a bit tingly.

"And how are things going for you?" Aliya asked, eager to take the focus off what the humans were doing, and how she was apparently affected by it. "You've been called out here to grant wishes, I suppose."

"I'm a Wish Fairy; it's what I do. These humans start wishing, so I sprinkle a little dust and give them what they want."

Aliya didn't need to ask what the human wanted tonight. She could feel it. He wanted to do things with his female—things that made him forget his pain and numbed him by those exotic human sensations. Sensations that would then be transmitted through the waves.

Sensations that a mermaid had no business being curious about.

"It's good to know your Fairy Dust is so reliable," Aliya said. "But he's probably done wishing for the night."

"Him? Maybe not. Seems like he's got extra stamina or something. Not that I'm any kind of expert on this sweaty human recreation."

"He's extra lonely."

"What do you know about that? You have some dealings with this human?"

"No…not at all. It's just that I've seen him out here on the lake before. I can sense how alone he feels, that's all."

"Well, you'd better keep that mermaid telepathy to yourself. The Fairy Council has been cracking down lately on questionable interactions, and I know they're generally in close agreement with the mermaid leadership. You don't want to find yourself being accused of anything, Aliya."

"I haven't done anything! I am careful around humans."

Mostly. There was something so alluring, so out of the ordinary about this human...

"Well, just be careful that you don't...shh, someone's here."

Aliya glanced up in the direction of Raea's quick gaze. A faint red-gold light reflected off the water. It appeared roughly the same size as the Wish Fairy's pink glow and was moving toward them. Another fairy. Great. What could have drawn this one out here?

"It's Kyne," Raea said softly. She didn't seem particularly pleased about it, either.

"A friend of yours?"

"Hardly. He's in league with the Fairy Council, spying on us, keeping tabs on how we do our jobs. You'd better go. As you can see, everything is fine on the boat. No sense getting mixed up with Kyne."

Aliya knew the fairy was right. She'd never been one to pay much attention to Forbidden Realm politics, and she was happy to remain blissfully uninvolved. If this Kyne was some sort of spy for the council, trying to make trouble, she wanted no part of it. As far as anyone needed to know, she'd been simply doing her job, keeping the Veil secure and separating the human's mundane world from their own.

The Veil was a magical force that ensured protection for creatures like fairies and mermaids. Humans had no idea it even existed, and that was the way it had been for millennia. If she were suspected of allowing a human to see through the Veil, to become aware of their Realm...well, that would certainly upset things.

"All right, I'll go," she said to the fairy. "It was good to see you again, Raea. Enjoy the rest of your wishes tonight."

The fairy nodded and shushed her away. Aliya sank into the dark waters. She would leave. It was the right thing to do. She would swim away and pay no more special attention to the man on this boat. She'd go about her duties, keeping things quiet and secure out here in her section of the Great Lake. She would ignore how he reached out to her, would ignore the forbidden things that her body felt when she was near him. She would go and never come near him again.

At least, she would do that after a little while. It certainly wouldn't hurt to stay nearby right now, just in case Raea's wishes were not strong enough to bring the man the relief that he wanted. What if he recalled what he had seen before his woman had pulled him back to the mundane? What if that woman was not proving distraction enough and he started snooping around? It was her duty, of course, to keep track of these things.

Best keep track of things out of view from the fairies, though. She dropped deeper into the water, watching the fairy glow fade above her. The dark silhouette of the boat loomed and she could still feel those sensations emanating from the man on board. Slow and rhythmic, gaining in momentum...she closed her eyes and let the feelings, like a torrent, envelop her.

Chapter Two

Raea watched her mermaid friend disappear. Good. Aliya had not asked why she'd been here, spying on the humans long after the man's carnal wish had been granted and he was well on his way toward the satisfaction he craved. Aliya seemed sweetly unaware of what was transpiring. With Kyne, however, Raea was not likely to be so lucky.

"You've been watching them go at it again, haven't you?" he asked as he came closer.

His accusation made Raea glow even pinker than usual. She spun around, turning her back to the boat. There was no way she could deny what was going on inside of it, though. The steady thumping of those nearby—and naked—humans played loudly against the silence of the lake. The heavy breathing of the couple inside could be heard through the open window, and sounds of passion echoed over the water. Anyone with half a brain could not help but know what the humans were doing. And realize that Raea had been watching.

Great. Of all the fairies in the Forbidden Realm, Kyne *would* be the one to show up now.

"You like watching, don't you?" he asked.

"No, I'm not *watching*," she replied, purposefully snippy. "I was *overseeing*. It is my job, after all."

He gave her a smile that was half sneer, half dazzle. "Funny, but it didn't look like overseeing. It looked like watching."

"Well, it wasn't. I was simply doing my job; granting wishes and making sure the humans are minding their own affairs."

"Yes, it seems like you keep them minding one affair after another. Seems to me you must like it."

Oh, but he irked her. He was always making snide comments like that, not quite accusing her of overstepping her bounds, but still...she felt uncomfortable around Kyne. And she really felt uncomfortable having this conversation right here, right now.

Based on human behavior she'd noted in the past—noted for purely academic purposes, of course—at any moment the sounds of rasping breath and shifting mattress would turn to animal moaning, guttural grunting, and maybe even a cry out to their deity. She recognized the pattern; the intensity of the man's passion, the woman's writhing, then the inevitable climax. Kyne was just in time for the fireworks.

She needed to end this discussion and get away from here. Now.

"What are you doing out here anyway, Kyne?" she huffed, barely remembering to use her Veiled voice to keep hidden from the humans, just one open window away.

"You mean a measly Summer Fairy shouldn't be rubbing elbows with such a grand and respected Wish Fairy?" he drawled, golden eyes flashing under their long lashes.

His wisping, flamelike wings stroked the air lethargically, but Raea knew better than to trust his calm exterior. Kyne was just as fiery on the inside as he appeared on the out—quick to react and burning with ambition. He was not one to ignore a perfect opportunity that might benefit his position. Somehow he'd managed to benefit himself right into a position working directly for the council, along with his usual summer duties, of course. He'd done that even with all the wild rumors that circulated about him.

Rumors that hinted Kyne might just have reason to know much more about humans and their lustful behaviors than normal fairies like Raea could ever dream of knowing.

"You know that's not what I meant," she said. "Did you follow me out here to spy on me for the Fairy Council?"

His wings flamed brighter and he fanned them with purpose. The whiplike tips cracked in the air.

"I'm not their puppet, despite what everyone says."

"Then you have no reason to hang around and pester me, do you?" she asked, happy to turn the focus on him.

He shrugged. "I thought maybe you wanted some pestering."

"What I want is to be left alone to do my job."

"Which is to watch humans have sex, apparently."

"So your job is to assume the worst about everyone?"

"And I'd love nothing better than to be proven wrong."

She doubted that. The council didn't want to be wrong, why would Kyne? He may not be their puppet, exactly, but with all those rumors swirling around about him he needed to keep on their good side. He had too much to lose. Raea knew better than to believe rumors—especially rumors like these—but Kyne didn't make them easy to disregard. His blistering aura and off-putting habit of turning up in unexpected places certainly didn't engender trust.

"I'm sorry if I seem unfriendly," she said, eager to get away from the boat and what was developing inside. "I'm just not used to the council sending lackeys to keep track of me."

"Who said the council sent me out here?"

"I don't see any flowers that need pollinating or dancing sunbeams you need to direct. Why else would a Summer Fairy be out here at night? Besides, I saw you going into the Council Hall again this evening. I know you're working with them."

"And you have some reason to dislike the Fairy Council?" he asked in his unfairylike deep voice.

She didn't bother to answer him. Why should she? It would just encourage him to launch an interrogation about the various wishes she granted. She really did not need that. What she needed was to leave this place, put these humans far away from them before things got…awkward.

"I simply think the Fairy Council needs to back off and give us more freedom."

"More freedom?" he asked, occupying what would be her flight path. "Is that what you really believe?"

Had that been the wrong answer? She made a halfhearted attempt to push him out of the way, but he didn't budge. Those bright, vapor-thin wings of his were stronger than they appeared. He hovered securely in place, blocking her. If she wanted to escape, she'd have to swoop down past the window on the boat—fully in view of the humans inside.

True, she was still in her usual stealth form, no bigger than the palm of one of those human's hands and fluttering in frequency unlikely to be detected by them, but an unsanctioned sighting was the last thing she needed on her record. The paperwork alone would take her forever.

"I need to get back to work now," she insisted.

"What do you mean about freedom? What would you do with more freedom?"

"I would do my job without need of you looking over my shoulder."

"Then you'd be free to find more horny humans so you can watch them go at it."

"I grant wishes that keep humans content," she declared, as if he needed a primer on what Wish Fairies did and why. "I can't help it that they're such raging animals and sex is what they all wish for."

"Only because you make it so easy for them to get it."

"That's what I do! I make sure they get what they wish for so everything stays neatly in balance, the Veil kept strong and secure."

"There must be hundreds of other wishes that could keep the humans safely in their place. Why are you so fixated on granting wishes like these? What these humans do with each other is vulgar and foul. Any true fairy should find it distasteful."

To punctuate his point the couple on the boat chose that very moment to break into the hoarse cries, gasping groans, and loud exclamations of pleasure she'd been afraid of. Raea cringed. Kyne's wings flapped more forcefully and he peered past her to see in through the boat window.

"No wonder you like to watch. By fate, they certainly do go at it. Beasts."

"If it bothers you so much, leave," she said. "Unless maybe it *doesn't* bother you."

"It bothers me. A lot."

"Fine. Then let's get out of here. Sometimes after they couple like that they're a little more open to seeing us, you know. I don't want to have to write up a Viewing Report tonight. My shift's almost done."

She shoved past him and took off. So what if her wings smacked him in the face? Maybe the other fairies thought Kyne and his light amber eyes, deep, dusky voice, and annoying little smirk were good company, but she didn't. Not right now.

He ought to be back over land changing a caterpillar into a butterfly, nurturing bees, or whatever it was those Season Fairies did. He had no business out here interrupting her while she was working.

Instead he was following her. She stopped and whirled to face him. An angry poof of Fairy Dust escaped her and glittered in the air around them. Fortunately, the boat was a distance away now, so she wasn't overly worried about being spotted. Her wings turned the dust into a sparkling whirl.

"Leave me alone, Kyne. I can't...I can't think straight with you here."

"I'm just flying in the same direction. What is it you plan to do out here that my presence makes you so nervous?"

"Nothing. I mean, I plan to do my job. I don't need a babysitter."

"You want me to leave you alone, to let you be free to go about your business?"

"Exactly," she said, relieved that he finally got it. "I'd like a little freedom."

A slow smile moved over his lips. The breeze turned warm and for just a moment Raea felt as if she couldn't quite catch her breath. Kyne's eyes held on to her in a manner she'd not known before, and she couldn't move away.

"What would you do, Raea, if you really were free? If you didn't have to dance to the whims of these humans, if you didn't have to worry about so-called babysitters from the council? How would you be *free* tonight?"

His question rolled over and over in her mind. What was he asking her? His words made no sense, yet something about them touched a place deep inside her. *Freedom.* What did it mean? She could hardly imagine a life where she didn't have to grant wishes, to be at the beck and call of frustrated humans, or under the watchful eye of the council.

What would she do if life wasn't that way? What would she do right now, right here, if she really were *free*?

The heat and the glow coming off Kyne felt like sunlight on her skin, familiar and enticing, as if she could let down her guard and let go of duty and responsibility. For a moment she almost thought about giving in to the feeling, finding out just what it was she *did* feel inside. A fish splashing below brought her back to reality, though, and she was glad for it.

If what Kyne was making her yearn for was freedom, then freedom was terrifying.

"Fairies *are* free," she said sharply. "We've managed the humans this way for centuries. Who are we to say things ought to be changed?"

"I bet you'd change things if you didn't enjoy granting these kinds of wishes so much," he said with a warm, smoky laugh.

Infuriating.

"Leave me alone, Kyne. You've sprouted too many daffodils, or something."

"I don't do daffodils. I do *summer* flowers. If you weren't so busy helping humans copulate you might notice the difference."

"I grant wishes. It hardly matters to me whether they're for an hour of sweating and strange noises or for a new pair of shoes."

"I've never seen you peeking through windows to watch shoes, though."

She glared at him, wondering how he could be so beautiful and so annoying all at the same time.

"I grant the wishes they want, Kyne. I follow the Great Code; I keep our laws and protect the Veil. You can go back to the Fairy

Council and tell them that. The Forbidden Realm is safe because I keep the humans distracted and content."

"And sex is the only thing that will do that for them? Surely they must have some higher qualities."

She shrugged. "Not that I've noticed. The males seem especially single-minded."

"You sound just like the council," he said, nearly hissing his words. "Humans are base, brutish creatures, they say, and we must dedicate our lives to managing them. Well, I say there's another way. There's got to be some other way."

"They're earth creatures, Kyne," she said gently, hoping to soothe the new fury that radiated off him. "They're not of the air, like us. Since their animal lust doesn't affect us, what does it matter what wishes we grant?"

"Are you sure their lust doesn't affect you?" he asked.

"Of course it doesn't."

He stroked the air for a moment, then pinned her with his eyes.

"Well then, I propose a bet. I say you have exaggerated the importance of this human need for passion. I say you grant the wishes you wish to grant. Humans are more sensible than you give them credit for being. When not distracted by moonlight and Fairy Dust and your sordid curiosity, they would make a more rational wish."

"What? All right, Kyne, I'll take your bet. Now how shall I prove that you don't know the first thing about human sexuality?"

"A virgin."

"A what?"

"A virgin," he repeated, still smiling. "I take it you don't see too many of those."

"I most certainly do." She smiled back. "They are some of my most ardent wishers!"

"Then this should be a fair test."

"Don't be ridiculous. All it will prove is what I've been saying all along."

"Maybe, and maybe not. As long as you follow the rules. Are you sure you want to do this?"

"Oh, I wouldn't miss it for the world. Tell me your terms."

"It's simple," he said. "If you can find one of these virgins wishing for a partner, offer her this option: you'll grant any three wishes in the world—money, good health, popularity, whatever—or you'll grant her one night of physical coupling with the partner of her choice."

"You want me to be seen by a human? But that's…forbidden!"

"Is that your excuse for backing out?"

"You're just trying to catch me breaking the rules so you can go running to the council."

"Maybe I ought to do that now, since you obviously can't defend your claim that all these disgusting wishes are necessary…"

"They are! It keeps humans out of our Realm. Very well, I'll play your games. I'll give the virgin your option. I suppose you won't turn me in if I use some Forgetful Dust on her afterward? I won't put the Veil in danger of detection just for your stupid bet, Kyne."

"Agreed. Once the experiment is completed, your virgin can't have any memories of magic."

"It's a stupid bet, Kyne. You'll lose for sure."

"No, I wasn't finished with my terms. There's a stipulation. If your virgin takes the other wishes, she gets them free and clear. If she takes the animal passion, all she gets is twenty-four hours. After that, she is wiped from her partner's mind and she goes back to her normal, clueless life, dull and passionless as it was before."

"But…"

He gave a fiery grin and hovered over her.

"No buts, Raea. *This* is my wager, and I'll give you a whole week to accomplish it. Do you still say you've been granting the right wishes all along? Or are you ready to admit your motives are less than pure?"

"I'll take your stupid wager, Kyne. So what do I win when you lose?"

He thought for a moment, smiling that lopsided, sizzling grin that was really starting to bug her. His golden eyes studied her carefully and his skin was taking on a bronze shimmer under the starry sky. Was the night air getting chilly? It must be, although Raea could never remember being affected by weather temperatures before. But something was making her skin prickle.

"If you win, I'll give the Fairy Council a glowing report about you," he said.

"You ought to do that anyway."

"You're pretty sure of yourself."

"I can afford to be," she said, giving him a heated grin of her own.

"And you're not the least bit worried what I'll expect on the off chance I might win?"

"All right, tell me. What would you expect me to do if—by some miracle—you win?"

"Grant a wish, of course."

By the Skies, what was he up to, asking for wishes? Not that it mattered, of course. She was going to win this without half trying. Kyne and his stupid wager were doomed.

She nodded and held up her hand. "All right, the bet's on, Kyne."

He smiled and laced his fingers through hers in the familiar Fairy Covenant. It didn't feel like the usual covenant grip, though. She wasn't sure what it was, but darned if more strange prickly sensations didn't start out in her fingers and travel through her arm. To her surprise, in seconds her whole body was tingling and warm.

Well, so much for blaming it on the cold night air. Parts of her were positively burning. What was wrong with her tonight? She pulled her hand away quickly, throwing off her balance so that she tottered a bit.

"I need to get back to work," she said, fluttering madly to regain equilibrium. "I'll see you later. When I watch you deliver my glowing report to the council."

"Or perhaps when you're granting my wish," he said, searing her with a smoldering leer.

"Enjoy the rest of your night, Kyne," she said as she spun and headed off in whatever direction would take her away from him.

"I've enjoyed it so far," he called back behind her.

She ignored him and shook her head, trying to be rid of the feel of his eyes on her. Was there something off with the moon phases, perhaps? She felt strange.

She waited until she was nearly to shore, then glanced backward to watch Kyne dart off, his form so much more solid and defined beneath his orange glow than she was accustomed to seeing. He was not like other fairies. Maybe that explained why she had such a hard time figuring him out. Kyne was somehow… different.

Not that she was prepared to speculate on what that difference might be. Her mind was just running away from her, that was all. She was not about to let herself wonder if maybe, just maybe, those rumors about him could possibly bear any truth. They were ridiculous, after all. No one could possibly take any of them seriously.

Kyne—it was said—was half human.

Chapter Three

Aliya gazed up through the dappling of the water. Nighttime made it dark, but her eyes were well suited to the lake. She could still make out the shape of the boat high above her, and she could see the pink and orange glow of the fairies as they fluttered off. She was alone now, unseen by anyone. The waves comforted her with their movement, like a breeze in slow motion. The water was soft and cool but her sheen of velvety scales protected her from any hint of chill.

Slowly, she snaked her way upward. Passion, emotion, yearning…they still transmitted to her from the boat, softer and calmer now than they had been. She ought to go, she knew that, but she just couldn't make herself. Carefully, she scanned the starlit sky above, staying safely just below the surface. Not that she didn't trust Raea, but there was always the risk that her friend might return. And that other fairy…Aliya did not know him and would rather not make his acquaintance here tonight. He had not seemed someone Raea was especially fond of.

What had they been arguing about? She hadn't been able to hear their words as she waited deep beneath them, so she'd reached out her mind. Air, however, was a poor transmitter of mermaid telepathy, and she could learn nothing. Besides, every part of her being had been fully absorbed in what was being transmitted from the boat.

She moved toward the vessel, reaching out to it and hugging close enough to be buffeted by the ripples of water lapping at its sides. The boat pressed its wooden form into the water, and the water pressed back. Aliya imagined the humans doing much the same, dry in their human shelter above.

If she stayed very still and shut her eyes tight, she could actually feel them. They were moving again, the steady rhythm of their bodies speaking above her in the heat of the air and brushing her with their vibrations. They were chafing against each other in that odd human dance. It made her feel things foreign to her, things that she wanted to know better.

Instead, all she knew was the familiar embrace of water. The tiny, satiny scales of her lower torso prickled with anticipation as she strained to feel each tiny tremor that could be transmitted to her through the earthy hulk of the boat. She knew she would find it, just the right sequence of undulation in the water. And there it was. She pressed tighter against the wooden frame and her tail fin rolled contentedly as her senses latched onto it.

Ah, that's what she was looking for. The constant drumming pulse that came from the humans' fervent motion. She shut her mind off to everything but that, giving her body over to float helplessly in the current of that gentle sway. And she thought of *him*.

He lived on the dry land and he breathed only dry air. He walked on two legs. She should not be so very aware of him. Vigilant in her capacity of Sentinel, yes, but not so very *aware*. She was supposed to monitor human activity on the lake, not grow to actually care about it. That was not a part of her job. She was not to be reveling in vibrations of human copulation like this.

Once again, however, here she was. Reveling. It was wrong. She should not let herself feel this, not give herself over to the movement. This was between the human man and the female he had brought out onto his boat tonight. A mermaid should avoid getting swept up in such things—it was one step closer to detection, to breaking the Veil that kept them all safe.

But how could she not be swept away by it? How could she not feel all of this in her body as the steady beat of human motion began to change? The vibrations became stronger, quicker, almost desperate in their cadence. Her watery environment caressed her, slick and soothing.

She responded so easily to the human's passion. She was a creature of magic, though. Passion was unknown in her world. How could her body crave such a thing as if it were familiar? While her velvety scales tingled at her sensations, the milky skin of her torso, her arms, and her breasts pricked with anticipation. Her nipples puckered and a fire kindled deep down in her core.

She stroked her hands over her skin, over her breasts as they were buoyed by the water, the nipples taut between her fingers. The action made her weak. She pressed her body tight against the boat, its surface smooth from the human's diligent care of it. This boat felt almost an extension of the man and she rubbed her fins over it, letting the water hold her as she cupped her own breasts and wondered at the heat welling up inside them.

She writhed as she felt the humans on board twist in each other's arms. Her hair wrapped about her, binding her arms and blinding her eyes. The vibrations were coming stronger and she could feel the full force of them. Once more, nothing else mattered but touch and sensation. She rolled in the water, feeling every molecule wash over her scales, permeate her skin, and surge through her lungs as her body drew oxygen and nutrients from it. She struggled not to cry out, to make herself known to the lovers above.

The release would come soon and come hard. She expelled her last draw of watery breath and floated free, her nerves singing with anticipation, waiting for the slightest message to arrive in the tremulous sea around her. Her body undulated, burning from her own caress and desperate for the delicious torrent to finally be over. It was terrible and wonderful. Familiar and forbidden.

When she thought she could stand it no longer, at last the end came. The panting rhythm surrounding her pounded to a fury, then came crashing to calm. The water stilled and she knew the humans were left clinging to each other and gasping for air. Their dry air, where she could not go. Aliya was alone in the chill water below, her body sagging but not satisfied, forever separated from whatever it was these vibrations made her seek.

She pressed her pale hand against the boat to steady herself and get her bearings. The humans were still, the man undetectable to her now. The boat was merely a cold, barnacled thing; a piece of the dry that invaded her world. She felt empty and drained. And sad. The sadness that human carried with him, she felt it wrap tightly around her now. She understood his hopelessness, how alone he felt.

She should not have done this. She must leave them now and go back to her work. Her folk counted on her to keep all things human from ever encountering them. There was nothing for her here and never could be. She had done her duty to make sure everything was well, and it was. Being seen lingering near a boat would only get her into trouble.

To be on the safe side, she gathered her composure and made

a quick inspection. Indeed, the boat was sound and the humans had nothing to worry about. A stranded or sinking vessel, after all, would bring all manner of humans out onto their waters. Her folk needed to know if they must vacate the area, didn't they? She tried to convince herself she was merely doing her job as she made another circle around the boat, watching, listening, seeing.

There was nothing worrisome, though, to be seen. She did, however, see *him*.

The human male had come back out onto the deck. She could see his form looming above, gazing down into the water. She was foolish for it, but she did not dart away as she should. Did he recall her? Was his mind reaching out for her, craving another touch, another glimpse with his eyes?

She must be a fool. No true Sentinel would endanger herself this way. She needed to think about her Realm, the damage that could be done to the Veil if humans became aware of them. There were repercussions and consequences to her actions; she knew all that. At the same time, she knew she could not ignore what she felt.

His pain. It cut through the water and begged her attention. Since the first night she had encountered him, she'd never been able to ignore it.

It was a pain that consumed him beyond conscious thought. He felt things in a way that most humans she'd encountered did not. Night after night he'd returned to this same spot while he tried to drown his emptiness. He immersed himself in passion, distracted himself with carnal enjoyment, yet that torturous pain never fully left him. Aliya had been transfixed, trying to make sense out of sensations.

But she was beginning to realize there was no sense to be made of it. She should not have tried. The pain this man felt had gradually transferred itself to her. After all her time spent watching him, touching his mind when she knew she should not, now his grief echoed in her own heart. The man's hollow yearning for what he had lost had slowly become hers. She would have wept for it if she could have.

But for the fact that mermaids were not able to cry.

* * *

Devin stared out over the water. There was a slight chill to the wind, but he didn't need clothing. There was nothing and no one around for miles, just water. The way he liked it.

His companion slept soundly back in the bunk, but he was restless. He was always restless, especially on nights like these, however that could be possible. By rights he ought to be exhausted after the gymnastics with Stacey. He hoped he remembered her name right.

He'd done that girl twice already tonight and she'd been worn out after. He'd met her last week at one of those boring fund-raising banquets his firm always supported. She was interning for a colleague and probably thought by coming out here tonight she was giving herself some advantage when it came to landing an actual job. Yeah, he'd put in a good word for her with his human resource department. She was not the most inspiring lay he'd ever had, but he couldn't really fault her enthusiasm. She'd put some effort into screwing tonight and he'd taken full advantage of it, for all the good it had done him. He hoped she didn't realize how uninvolved he'd really been. It wasn't her fault she hadn't been enough for him.

When would he ever learn? He kept expecting the pain to go away, hoping, praying, wishing for lust and desire to somehow swallow up the ache. Every now and then his wish almost came true, but it never lasted long.

Sure, for a while he could distract himself with the sex. Sometimes it was nearly good enough. But after all the thrusting and panting, he was always right back where he started.

Alone.

Judith was gone and he was alone.

He could nail every hot young thing on the planet and it still wouldn't bring her back.

Sleep was no retreat, since that was when he relived the tragedy. Every time he closed his eyes he was back there again. He'd see the flames, hear his wife's scream. Then he'd wake up to cold reality. All he had left was wishing he could forget. He would run away to the cool, wet safety of the lake and bury himself and his memories in some warm, willing female.

And there were plenty of them, he'd found. His money attracted them like flies. Everyone wanted their night with Devin Sandstrom. By day he was the CEO of Sandstrom Industries, making deals and negotiating takeovers. By night he was just another man who used women as playthings and didn't bother to remember their names. He didn't need to remember—when he was done with one, there was always another waiting for her turn to warm his bed. Hell, they never even complained. It was like people expected this from him. He had power, position, and wealth enough to get anything he wanted.

It hadn't been enough to save Judith, though, had it? No, it hadn't been. In the end, all his money was little more than kindling. It could do nothing to put out the memory of those flames that turned his heart into ash every day.

And so here he was again, on the lake with a woman who didn't matter and couldn't help him. All the wishing in the world wouldn't change that. Still, he kept coming back. It seemed like the only thing that could douse those flames licking at his sanity was this big, cold, uncondemning lake. But it didn't seem like that was enough anymore, either. Lately he'd felt his sanity slipping.

Hell, he'd thought he'd seen a freaking mermaid earlier, hadn't he?

Proof of that, the water beside his boat shimmered and parted silently as a pale figure appeared there. Fair hair flowing out into a liquid halo, skin that glowed under moonlight, and the face of an angel.

Yep, not much of that sanity left.

But he smiled just the same.

"Hello," he said.

His apparition smiled in return and he more *felt* than heard the gentle sigh she made. He'd felt it earlier, too, when she visited him. Or rather, when he imagined her visiting. Of course he knew she couldn't be real. His desperate, depraved mind had invented her. A fantasy. A mermaid.

"Hello, Devin," she said, her voice drifting around him and making him dizzy.

Hell, he sure had one active imagination. She was so perfect in every way. He might be insane, but he was a genius along with it. To have invented such an elaborate, amazing daydream!

Maybe he should write a book.

"You can't sleep again, I see," she noted.

He felt as if she were caressing him even from this distance, but that was all just a part of the wonderful illusion. It was as if she actually knew him. She'd even called him by name! It seemed perfectly natural to be sitting here naked, having a conversation with her.

"I can't shake the dreams," he replied, knowing she'd understand.

She was his own invention, after all. Of course she'd understand better than anyone ever had. Her sigh drifted up from the water and embraced him. He would have closed his eyes and reveled in the feeling, but then he would not be seeing her. Experience had taught him that fantasies never lasted long enough and he refused to miss any of it by giving in to the loneliness.

"The dreams are getting worse, aren't they?" she asked.

He nodded. Even his therapist didn't know that, but she did. His own private mermaid.

"Devin," she began softly. "How can I help you?"

"Just let me look at you."

Okay, so maybe that was a standard pickup line, but this time he meant it. Watching as she floated there, wrapped in waves of her long beautiful hair and glinting blue sparks off her shiny body, he had to admit the emptiness faded just a bit. Somehow, this crazy fantasy made him feel better. He couldn't explain it. He must be going full-on insane, but he sure did like looking at her.

Her eyes were deep and endless and green, like the water at daybreak. She floated there, her perfect breasts buoyed and bobbing slightly with the waves. The moonlight made her nakedness glow. She let him stare to his heart's content. No self-conscious blushes, no nervous shifting, just an easy and sensual smile meeting his gaze.

She was everything he wanted. She was kind, she listened, she didn't ask for anything, plus she was flawlessly beautiful. And she was a being of water—that was the best part of this fantasy. Fire could never touch her.

That damned, ravenous fire. God, why had he not been able

to stop it? It had kept coming, devouring everything in its path. He'd beat it back, his own hands were scorched, but nothing worked. He'd failed. He lost everything that mattered to him that day.

"Devin," the mermaid said. Her lilting voice pulled him out of the hole he was slipping into.

"Come into the water with me."

Like waking from a dream, her invitation washed over him, drenching those terrible memories. She wanted him to join her in the water. Well, it was stupid to question his own daydream. If getting into the water with her was an option, he was all for it. Hell, he was already getting hard just at the mere thought of it.

He moved to the ladder and lowered himself into the water below. It was cold. He welcomed that, though. Maybe the wet and the chill would help clear his thoughts. He plunged his naked body into the water, letting go of the railing and pushing into the lake. The chill ran over him, through him, but he ignored it and willed himself to regain his grasp on reality.

Not that he wanted this slick, tempting mermaid to be gone, but he recognized his fantasy was becoming more real by the moment. As much as he wanted to escape his reality, he knew it would not be right. He shuddered from cold and burst up through the surface, expecting to see nothing but moonlight and the usual loneliness all around him.

But she was still there. Damn it, his imagination was running wild tonight. She was right there, snaking through the water with her shiny wet body and watching him with her strange watery eyes. His cock throbbed even in the cold. His gaze raked over her as if she were the first woman he'd seen in a year.

And she wasn't even a woman, was she? She was a mermaid, of all things. Yeah, he was losing it, for sure.

"I'm Aliya," she said, her words drifting like mist over the water.

It was a beautiful name, but not one he'd heard before. If she was a figment of his imagination, how had he come up with that name? Not that he was complaining. He could think of nothing better to call this beautiful, surreal creature before him.

She drifted toward him, slowly, hesitantly. Did she fear him? No, of course not. She was his fantasy, after all. She wouldn't be afraid. It almost seemed as though she was moving cautiously so as not to frighten *him*. That made him laugh. Even his own daydream knew just how close he was to going over the edge.

"You are laughing, Devin?" she asked.

"I've never been swimming with a mermaid before," he said.

"You have," she said with a soft smile. "You simply were not aware of me."

"Well, I'm aware of you now."

"And I'm well aware of you, Devin."

Her eyes were unblinking. She moved close enough that he could see water droplets collected in her pale eyelashes. God, she was gorgeous. He'd never seen skin like hers and he was aching to touch her.

Since she didn't seem to mind, he stared unashamed. Her face was human and as perfect as any woman he could have imagined. Her neck was long and slender. A man could spend hours just working that neck and those perfect shoulders. And the breasts.

Good God, what breasts.

She was aware that he was staring, but instead of slinking away she actually rose up higher in the water before him. Rounded breasts heaved with the water, floating just at the surface a couple feet from him. Her nipples puckered.

His cock throbbed, aching for satisfaction. Again? In the cold lake water? This was the perfect fantasy, after all. *She* was perfect. No man could remain unaffected by Aliya.

Below the water's surface her woman's body subtly tapered to something…different. The pale of her skin gave way to a glistening fishlike body. He could see her moving back and forth down there, a graceful dance to keep her upright and above water. It was tantalizing.

"You have so much pain," she said finally.

"I want to touch you, Aliya."

She smiled and glided toward him. The sound of water lapping against their bodies was seductive. He involuntarily moved back toward the boat and clutched the ladder with both hands behind him.

God, he did want to touch her, though! But she wasn't real, nothing more than a desperate fantasy he'd dreamed up. What would happen when he reached out? She'd evaporate, disappear. His fantasy would be gone and he'd be the fool, alone in the frigid water with his own guilt and stupidity. And the hard-on to end all hard-ons.

"I want you to touch me," Aliya said. "Please."

Her timid half-smile was pleading with him and he could see the desire in her eyes. Did he dare? Was he ready to reach out and ruin this beautiful dream? Then again, this was his fantasy, wasn't it? Maybe he could imagine that she wouldn't disappear. Maybe he was lunatic enough by now that he could make her feel real. Hell yes, he was going to touch her.

One hand on the ladder, he stretched his arm out. Farther, farther…nearer…he touched her. By God, she didn't disappear. She let out a breath that was a combination sigh and caress. He brushed two fingers across her face. Damn, she felt so real. She came closer.

He cradled her face in the palm of his hand. She felt as soft and solid as any woman. And ready. Her tender moan sounded perfectly real, and perfectly willing. She slid her body up against his and she felt so good it was all he could do to keep his head above water.

For the sake of survival, he was forced to keep one hand on the ladder. But she still remained tight up against him, still sighing as he touched her face, her neck, the slope of her shoulder. This was *his* daydream, *his* mermaid. He wanted her. What was to stop him from taking her?

He leaned his head toward the water, where her full breasts with those ruby nipples lay at the surface. He let himself sink slightly into the water, cupping one of those moon-kissed breasts. It was warm and soft as silk. He dipped his head and caught her nipple in his mouth.

She drew a quick breath, making a sound almost musical in nature. It filled the air and water around them. Its vibration reached into Devin's bones and rocked his soul. His own nipples tingled with sensation. He pulled her closer, higher. His mouth covered her areola, his tongue worked her nipple.

And he felt her response in his own body.

It was an odd sensation, but he knew immediately that he was experiencing what Aliya was feeling. For every move he made, every gentle sucking motion or caress, he felt it. The experience was irresistible and he wanted more.

She moaned and the sound became the wind, warm and encircling them. This was new to her, he could feel that, too. Whatever it was merpeople did with each other, it was not this. At least, Aliya never had.

The realization stoked his heated passions. It didn't matter anymore whether she was real or fantasy. What they were both feeling right now was very real, and he couldn't let it stop. He wanted all of her, needed all of her.

And she felt the same. She was skimming her cool fingertips along his arms, his back, and down toward his hips. The combined sensation of his reaction and hers was driving him wild. As much as he wanted this to last all night, he knew he would never let it. He needed release soon. For both of them.

Her ragged breaths were like the gales that fell and twisted from the sky, swirling around them in sound and emotion. He teased first one nipple, then the other, and let his kisses trail back up to her neck, where he nuzzled her ear. The area there was especially sensitive for her and she arched under his assault.

Then he captured her lips. Salty, sweet, unlike anything he'd ever felt. She was warm, but it was tempered by the water. She was firm, but her body seemed to mold itself to him, wrapping her fishy tail around his legs. He parted her lips with his searching tongue.

She greeted him eagerly. As he showed her the way, she began tasting him, toying with his mouth. The surge of current through her body was mirrored in his own and his muscles began to weaken under the strength of their passion. He gripped the ladder, fighting to keep from giving in to the desire to leave reality behind and become one with Aliya.

But it was too late. His need overwhelmed him and he let go, grasping her to him with both arms and feeling the water draw him down, closing over his head. He hardly paid attention, though.

Aliya was writhing against him, the lower part of her body a sleek, textured form of muscle and nerves. He felt as she felt when he slid one leg around her to hold her there, keep her with him. Her lower skin was even more sensitive than the skin he had been feasting on above water.

He could feel that his legs brushing against her were shooting spasms of pleasure through her entire body. And she had deepened their kiss. It was as if something were flowing back and forth between them, as if he had somehow begun sharing his very soul with her.

Then it dawned on him; he was underwater. Aliya was breathing for him! They were drifting free, several feet below the surface, and Aliya was breathing for him. Their bodies twined together in blinding pleasure. Thank heavens. If she could breathe for him they might go on this way forever!

His throbbing cock begged for Aliya's body and he pushed against her. The anatomy was different from what he was used to, but none of that mattered just now. She rocked with the pleasure he was giving her by simple contact with her skin. Still, he sought a way to merge.

Suddenly he felt her stiffen. He broke off the kiss to try to see her face, but the darkness and the murky water made it impossible. Her body began pulsing and he realized she was swimming, propelling them to the surface. Damn, he didn't want it to end.

They broke through the surface very near the boat, beside the ladder where they had begun. He noticed a dull ache in his body before he understood that it was actually Aliya that ached. Oh God, oh God! Had he hurt her?

Chapter Four

He grasped for the ladder and wrapped his free arm around her waist to support her. What was wrong? He understood this was new to her; had he been too forceful?

He hadn't entered her; hadn't found a place for it. But it hadn't been for lack of trying. He'd wanted her badly and he knew it had shown.

"Aliya…," he started, only to be silenced by one of her fingers pressed to his lips.

She smiled, the dappling of moonlight on the lake only making her more tempting. But her smile was sad.

"I'm so sorry," she said. "I didn't know how it would be for you."

She must have read the confusion on his face. He sure felt it inside, and cursed himself for not being more sensitive to her.

"Your appendage. It's supposed to be involved more, isn't it?"

It took half a second to understand her meaning, then he had to restrain a laugh. She'd never encountered an "appendage" before!

"Yes, I guess you do things differently where you come from."

"I didn't know what to do!" she said and looked honestly disappointed. "I really want to make you happy, Devin."

"Aliya," he managed. "What you did to me...well, I was more than happy, trust me. I feel things with you that I haven't felt since...damn it, Aliya, I can't even explain. This is like nothing I've ever felt before."

"But there's more. Tell me what to do for you."

He wanted to go back underwater. He wanted to kiss her again and feel her desire spike as he rubbed against her skin. He wanted to show her there was indeed more.

Instead, she needed affirmation. Well, he could do that for her. What kind of fantasy had he created here, anyway?

"We—people, that is—have different bodies," he began. It felt awkward to have to explain this right now, but it was the least he could do for her. "Males have this appendage, as you call it. Females have a...well, they have a place to insert the appendage."

She contemplated this. Her sculpted face twisted into a cute little frown and she stared off into the distance as she pondered his words. Her breasts dipped below the surface and bobbed there to torment him.

Man, this fantasy was getting more and more creative all the time. How was he doing it?

"So, that's what you were looking for? A place to put that?" she asked.

"I'm really, really sorry if I hurt you."

She gave him a timid, but sly, smile. "No, it didn't hurt. Far from it, actually."

"You liked it, didn't you?" he said, touching her again. "I know you did. I could feel it."

"Yes, and I could feel you, too. But that was unusual for you, wasn't it?"

"You mean it's always like that for you? Sharing someone else's feelings, and all that?"

She smiled and slid up to him. Her body brushed his length and the desire that had gone unsated reared up immediately.

"We live underwater where vocal communication can be difficult. It helps to be able to share thoughts and feelings without speaking," she explained.

"Oh," he said, as if it made perfect sense. "So I invented telepathic merfolk, did I? I'm better than I thought I was."

"What?" she questioned.

He pulled her to him again to taste the smooth, salty skin of her neck. "Too bad I wasn't smart enough to think up something to fix that no-place-for-my-appendage problem."

But she pushed away to look at him. Her big green eyes were wide and full of questions.

"I'm not certain what you're saying, but it feels to me that for some reason you think I'm not entirely real?"

He didn't know what to say. Was he supposed to humor her, his own imaginary mermaid? Maybe his subconscious was struggling to hold on to any last shards of rational thought. That must be it. He was creating dialog to justify having sex with a nonexistent fish-tailed virgin.

She must have heard his thoughts. Maybe he shouldn't have made her telepathic. Dumb idea. She pushed away from him.

"You don't believe this is true!"

He reached for her and sank to his earlobes when his hand slipped off the ladder. His body was still too taut with desire to be able to tread water with any reliability.

"Aliya, wait," he called. "It's not that you're not real to me. No, I promise this is the realest thing I've done in two years."

"But I can't understand your feelings. You want me, don't you?"

"Oh, hell yes!"

"But you don't think I am real."

She seemed to think on this for a moment, but then a brilliant smile returned to her face. She came closer to him, gently pushing him with her body as she scratched her fingers through his hair. He bumped up against the ladder again and grabbed it. Her breath hit him like sea spray.

"Perhaps I'm not real, Devin," she said and came up to kiss him on the lips. "Perhaps this is just a dream and you won't remember any of it in the morning. So we can enjoy ourselves now and forget everything else."

Yes, that would be perfect. He kissed her, tasted her, traced the soft contours of her body. Damn, when he dreamed he sure did it right. If only... if only he could have more. Again he felt that desperate wanting, that longing for more than imaginary kisses.

He blocked the thought from his mind and held her tightly, searching her mouth with his. Searching for what? For his soul, he assumed. That's what it felt like. Moments ago Aliya had given him life with her very breath. Now he wanted more. Needed more.

He cupped her breast with his hand, felt the nipple grow tight between his finger and his thumb. The waves of her own emotion and need swept over him as it had before. She was as desperate for him as he was for her. Still their mouths possessed each other.

His hand slid from her breast down to her hip. He studied how her skin changed, smooth as silk going down, but with tiny scales when he brought his hand upward. He stroked her there, up and down, and rode the thrills of sensation with her. His erection danced with the tempest of near ecstasy inside him.

He wanted her so badly and she was so willing, so very giving toward him. It was nothing short of cruel that they were so different and he could not thrust himself inside her as he ached to do. He would plunge into her for all he was worth, driving to the core of her being. She would take the full length of him if she could, he knew it. And she would know that this was more to him than the shabby one-night stands he'd been trying to hide behind.

He groaned and almost came. But he stopped himself, moving away from her enough to calm the flaming sensation in his loins. He had not found a way to pleasure her fully yet and he was determined to do that.

"What is it?" she murmured.

"I want to make you happy, Aliya. How can I give you pleasure?"

He stroked her lower portions as he said this, running one leg up and down her side as his hand followed the line where human became fish. And he knew the answer in his own body.

"Like that," she breathed. "What you're doing. It's wonderful."

So he continued, and kissed the side of her neck where she had shown particular reaction before. Again she arched toward him and her head fell back, draping his arm with her flowing hair. He wished for special powers to be able to let go of the boat and devote himself fully to serving her.

She was so responsive and so honest about how he was making her feel. He let himself feel it all with her. It was like no sex he'd ever had before. Touching her, experiencing her, was breathtaking.

Giving over to temptation, he let go of the ladder and let his body slide down into the water, keeping as much contact with her special skin as possible. She twisted in his arms, at first resistant to seeing him disappear below the surface, but then welcoming his ministrations.

Running on sheer adrenaline and force of will, he ignored his body's craving for oxygen and let his hands and mouth have free run of her remarkable body. He noticed that her reaction was strongest just below her waistline, where the tender skin of the woman transformed into the satin skin of the sea creature. He kissed her there, nipped carefully with his teeth.

Then both hands found their way back to her breasts, and she was undone. He felt her body writhe and her emotions soared above the mountain of sensation to come crashing down into the lake. She thrashed once, twice, and their physical contact was broken. He was shoved away from her, into the darkness of the water.

But he didn't have time to worry for his own safety. In a heartbeat she was against him, cradling his head and finding his lips with hers. She gave him the air his blood cells were crying out for and again they were sharing their very existence. It was more than just breathing or staying alive. This was *being* alive deep down, all the way into his dark soul where he had felt dead for so long.

She swam them to the surface. He came up into the night air gasping, aching, and too amazed for words. He had felt her come, lived her orgasm as clearly as if it had been his own. But as her body brushed against him he was fully aware that his own need had not been satisfied.

He was still as hard as a rock and aching for fulfillment.

But she sagged against him, weak and drained. He held her to him as a lover would. He kissed her head. In that instant he felt full. The emptiness was gone; the pain that held him prisoner was released. His body was straining from desire, but his heart was free.

"I have never known such a thing." She sighed, contented.

"Me neither. Nothing like that."

For minutes he held her, controlling his breath and waiting for the pulsing ache in his own body to go away. It was hard to concentrate on not being aroused when her body was nestled so tightly against him. The surge of afterglow in her body was coursing through his and only serving to keep his senses on high alert.

He'd been truthful. Never had he known such a thing as these few minutes with this woman.

Finally she lifted her head and smiled a dusky smile for him. "You are waiting for something."

He knew it was time for another biology lesson. But how to explain what was going on in his own body without making her feel in any way inadequate? She had been perfect. He had gotten so much pleasure from seeing her, feeling her reactions. It was so nearly enough.

"Honey, you've got me so hard and so hot, I can't seem to quit wanting you."

For a moment she considered his words, maybe even considered his thoughts. He knew she could read them. If she thought he was in any way displeased with her...

But she smiled. "I see. Your mind tells me what you want."

"It's going to take me a while to get used to you reading my mind."

He wouldn't be surprised if she swam away in terror, reading his thoughts right now with all the erotic images flooding his brain. He wanted her every way possible, ways that the both of them knew she wasn't capable of. Damn, but if she were, he'd have her up against that smooth hull and plunge himself so deeply into her, riding her with every wave until they both ended up begging for mercy.

Her breasts were just so damned full and round, and that sexy little dip in the small of her back called out for him to grab her and pull her up tighter against him. And that mouth...with those red, pouting lips...

"I *can* read your mind, Devin," she cooed. "And perhaps I can help you."

Silently she dipped below the water, letting her body glide against him. He felt her breast graze his penis, then felt her hands on him. She took him gently, studying him. He drew breath in through his teeth as he realized just how much that added to his arousal. She liked what she was finding there.

She touched him carefully, trailing a finger from the thick base of his erection out to the end. She was getting him so out of control he worried he might slide right into the lake. To prevent that, he hooked his arms behind him over the closest rungs of the ladder.

It was just in time. Without warning, Aliya had taken his cock into her mouth. By God, she *could* read his mind. He stifled a groan. The pleasure she was giving him just from the slightest touches was almost unbearable.

He sank as low in the water as he could, just barely able to breathe. He closed his eyes to block out any unnecessary stimulation. All he cared about right now was Aliya and what she was doing to him below the surface.

Her lips closed around him and very slowly she began drawing her tongue in circles around the head of his penis. So good, so perfect. He could die a happy man from torture like this.

Then she was timidly sucking. Oh God, that was going to do him in. How could she know to do this? He was helpless to stop her. With his arms wrapped around the ladder and the rest of his body floating below he was completely at her mercy.

But she took none. She must have been able to tell what she was doing to him because her efforts intensified. She wrapped two fingers around the base of his penis and gave gentle pressure there. All the while she was still holding him in her mouth, sucking in earnest.

Then he could feel her in his mind. She was loving him in his mind, holding his emotions, tending to the old wounds, seeping into the places he thought no one could ever go again.

And he came.

The force of it was startling. He jerked his arms free from the ladder and sank beneath the water. He knew she had dragged a scream out of him and he was determined to muffle it under the cool, dark water. If he drowned tonight it would be okay.

But she was holding him, keeping him from sinking deeper. In her hand she still cradled his penis as it continued the spasms she had evoked. Her other hand was buried in his hair and brought his mouth to hers. Air. She was bringing him air.

He gasped for it, sucking from her just as she had done from him. She was keeping him alive.

No. She had made him alive. For the first time in two years he was alive again. He relaxed in her care and let her take him to the surface again.

"That is what you wanted," she said quietly.

"My God, Aliya," was all he could get out.

"You taste sweet," she said, licking her lips.

He had about an ounce of energy left and used it to latch onto the ladder again and clasp her to him.

"That was incredible. I don't care what happens now."

She smiled at him. "Then I've made you happy?"

"Amazingly happy," he said and kissed her.

"Then you should sleep well tonight."

"Hell, I'll probably sleep for two days after all that," he said.

But it dawned on him that she would not be there. He would

go to his bed without her. He would go back to his reality, and she would not be there.

She knew what he was thinking and touched his face.

"We each have our own world to go to, Devin."

"Damn it, Aliya." He sighed. "I don't want to go back to that world. I like this one."

"But you're a creature of the dry. You need the air. As much as I hate to see you go, you know you have to."

He knew she was right. He hated it, but she was right. Tonight she had given him his life when for so long he had given it up. He wanted to sink under that cool, clear lake and just fade off into eternity with her, but he knew he couldn't. He had to get up on that boat again.

"I can come back," he said. "I can come back here and imagine you all over again."

She kissed his chest and stroked the curling dark hair that grew there.

"You didn't imagine me, Devin. Can't you believe that? This is real. I'm real. And now we have to say good-bye."

"No, damn it!" He grabbed her and kissed her mouth, seeking the same connection they had shared underwater. But she turned away from him.

"No, I've stayed too long with you. It's not allowed; they'll find out. There are rules about this sort of thing, Devin. There are forces you don't know about. We have to go."

"But you're not even real. Why must you go?"

"Hush. You know every dream comes to an end."

He opened his mouth to protest, but suddenly she was listening to something in the distance. She held up her hand to silence him, then slowly turned her face back to his. He knew it was pointless to argue.

"I have to go," she said.

He released his hold on her. She slipped away from him, sliding deeper into the water.

"Will you be all right?" she asked, though he wasn't certain if it was aloud or in his mind.

"Yeah, I'll be all right."

"I'm glad I made you happy, Devin the human. At least...in your dream."

Then she was gone. The water tracked out in dark ripples, but other than that and his achingly spent body there was nothing left to say she had ever been there.

That's how he knew beyond all doubt Aliya was real. If he had created her as a sort of fantasy, if all this had been just his imagination, she never would have gone. He'd have found a way to keep her with him forever.

She made him happy? Hell. More like she ripped out his heart.

Chapter Five

Kyne buzzed over the tree line that bordered the banks of the Great Lake and followed the crowded roadway there along the shore. He'd spent the night on the distant, deserted shore, avoiding Raea and all others of his kind. It was better for everyone that way.

But now it was morning and he had his work to catch up on. He had to monitor the seasonal progression of local plant life, insect activity, air currents, and other things that humans so easily took for granted while they bumbled along in their daily lives. They were such busy creatures, always coming and going somewhere. The start of the day seemed to be especially full of activity for them as they bustled here and there, caught up in their lives and oblivious to so many things around them.

A flash of pink sparkle caught his notice. By the Skies, what was...could that be Raea? Yes, as a matter of fact, it was. She came skimming long the tree line from the opposite direction, moving with definite purpose and aim. Kyne ducked into the leafy shadows and watched as she came nearer, then left the relative safety of the tree line and zipped up high, soaring toward the very top of a nearby tall building.

What could the Wish Fairy be up to, glittering in the early sunshine and putting herself in such a position where she might possibly be seen? The Veil protected them from most human view, but every now and then someone was not caught up in mundane life. Every now and then some human was unexpectedly searching for magic, opening his eyes to the possibility of more than just what he knew. Those were the humans to watch out for. Those were the ones Wish Fairies like Raea were supposed to be keeping distracted.

Is that what she was doing now? She moved so rapidly and seemed so sure of her direction...he thought maybe he ought to check it out. This was exactly the sort of unexpected behavior the Fairy Council had asked him to be on the lookout for.

Not that he was the spineless little patsy they seemed to think him. When the leaders from his previous region had transferred him here, he hadn't raised up a fuss. When he was called before the council and told that he was under investigation on interference charges that he knew for a fact where purely invented, he'd played the part they all wanted him to play. He let them think he was afraid, but he wasn't. He was simply keeping his boiling rage under control.

The Fairy Council was using him. They'd heard the rumors of his unusual birth and they'd sought him out. He'd been investigated relentlessly, the council hunting until they found some so-called discrepancies in his behavior that they could use against him. To avoid punishment for them, he must follow their orders. They demanded he act as their spy.

They wanted him to track other fairies for them and report back, gathering bits of information they could use to turn more well-meaning fairies into their cowering cohorts. If he did not do as requested, it was clear what the council would do. They would punish him by making his background known and expelling him from the Realm. Then they'd simply find the next willing sap to dance to their bidding.

By the Skies, Kyne had lived with rumor and suspicion all his blighted life. He was practically an exile already. Whether the council humiliated him or not made little difference to him. What he couldn't abide, though, was the knowledge that his own kind could be so ruthless and duplicitous.

Everyone knew humans were capable of such barbaric behaviors, but fairies were supposed to be beyond such pettiness and schemes. They were not governed by the same animal passions as humans. They were above greed and envy and power-lust. He needed desperately to believe this, to have hope that a half-breed like himself might overcome the base instincts he inherited on his human side.

But if it was true that fairy nature was above all that vulgar humanness, why was the council so worried about fairy behavior? Why did they need to blackmail him into betraying his own kind?

The whole purpose of the Fairy Council was to defend fairies, to guide them in ways that built up and strengthened the Veil for their own protection. He'd always admired the council for that, he'd trusted them and been a stalwart supporter of the firm barrier between the mundane and magic. He, more than anyone, understood the need for such a thing.

But now it seemed not even his own kind could be trusted. The council was suspicious of those it purported to protect, and he certainly was suspicious of the council. Now here was Raea, a well-respected fairy he'd seen on numerous occasions buzzing about places he was sure that she had not needed to be.

Maybe the council was right to have their suspicions. Not that they'd ever seemed to notice Raea for anything...yet. Kyne had noticed her on his own. Something about Raea had attracted his attention from the first day he'd seen her.

She always had such a spark, always put so much of herself into her work. He liked that. He also couldn't deny he liked looking at her, but that was nothing he was particularly proud of. Not only did he notice and respect Raea for her excellent fairy qualities, but there was something in her that appealed to his human side, too. And that was reprehensible.

He had a hard enough time keeping his human side under control; the last thing he needed was to torment himself by trailing around after a fairy he found...well, he found her attractive. In *that* way. A *human* way.

The way that made him go hot and uncomfortable in his over-size, over-, overly humanlike organ.

Thank the Clouds that the council had never asked him about that. He would have certainly incriminated himself if they had. All his life he'd carefully governed his actions, his appearance, even his thoughts. He'd been a full fairy to everyone who had met him. Deep down inside, though, he knew the truth. Even his own mother never knew how fully human parts of him were. Magic helped him somewhat, but mostly he stayed in control purely due to his single-minded determination. For the rest of his life, he intended to keep it that way.

It wasn't easy, of course. Especially around Raea. Sometimes— like last night—after being near her he needed some time off on his own before he could get himself under control again. Especially when he encountered her granting one of *those* kinds of wishes. By the Skies, if only he weren't so damned sensitive to noticing those human passions. And her.

Life would be so much easier without those aspects of his

being. He wished he could avoid everything that brought out the worst in him. He tried hard every day, but sometimes he failed and let himself be drawn to things that brought only torment. Like passion. And Raea.

Despite his internal chastisement, though, he didn't think twice about following her now.

Toward the top of the building she paused. The interior space of this high-rise facility opened to a marble-and-tile balcony. Apparently humans enjoyed viewing their domain from high places, and this would certainly provide quite a view. The double doors leading into the building were open on this sunny day and Raea found a sheltered perch on a nearby potted plant.

The natural state for fairies was small, of course, and fortunately so. While mermaids tended to be every bit proportionate to humans in their size, and some magical creatures, like dragons, were positively huge, fairies were small. This made it much easier for them to remain hidden beyond the Veil, and Raea was taking full advantage of this now.

Kyne hoped it would work for him, too. He was slightly larger than most fairies, and no one else realized how hard he had to work at forcing his body into this tiny form. It seemed his human traits weren't limited merely to forbidden inclinations and one reactive private body part. One of the reasons he needed seclusion at times was because it took so much of his energy to maintain this size. Too much energy, in fact. Plus, it used up quantities of his Fairy Dust that might make the council ask awkward questions. Sometimes he just couldn't do it. He would go off on his own and let his body simply do what it would.

So far, fortunately, no one had ever caught him in his larger state. Today would be no exception. He was fully in control of his human inclinations and tucked himself behind a large concrete urn. He could see Raea clearly, though he could tell she was blissfully unaware of him.

All her attention was on the man pacing nervously just inside the doors. He was mumbling to himself, too, though Kyne could not hear his words. They were enough to make Raea noticeably nervous, though.

She listened, put her fingertips to her lips in a most distracting show of distress, and then buzzed her wings almost to the point that Kyne expected her to be heard. What was that man doing or saying that was causing her so much agitation?

Kyne moved nearer, positioning himself behind a sturdy wooden chair. He could see the man clearer now, but some sort of human heating and cooling device was too close for him to hear the man's words. He could see his face, though, and it made him buzz his own wings in agitation.

The man from the boat. Yes, Kyne recognized him, even wearing clothes and not pumping his body over some female. He was dressed in the sort of attire often seen on men of business. Given the apparent quality of this man's clothes and the obvious affluence of the building around him, Kyne determined he must be a man of some power or wealth, at least by human standards. They gave too much credit to such things.

But why would this man cause Raea concern? Were his wishes as distasteful to her as she had claimed last night? She certainly hadn't seemed uninterested in them, or the dozens of other such wishes he'd found her granting when he let the passion those humans emitted lure him out to watch. Why was it usually her and not any of the other Wish Fairies assigned to this region? He still felt she had not been entirely truthful about her interest in such things.

All the more reason he did not regret that stupid wager he'd made with her. Did this have something to do with that? Was she here with this man in hopes of finding some way to win at their bet? If she was it did not appear things were working in her favor.

Good. Kyne was right to insist she needed to take the Veil more seriously. All of them should. He would actually enjoy winning this bet and seeing the look on her face when she would acknowledge his point. He'd have to think long and hard on what wish he'd ask her to grant.

Long and hard. So very hard…and she'd beg him to wish it again, over and over and…

By the Skies, he was getting carried away. Damn it. He couldn't afford to think that way, especially not over another of his kind. He'd made that bet with her to prove a point, not to find a way to take advantage of her. Although what a pleasant thing it would be to finally take advantage of those luscious pink lips and that tight little winged body and…

He'd been getting carried away again and it almost cost him dearly.

The man was leaving the interior of his office space, coming through the doors out onto the balcony. Raea darted off out of view, and Kyne hurried to hide just beyond the jutting marble cornice over the building entrance. But a jet of air coming up from the heating and cooling device threw him off course and he lost his lift.

Unbalanced and unsupported, he tumbled over the side of the balcony, falling a good two stories down before he was finally able to catch himself. He probably wouldn't have been so out of control if he'd not been letting his mind wander as he had, but now he was righted. He dodged windows and made his way upward again, slowly rising above the high wall surrounding the balcony, careful to keep himself unseen. Given the human's erratic behavior and Raea's reaction to him, this human could very well be a danger to them. Clearly he was often touched by Raea's magic. Everyone knew the warnings about humans who required excessive magical intervention to keep them content. They were possibly the most dangerous kinds of humans.

Kyne would be wise to stay clear. Trouble was, though, as he hid off in a corner he could not view the full balcony area. Was Raea still here? Which way had she gone? He had no way to tell, and the longer he was here the more likely his chance was of being discovered.

When a human female voice called for the man from inside the building, it was obvious he was not alone. His companion would be joining him here on the balcony. Things were not safe. Kyne buzzed high overhead to see if he could spot Raea, but she was long gone.

Damn. He'd been trying to determine what she was up to. Was she granting another wish for this man? Were things just about to get passionate with the approaching female?

It was all Kyne could do to pry himself away, but he did. He left the building and the humans in it. He flew off, headed back toward the Circle, the gathering place of his own kind where he knew he'd be surrounded by calm, passionless fairies who might not quite understand him, but who would do nothing to make him crave things he should not.

It took everything he had to leave that human on his balcony, imagining the actions that might be unfolding behind him. Passion, heated coupling, the cries of satisfaction when they reached that illusive climax. Kyne's body craved the feeling he got when he came near humans engaged in such actions, but he knew it was wrong. These things were not for him. He was a fairy, not

some base human creature. Always he was at war with himself.
It was maddening.

Let the Fairy Council believe he feared them, worried about
what they held over him and what they could do. He didn't fear
them one bit. No, he had someone much more terrifying to
worry about.

Himself.

Chapter Six

Devin left the plush confines of his executive suite and stepped out into the morning sun on his balcony high over the city. He wasn't seeing the spectacular view sprawling around him, though. He wasn't hearing the traffic or the din of daily life below. No, his mind was full of Aliya.

He could see her, feel her, taste her as if she were still here with him. As if she were *real*.

Of course she was not. He knew that. Mermaids weren't real. All his life he'd been told that. Hell, Judith had even mentioned it once when she found him ogling a painting in an antique store. An art deco masterpiece with mermaids frolicking in the sea spray—it was priced way too high but he was ready to pay it. He would have hung it over their bed if she hadn't put her foot down.

To this day, the painting over his bed was a portrait of her. Not that he actually slept in that bed. No, he'd been in the guest room ever since that night when...when he hadn't been able to save her.

God, why couldn't he let himself get past that? There was

nothing he could have done. Everyone told him so; the fire marshal, the EMTs, the cops on the scene. Everyone was so very sorry for him, but it was time for him to move on. Even his therapist seemed tired of his constant fixation on the subject.

But the truth was, he could have saved Judith. He could have forced her to take some time off, not to push herself so relentlessly. He could have talked her into going home with him that night and not driving in to work during such a bad storm. He could have made her love him enough that she would have wanted to go home with him.

He paced, wishing Aliya could be here to help him drown out the pain. He could have saved Judith if he'd have been enough for her. But he wasn't.

She'd wanted more than he could provide. She'd wanted success and everything that went with it. She'd told him over and over that he was going to make it big, that his designs would change the world. Right from the start, she devoted herself to making that a reality.

He'd been a wide-eyed kid at MIT when he met her and she made him believe his renewable energy innovations weren't just crazy ideas. They were going to make him rich, she said. They would become famous, she said. All they had to do was give everything they had to finally make Sandstrom Industries a reality.

And of course he'd wanted that, too. But every success they'd achieved just seemed to make her eager for more. She encouraged him to push harder and harder, never to sit back and enjoy their accomplishments but to keep striving for more. Even on their days off, she insisted on spending most of her time in her office, going over marketing plans and drawing up proposals for yet more research grants.

They'd been busy at work until late that last night. A storm was rolling in and they knew that, but she was determined to finish her project. He tried to tell her that inventory could wait; another day or two would have hardly mattered. He asked her to go home with him, to get some sleep. To spend some time as a couple, not just as coworkers.

She'd refused. Frustrated, he'd left. She said she would drive herself home later, so he'd gone and left her there. Alone. With a storm on the way.

It hadn't been expected to be severe; they'd had the radio on in the workshop where she was scouting through miscellaneous equipment trying to update her parts lists. Why did that have to be her job? Why couldn't she have let someone else do it? Why couldn't he make her believe he was on top of everything?

Damn it, if he'd just done things differently he could have saved her. He could have made her go home with him that night; he could have been more important to her than their work. Why couldn't he have made her love him and convince her it was time to start that family they'd always dreamed of? But she wasn't ready for a family, wasn't ready to go home with him that night.

So she'd stayed and she'd worked. She was all alone there in that back workshop when the lightning struck. The power blew out and the interior alarm must not have worked. She'd been trapped there when the fire started.

He'd felt guilty on his drive home so he called her to apologize. When she didn't answer her phone he was worried. He turned his car around and drove straight back to their facility. He got there just as the first of the fire trucks pulled up out front. The police held him back as he heard his wife's screams from inside, heard her crying for help. They kept holding him back when those screams finally stopped.

They never did let him go to her. The fire was like nothing they'd seen before. It raced through the building, devouring everything. The roof collapsed, the walls caved in. The responders could do little but stand with him and watch. In the end, nothing was left of that first Sandstrom Industries building but a pile of unidentifiable ash.

He didn't even have Judith's body to bury.

After that, work had been the only thing that mattered to him. He would be the man Judith wanted. Nothing stood in the way of advancing his company. He built Sandstrom into a world leader in the energy field, and he tried not to care about anything.

When it all got to be too much, he went out on his boat. He felt safe there; he could breathe there. The air was fresh and cool, the water would never let fire take anything from him. And hell, the moonlight on the waves was a great way to get women hot and in the mood. He could distract himself with them for hours. Water was always good for that.

Now, unfortunately, the water seemed to be keeping him from the only thing he'd truly wanted in years. Aliya. He ached for her in every way possible.

How could she be nothing more than a fantasy? He couldn't have imagined her, what she'd done to him last night. And his response to what she'd done...he sure as hell hadn't imagined that.

He wasn't imagining his response now. He wished she were here to put out the fire burning inside him right now. The way she had taken him into her mouth, the way she looked at him with those huge, innocent eyes...he wished he could live all those moments with her again, over and over.

He wanted her, there was no doubt about it. He wanted her in a way that was more real than anything he'd ever felt. She had to be out there, waiting for him. Somewhere. Why was he here when Aliya was out there?

"Mr. Sandstrom?"

It was his secretary. She'd said something from inside the office but he hadn't been paying attention. She followed him out onto the balcony. Damn. It was as if he'd forgotten she'd even existed. Not a good thing, considering that on more than one occasion she'd been the one he'd taken out on his boat.

"Everything all right today?" she asked him.

"It's fine, Miranda. I'm just…distracted."

"Anything I can do about that?"

He knew what she meant. Her eyes, her voice, the sway in her hips as she approached him, told him exactly what she meant by her words. She would be happy to help with his distraction. She was pretty good at it, too, as he recalled.

She liked their occasional trysting and she never expected anything more. Maybe she had demons of her own and he helped chase them away, just as she did for him. Maybe she felt sorry for him and did what she did out of pity. Or maybe she just liked screwing the boss. It never crossed his mind to ask why, he just knew she was a hot lay when he needed it.

He needed it right now, too. They'd never done it here at the office, but maybe that's just what he needed. He could take her on his desk, or right here in a chair, or up against the cold marble wall. He could lose himself like he did on the boat. Then maybe he'd forget about mermaids, he could come back to reality, and he could finally think straight.

But no. One look at Miranda's willing smile and he knew it just wouldn't work. He didn't want her.

His cock still throbbed, but it was not Miranda's touch that could soothe him. He was aching for Aliya. He needed her lips and her hands. His skin itched to rub up against her, feel that velvet-soft sensation of her snaking around him, touching him, exploring him as if he were the only man in the world.

That's what he needed. She had loved him with a part of her he'd never encountered. She knew nothing of business, his widely acclaimed success, his net worth, or his car. She only wanted to put her hands on him, to give him what he wanted, to know *him* any way that she could.

That's what he wanted. And of course that was insane. Mermaids weren't real. He needed some water, all right—to throw in his face and bring back his sanity.

"Thanks, Miranda, but I'm okay," he said finally. "Why don't you head down to engineering and see if you can remind the guys there I'm still waiting on that report for the new geothermal project."

She didn't even look disappointed. All she did was shrug. "All right, if that's what you need."

"It is. Thanks."

Her bright red stilettos clicked on the marble as she headed back into his office. It wasn't all he needed. Not by a mile. But he wasn't quite lunatic enough yet to send his secretary off hunting mermaids.

He half wished he were crazy enough to go do it himself.

* * *

"So, Aliya," a twinkling little voice above her asked. "What have you been up to?"

Aliya didn't answer right away. She blinked up into the midday sunlight and tried to read the Wish Fairy's pink expression, but the glare was too bright. Usually Aliya enjoyed her visits with Raea, but today something seemed different. She hoped she could not guess what.

"Just the usual, Raea," Aliya answered her lightly.

But Raea's eager fluttering said she didn't believe it.

"Come on. You can tell me."

"Tell you what? I found a fishing boat with the net tangled in its motor, so I corrected that this morning." Aliya shrugged, water lapping at her shoulders here in this secluded cove where she had gone to be alone with her thoughts.

"And that's all you've done?" Raea questioned.

"Pretty much. Nothing out of the ordinary."

"Really? So, it's perfectly usual for you to go swimming around down there with one of those humans?"

Aliya frowned. Raea knew about that? She couldn't. Could she?

"Oh yes, I know about that." Raea laughed, swooping annoyingly overhead and dipping her pink toes into the water.

Aliya sent up a little fountain of lake water. But Raea just fluttered her wings dry and grinned.

"Now, be nice, little fish. I'm not telling anyone what you were doing last night, so your secret's safe with me."

Aliya flashed her tail angrily. She should have known making friends with a fairy—the driest air creature imaginable—would be troublesome. This was all she needed, Raea and her busybody ways informing everyone from mermaid to dryad what Aliya had done last night. With a *human*.

Oh, and what she had done! At the merest memory of his body, his taste, his raging emotions…it brought a wave of sensation to her skin. She sank deeper into the water so Raea might not notice the heated flush that crept over her body.

"I swim with humans occasionally, I admit it," she said as casually as she could manage. "The clumsy creatures are practically helpless underwater and of course we don't need anyone having an accident, drawing all sorts of attention out here."

And it was perfectly true. Everyone knew a living human would come out into the lake, pass the time for a while, then simply go home to the dry without so much as a thought about mermaids. It was a fact of life that had kept the underwater world alive and well for centuries.

On the other hand, a drowned human would bring all manner of boats and humans in funny suits and silly breathing apparatuses. Whole societies of merpeople had been uprooted and forced to scatter barely one jump ahead of humans in terrifying rubber masks, searching for one of their own. They would come in droves, their unnatural costumes spewing mind-numbing bubbles out in all directions. Their ships were loud and left slicks of poison in their wakes. It was bad when humans went missing on the lake.

"It's part of my job to help humans every now and then, to keep them out of our hair," she said, playing with a shimmering school of minnows who happened by.

"It looked like more than just your hair that human was getting into last night," Raea quipped.

"I couldn't very well let him drown, could I? I...I think he was drunk."

"Drunk on mermaid, if you ask me."

"I don't care what it looked like to you. I was helping him. Nothing more."

Raea giggled. "Oh, don't be so nervous. I'm just teasing."

"That's not a very nice way to tease. If anyone should hear you..."

"Relax," Raea went on. "You're not in any trouble. You have caused quite a commotion, though."

"What are you talking about?"

Raea flitted back and forth above her. Sheer fairy wings whizzed in the air and stirred up the water. "I don't know everything you did with that sex-crazed human, but he's been monopolizing my day."

"What?"

"Oh yes! Maybe you didn't expect him to remember you, dearie, but I've got some news." Raea paused for dramatic effect and shook her shimmery pink hair. "You're all he can think about."

"What?"

Raea dipped so low Aliya had to back off from the drying effect of those wings.

"He's been wishing for you."

It took a moment to sink in.

"He's been *what*?!"

"Oh yes. I've been unable to hear other summons, his wish is so strong. From sun up this morning, wish wish wish wish."

This was bad! Oh, this was sooooo bad. Devin hadn't forgotten her! She thought that he would—they usually did. Humans counted all things they couldn't explain as pure error or imagination. When she'd read Devin's thoughts, he clearly thought that's all that she was. They had enjoyed each other and he had lost some of his emptiness. But he still thought her merely a dream, just part of his imagination, didn't he?

She'd watched him leave, sail his boat back to the dry. Everyone knew once the humans were back on the dry, once the moonlight was gone and they were back to their mundane lives, all dreams faded away. She'd expected him to forget her. But could it be true? Did he remember?

"But I saw him leave. I was sure he'd gone back to the dry…"

Raea nodded. "He did. That's what's so odd about it. He went back to the city, sent his clueless companion home, and headed off to work this morning—he's pretty important there, you know—but all day long he's been wishing."

"Oh no."

"Oh yeah. I don't get many calls quite so powerful as his, let me tell you."

Aliya understood. Raea knew about wishing.

The delicate balance of all creatures who shared the planet had to be maintained, of course, and often the best way to accomplish that was to keep the humans satisfied. Give them what they needed, and just a little bit more to keep them busy. Grant wishes.

They were odd creatures, these humans, and grew restless. The fairies were integral in keeping humans in their proper places, keeping them from ruining things for everyone else.

But Devin was wishing...for her! That was dreadful. He should have forgotten her, but he did not. Now what was to be done?

Of course Raea couldn't grant his wish. It would upset the balance, disrupt the course of nature, reveal the Forbidden Realm. It simply couldn't be.

But if his wish was as strong as Raea had said, then things could get ugly. He could draw attention—he could begin to search out things he had no business searching for. He could put himself in danger. He could call up the Old Revenge. And it would be all Aliya's fault. How awful.

She never meant for this to happen. Never in three lifetimes would she have wished the Old Revenge on Devin! Never had she suspected she could be the cause of it. What was to happen to him? Already he had not forgotten her—that in itself was disturbing. But if he were as obsessed as Raea indicated, that could only mean things were worse than she imagined.

Was it possible that, without ever meaning to, she had visited him with that ancient curse? In former times it had been used against humans whose persistent interference posed a threat to the Forbidden Realm, but no one had required it in ages. Still, everyone knew it was there. In the days when humans and magical beings still vied for supremacy in the world this form of revenge had been used; the Old Revenge, it was called. A human who refused to simply forget his encounter with magic, who would fall into obsession and could not go back to the mundane, could be judged a true threat. He would fall under the Old Revenge and meet a terrible end.

He would be driven mad; he would give up his life and…No, she couldn't even think it. That was something from years gone by, when humans were first invading the seas and merpeople hadn't yet learned to manage them. Some of the defense tactics used then were barbaric. She really, really could not have brought that on Devin, could she?

Then again, she knew what she'd done to him. She'd felt what he felt, she'd ridden the waves of passion that rolled inside him. She'd felt those holes of aching emptiness fill as she'd wrapped him in her arms and poured her soul into him. Yes, if she would be honest with herself the answer was obvious.

She had loved him, and in so doing she could quite possibly have made him love her. The realization dawned on her as both pain and ecstasy. Devin the human might love her.

But for a man to love a mermaid was to bring his certain death!

Chapter Seven

Raea hovered over the mermaid. Aliya sank deeper into the water as her expression showed worry. The poor little fish creature certainly was taking this to heart. Well, no sense letting her friend suffer any longer than she needed to.

"Hey, get back up here where I can talk to you," she admonished.

"Oh Raea!" Aliya moaned, like a cold shift in the wind. "Do you know what I've done?"

"No, as a matter of fact, but I've been wondering about it all day. Some of the things that guy keeps wishing for just don't seem logistically possible, if you don't mind my saying. I mean, you are a fish, right? At least, certain parts of you."

Aliya was clearly not listening to her. Her gaze was a hundred miles away and her words came out hushed. "But he...I thought...oh, what exactly is he wishing for, Raea?"

Raea didn't bother to hide the smile that crept over her face. Ah, Aliya was such a sweetheart, so eager to be helpful. She might be so willing that she could help Raea win a certain bet with a Summer Fairy. Yeah, this was going to work out just fine. For all of them.

"He's wishing for things that I know you haven't done with him!" Raea laughed. "But that's just the point. Even if I thought it might be a good idea—and it's not—there's no way I can grant his earthy wishes."

Aliya nodded, her head dipping into the water. "I know. But what am I to do? You know what they say can happen!"

"You can't seriously believe all those stories about the Old Revenge? Is that what you're worried about?"

"Of course I believe them; every mermaid does. We don't dare doubt it! Maybe you don't know, but long, long ago humans used to come out here and hunt us! The men thought we were like their women, I suppose, but…Oh, the stories sound just horrible!"

"So the Old Revenge was created to protect you."

"Protect us, yes, but also to punish the humans. It was intended they suffer."

"Then you'll just have to explain to your council—or whatever you call your head merfolk—that he doesn't need punishing. Tell them not to engage the Old Revenge on him."

"It won't matter. No one engages it; it engages on its own. When a human believes we are real, when he develops an obsession that will bring him to hunt for us, the Old Revenge engages itself. It just *happens*."

"What? Without Fairy Dust? I don't think that's even possible."

"What if it is? I should never have…but I didn't think that he would…and it seemed so…"

"Okay, now just paddle back up to the surface and calm down," Raea coaxed. "I don't think we need to let our handsome victim suffer his way to a watery grave."

"But they say that's what happens! We become their obsession; they no longer want to live. The Old Revenge will take over and he'll think of nothing but his obsession. He'll give up his life on the land and come out here to find me! But the Old Revenge makes him blind to us. I could be right there with him and he'd never know it! He'll search and he'll search without eating or drinking, until he breathes his last breath. Oh Raea, he'll die in the lake, and it's all my fault."

Raea risked touching her friend's wet hair. She didn't really like wetness, but she liked Aliya. Odd creature to make her friend, but they'd known each other so many years now she couldn't even recall what had first brought them together. Well, maybe she could do a good deed for her friend today.

"He won't have to die. Now pop back up into the nice, dry air and let me finish. I have a proposition."

Aliya's pale green eyes widened and she hoisted herself higher out of the water. "A proposition?"

"Yes. I don't usually go outside my boundaries, you know, but I'm not altogether powerless in the wish department."

Hope washed over Aliya's face and Raea was glad she could offer something positive.

"What is the best way—the only way—to cure a man's obsession?" she asked the bobbing mermaid.

Aliya shrugged. "I didn't know you could."

"Of course you can. I see humans do it all the time."

"Then how?"

"By giving it to him."

"What?"

"Give the man his obsession, and almost immediately he will lose interest in it and start wanting something else."

Aliya blinked at her, confused. Raea would have to go ahead and spell it out.

"If I give you to him—for one day—the obsession will be broken. He will go back to his life on the land and think nothing more of you. You will go back to your life here in the water and not have to worry about him. Everything will be just like it was, and no one will die. How does that sound?"

A bright smile lit up the mermaid's pale, translucent skin. She was really quite pretty, for a mermaid, and for just a second there Raea could maybe understand what this Devin guy saw in her. Aside from the fact that half of her was a fish. That still seemed a bit unnatural, but Raea had been granting wishes long enough to know humans had a lot of kinky fantasies.

"It sounds wonderful!" Aliya sighed. "But to do that, I'd have to be human, wouldn't I?

"Yes, that's how it would have to work."

"But I'm a mermaid."

"Right *now* you're a mermaid, but that could change…just temporarily, of course."

"What? Can we do that?"

"Of course we can. All you have to do is wish it."

"I wish it!"

"Not so fast; let's think this through. First, tell me very plainly what it is you are wishing. These things have to be precise, after all."

Aliya thought for a moment, then asked, "You say it can only be temporary?"

"Twenty-four hours. That's all I'm authorized to do on this sort of thing."

It was almost the truth, and she certainly wasn't going to mention the details of her bet with Kyne. After all, the annoying Summer Fairy hadn't exactly specified that she had to use a *human* virgin. He may have indicated it, sure, but really his word had been simply "virgin." Who could possibly be more of a

virgin than a genital-free half-fish mermaid girl? She'd get Aliya
to agree to this and get Kyne to admit he was overreacting in
his suspicions of her interest in those wishes she was granting.
Ha! Before the end of tomorrow he'd admit he was wrong and
he'd go off and spend time spying on other fairies. She wouldn't
have to look into those intense, golden eyes of his and explain her
actions ever again.

But Aliya seemed to be wavering. She'd seemed so eager to
make her wish right at first, but suddenly Raea could sense hesitation. Perhaps she'd pushed her too hard. Mermaids were con-
servative creatures, not given to risk or adventure. Maybe she'd
better let the girl get a little more comfortable with this outra-
geous idea, let things sink in a bit and let the desire for passion
have time to work on her.

Yes, Aliya seemed truly affected by the human's desire. She
cared for him, in fact. When asked to make an immediate decision she might shrink back and decline, but if Raea gave her some
time, she felt fairly certain the girl's curiosity and interest in the
human would win out. Raea just had to handle her carefully.

* * *

Aliya warred with her conflicted emotions. Could Raea truly be
offering her such a wondrous opportunity? She would be with
Devin in the way that he wanted! She could touch his soul *and* his
body, and he could be satisfied as he desired. His pain would abate,
and so would hers. She would understand the full ways of desire.

It was a terrifying proposition, of course. To be made human?
Completely against the Great Code. What would her mother say
if she learned of it? The consequences could be enormous. Aliya
could be expelled from the community.

But that would happen only if anyone found out. Surely she could hide things for just twenty-four hours, couldn't she? No one would suspect, so they'd never think to probe her mind for such a thing. And she could be with Devin, truly *with* him in every human way.

The fairy was offering something Aliya almost could not refuse. She wanted that human so badly...yet everything was at stake. How could she accept?

"But you probably shouldn't decide right away," Raea announced. "After all, perhaps you don't care for that human so much."

"I *do* care for him. I can feel him like no other human I've ever encountered."

"So you want to do this? Well, I can't let you. No, I'm afraid this wish is a bad idea, after all."

"No! Please, let me wish for this, Raea. I want to."

"Hmm, I'll tell you what. I want you to think about it for a while. Contemplate your life, cold and damp, swimming around alone all day in this big murky lake. Then consider what you'd be doing, how you would be joining that human in ways most mermaids can't imagine, experiencing all the pleasures of human desire. If that is truly what you want after you've thought about it, then I will grant your wish."

Oh, but the way the fairy described it was so tantalizing, indeed. She wanted Devin so badly she could taste him even now. Yes, she could carefully consider, but she knew already which way her desire was leaning.

"All right. I will think about it. When must I decide?"

"Tonight, just as the sun is setting on the horizon," Raea replied. "If his boat returns, meet me nearby. If you truly want me to grant you your wish, then I will consider. But remember, it is for twenty-four hours only, and then all will be returned to the way it should be. You will be a mermaid again, and he will forget his obsession and return to his life on the land."

"And he will forget about me? About everything?"

"Yeah, that's the deal. I agree it doesn't sound like a perfect happily ever after, but it will solve our immediate problems."

"He'll be spared from the Old Revenge. He'll have some hours of pleasure and will be released from his obsession. And you are certain he'll forget me? He won't waste away searching for something he'll never find?"

"Well, not thanks to this Old Revenge thing," Raea replied. "He's still a human, and they are prone to a lot of useless pining. No doubt he'll be right back out here with one of his females."

The thought of Devin with another woman cut into her, but of course she had no right, no reason to feel anything like that. Perhaps, though, if she gave him all that he wanted, his loneliness would be lessened even once she was gone. Perhaps he would not need so many wishes with other females. She would certainly keep that in her thoughts.

"Very well. I will contemplate all of this and will meet you at sunset to give you my answer."

"Fine. I will look for you then," the fairy said, then added off-handedly, "if you decide to come back."

"I will. I promise you that."

They said brief good-byes and Raea went off to grant more wishes somewhere. Aliya sank down into the water. The fairy had been right; it was cold and murky. Aliya did spend most of her days alone, just as she said. It was simply the way of things and she'd never thought anything of it. Not until now, at least.

Now that she'd met Devin. After feeling his touch, knowing what true warmth felt like, she could hardly feel satisfied with the life she'd always known. How could this be? Had her interaction with him already changed her in some way, even without the help of Fairy Dust? What could this mean for her future?

If she already felt so very changed, how would she feel after twenty-four hours experiencing him as a human? Would she be content to return to her life? Perhaps Raea was right and she ought to think long and hard about this.

The sun was sending bright beams down into the water now and she realized it was time for Morning Gathering. This was not a mandatory thing, but perhaps given the circumstances she ought to show up. Not only would it be a good idea to present herself and assure everyone that all things in her watch area were quite well, but the community would be less likely to notice if she did not show up tomorrow. Yes, she would present herself today and use the opportunity to truly evaluate her options.

Was this life worth rejecting Raea's offer, or would she dare risk everything for twenty-four hours of the sweetest imaginable wish?

She left her watch area and swam along the lake bottom. The upper shelf dropped off dramatically and she followed the sheer sides down, down into the darkest depths of the Great Lake. Sunlight couldn't penetrate here, but she had other senses that were every bit as accurate as sight. She could feel the rock formations around her as surely as if she could see them. Vibrations from currents and creatures resounded around her, forming detailed images in her brain so that she could maneuver as surely as if she had been at the surface.

The gathering was already under way. She could feel the minds gathered in the semicircular cleft of the deepest valley in this part of the lake. The erratic formations in this area made it the best possible place for those like her to make their home. Humans had no reason to visit this area, and their sensing devices were inaccurate when mapping the floor. The Veil extended around this area, made strong by the energy from mermaid minds, keeping their world perfectly hidden. They could gather at will and never worry about human detection.

She felt her mother's mind greet her as she moved into the circle. Mother was nearby, along with some of her sisters and aunts and several dozen other mermaids who were well known to Aliya. She sent a friendly greeting back to her mother and was glad to feel that heavy matters were being discussed today. Her mother was distracted by these and paid no mind to any of the things lingering deeper in Aliya's mind.

She turned her focus to listening, taking in the matters at hand.

It seemed one of her older sisters was being commended for rescuing a human child who had fallen unseen off a boat. If Teela had not been carefully monitoring, it could have been several more minutes before the family aboard even noticed he was gone. Acting immediately, Teela created a disturbance that alerted the humans to the child's distress and he was saved without anyone suspecting mermaid intervention.

What could have turned into a tragedy that brought entire fleets of search and rescue vehicles out here had been heroically averted. The child was preserved, the humans were happy, and the mermaids did not have to worry about being discovered. Teela truly did deserve her commendation.

Mother was exceedingly proud of her, as of course all of them were. When one mermaid acted honorably, then honor was brought to the whole community. Aliya sent her thoughts of pride and appreciation to her older sister, which was the proper thing to do. Teela gave a casual reply and the discussion continued.

Other matters were brought up—concern over a new human facility that was being constructed and would most likely mean the introduction of certain chemical compounds into the water, and a plan was decided upon for monitoring this. Mother was especially gifted in areas that dealt with things of this nature, so her opinion was sought and given. No further attention was paid to Aliya, and when the time for general reports was announced, she needed to do nothing more than send thoughts of peace and assurance.

No one asked her any questions and she was happily ignored beyond anything more than polite, superficial greetings. This was the usual way of things. No one had any reason at all to worry that she might have extraordinary things on her mind and she gave them no reason to probe. It was a typical Morning Gathering and she should have left the lake floor with a sense of contentment and belonging.

She did not. As the group pleasantly disbanded with the usual polite well-wishing all around, she took an extra moment to reach out for her mother. Somehow, she felt the need for that extra touch from one of her kind. Mother responded, quite pleased, actually, and even took the extra effort to move closer to Aliya so that she felt her presence almost tangibly in the dark waters.

"I am happy to find you here, Aliya," Mother said. "You are proud of your sister?"

"Very proud, Mother," she replied. "Teela is a credit to you."

"To all of us. As are you, of course. No doubt you will have your day of honor at one of our gatherings. All of my children give benefit to the community."

"Yes, Mother. I . . . we try to do right."

"All of my daughters make my name great in the community,

just as my mother's name is still revered to this day. It is good to connect with you, Aliya. I am happy you are well."

"Thank you, Mother," she replied, hoping the niggling worries of guilt in the back of her mind weren't obvious in the vibrations around her.

But Mother's mind was too caught up with Teela's success and the concerns of the community for her to notice the things Aliya was keeping carefully hidden. Her life here was good, and she was proud of her mother and the honor of her heritage. The community was peaceful and she could count on everyone to work tirelessly to preserve that. Everything was calm and predictable and just the way it should be. She had nothing to fear and a long, secure future ahead of her.

Was she really going to sacrifice all of that for twenty-four hours with a human? She was only a mermaid, after all. They were not a species known for courage and impulsive behavior. She knew nothing of passion and risk. Her life revolved around responsibility and honor; they were the only reasons she had been given life. How could she possibly consider anything outside of that?

* * *

Raea made another pass over the boat. Yes, the human had returned to the lake just as on so many evenings before. The sun shone as a huge, fiery ball resting on the horizon. The man's wishes filled the air around Raea and she knew he was in the full throes of his lustful fixation.

He wanted that mermaid. But where was she? Had Raea gambled too much? Maybe she shouldn't have let the girl swim away, to go off and think of things all day. It had only given her time to forget her desire, to remember who she was and what she was. Now Raea was left with a sex-crazed human and a wager that was nowhere near being won. How was she going to locate another virgin in the short time their arrangement allowed for?

But wait…what was that in the water? By the Skies, it was Aliya. So, the mermaid had shown up, after all. Raea darted down toward the glinting surface of the water to greet her.

"I was afraid you might not show up," she said as Aliya burst through the surface.

"I very nearly didn't. I kept thinking how my actions would dishonor my people."

"So you aren't going to make your wish? You can see the human is here, and I assure you, he hasn't forgotten."

"No, I can feel that. He…he is making his desires very well known."

"His desire for you," Raea added. "He's been sending up wishes all day long."

"And you haven't granted them?"

"He's wishing for you. And he didn't bring a female with him tonight."

"He didn't?"

"No. As we worried, he's truly obsessed. I don't know what else to do, if you won't help him through this…"

"I will help him! That's why I'm here."

Raea tried not to look smug. Things had gone her way, after all. She would win her bet and Kyne would give up his suspicions of her. She'd be doing a good deed for her friend, too. Aliya really seemed to care about this human. It would be a great relief to know that he would give up his silly obsession. Yes, all the way around she was pleased with her accomplishment.

"You're ready now?" she clarified.

"Yes. I'm ready. I can't leave him in his obsession, Raea. It's my fault for letting him see me, so it's my responsibility to help him now. You will grant me my wish, won't you?"

"Yes, of course. As long as you understand the terms."

"I do. Twenty-four hours, then everything is back to the way it should be. He is released and he won't die."

"Not from that stupid Old Revenge, at least. Go ahead; make your wish."

Aliya beamed. She held herself up very straight in the water and met Raea's eyes with a huge, confident smile.

"I wish to become human for one day and spend it with Devin so he can have enough of me and forget all about that terrible obsession and be safe from the Old Revenge."

Raea smiled. Ah, easy as cake. The wager was hers for the winning. Kyne was an idiot.

"Okay, sweetheart. Now, hold on to your gills because this is kind of a biggie. I don't think I've ever done a mermaid before!"

Chapter Eight

It was nearly sunset and Devin urged the boat to slip faster through the water. Ridiculous, he knew, but Aliya was out there. All day he'd tried to make sense of things and he finally ended up leaving the office early and heading for the boat.

He had to find her. Was she real or simply his fantasy? He had no idea. His body thought she was real. Did that make any sense? Absolutely not. He didn't care.

So here he was, sailing aimlessly out into the water, convinced somewhere in this vast expanse he would find a mermaid. A real one. Positively insane. But of course he couldn't stop himself. He had to find her.

How long had it been since he'd brought the boat out here alone? He couldn't recall. After he lost Judith he'd been afraid to be alone out here. It would have been too tempting to give himself over to the water and never go back, so he always came out only when he brought a guest.

And few of them ever got a second invitation. He hadn't wanted anyone to become familiar, hadn't wanted to get used to a face. It was better that way.

But not today. Today all he could think of was Aliya. All he could see in his mind was her face. Now, with the first hint of pink seeping into the late afternoon sky, hers was the only face that was familiar to him. Even Judith's features were obscured, tangled in his memory with pale skin and crystalline eyes that matched the lake.

Somehow his little mermaid had taken him over.

Had it been merely the physical connection? Possibly. That had been indescribable. But that wasn't the whole of it. No, there was more than just lust.

Sure, he wanted her. His body had been taut, tense, anticipating her all day. But there was another aspect he couldn't even grasp. Something inside her, that psychic thing she had going on. Her mind had managed to wrap itself around him and hadn't let go, not even after he'd slept a few hours, not after a day at work, and not now.

The fact that he would find her was as undeniable as the fact that he must breathe. Aliya was here. And he would find her. Eventually. Somehow.

"I just wish I knew where she was."

A fish splashed beside his boat. Light from the sun's sinking rays played like Fairy Dust on the water. And Devin's eyes shifted to a formless glow, some sort of shape that appeared in shadow just off to the north. It hovered over the water. No…his eyes were playing tricks. It was in the water. He hadn't noticed it before, but now he couldn't take his eyes from it.

A tree? Driftwood? Out here? Maybe, but there was something more, something far more precious than the floating bits of vegetation. He knew without thinking that Aliya was there. He wasn't sure exactly how he knew it, but the certainty was there. In a heartbeat he had scrambled the boat to port and glided toward the floating object.

It was a downed tree, weathered and gnarled, floating nicely on the glassy surface. He butted gently up against it and tossed out a rope. The knobby trunk snagged easily and with barely any effort he dragged it up close.

There, cradled in the branches all silent and limp, was a pale form with long, trailing hair wrapped like a blanket around her. Even the sunset failed to tint her face with color. His gut knotted as for an instant he worried she was dead. He secured the rope and slid down the steps on the side of his boat to reach her.

One touch, and he knew. She was alive. The breath caught in her chest and she arched in a sudden, desperate attempt to draw air. She moaned.

He leaned to scoop her into his arms. She was heavier than he remembered, but it hardly took any effort to pull her up onto the deck. He laid her out and knelt beside her, rubbing her and talking gently, begging her to come back to him.

And she did.

Those eyes slowly opened, and she smiled. He sagged with the relief of knowing she was all right. He touched her face.

"Aliya."

She put her hand over his and her lips parted to speak. But instead another moan escaped and he saw pain in her eyes. She looked down, her face showing something he hadn't expected. She was afraid.

She wouldn't meet his eyes so he followed her gaze. She was staring at her legs. Without thinking he skimmed one hand gently over them, seeking for injury.

"Are you hurt? Can you feel anything?" he asked.

Then he stopped. Reality dawned on him.

"My God! Aliya, you have legs?"

She smiled at him and reached one long, slender white arm up toward him. He let her caress his cheek.

"Hello, Devin. They're for you—my legs."

He had more than a few questions. What was happening? Her nakedness he had expected; somehow he'd never bothered to picture Aliya with clothes on. But legs! Holy shit, she had legs.

Gorgeous legs. Long, creamy, sculpted legs. Every curve, every muscle, was perfectly defined and oh, so soft. He was feasting his eyes on them. He was touching them. He was picturing them wrapped around him, capturing him in...

Oh God, she was a woman now, wasn't she? Gone was the tail, the satin fish skin he'd stroked the night before. Today she was a woman, human and hot and made just for him. Wisps of angel-soft hair curled at the juncture of her legs, and he knew that beyond he would find a haven of warmth just waiting for him to sink himself into.

He was ready now. Jeez, was he ready.

"I will serve you better this way, I think," she said.

Her voice was small, but her smile was warm. He dragged his attention away from the throbbing in his groin and the banquet stretched out before him only to find himself drowning in her eyes. Had she been this beautiful last night? How could she possibly have improved?

Still, he couldn't overlook the fear that lingered in the edges of her smile. She was afraid. Of him? Of what he was obviously planning to do with her? The idea sliced into him like a wound.

"Aliya," he said carefully. "You're safe with me."

"Oh, I know, Devin," she said and he heard the sincerity. "Come, there's not much time. Let me give you pleasure."

He was probably the most stupid man on the planet, but he decided to talk first.

"Wait, we have time. I'm not going anywhere."

"No, Devin. Please don't talk. Kiss me again. Kiss me like last night," she insisted.

Well, so much for talking. He'd done as much of that as he could. Aliya's arms slid around his neck and he was helpless against her. Willingly he bent to taste her once more.

There was no doubt in his mind, however, that once more would be far from enough.

* * *

He was being so gentle, so careful with her. She'd never known a human to be so kind. Generally they seemed too intent on their own goals, seeking to serve their own whims and desires. Really, though, her experience with them was limited. Devin was the only one she'd ever gotten to know this well. He was the first she'd ever wanted to.

And now she wanted to know him still better. She studied him, let her hungry eyes rove over his features. Here on the dry deck of his boat he was fully in his element. She could see the deep, deep blue of his eyes with little flecks of gold, like sparks inside them. She memorized the planes of his face, the tiny lines at the corners of his eyes, the way his lips curled and tensed as he spoke softly over her. And she longed to run her fingers through his thick, dark hair as the wind tousled it, teasing her. Would he welcome her touch?

Now that she was out of the soothing, encompassing connection of the water, she had a hard time touching his thoughts. Air was a poor transmitter for such things. She had to rely on her other senses, what she could see in his face or feel in his lips as he bent to kiss her. And that told her she was welcome, indeed.

Ah, but she loved his kisses. His lips were soft, and that had surprised her. He seemed so solid, so set. To find that his mouth was supple and pliable tuned her into depths she had not detected.

And today his kiss was something more than the careless passion it had been last night. Today he was convinced of her existence—he was seeing her as he would another human. She was not just a fantasy creature to him; today he cared about *her*.

That made the wanting even stronger. She felt his desire, not just the hardened flesh she could feel beneath his thin clothing, but she could feel desire in his hands, in his arms, in his lips. It matched her own.

Yesterday she had not understood. She had reacted to him primarily because of his own feelings being telegraphed to her. But today, in this new human form, she understood.

And she ached to have him even nearer.

She circled her arms around him. His mouth held hers captive and his tongue parted her lips. She gave him access freely, as she had done last night, but today there was no need to give him air. She was able to let herself get lost in the sensations.

And such sensations they were! As his tongue grazed the tender insides of her mouth, giddy, tingling jolts fired through her. They coursed from her mouth, down her neck, and spread across her shoulders. As Devin's mouth worked over hers the sensation flowed down and down, until her whole body flamed with wanting him.

Then he began his assault in earnest.

"You're so perfect, Aliya," he said.

She pressed herself against him, raising herself up off the floor of the boat as much as she could. She had to be closer to him, touching him with every part of her skin. But she felt clumsy and unsure in this new body, dry in the air and out of her reassuring water.

He must have realized her distress because his kiss ended. It was not abrupt, but she felt his departure from her mouth as a sort of ache. She needed him touching her, didn't he know that?

"I'm not a very good host, am I?" he said with his beautiful smile. "You cannot be comfortable out here."

"I'm comfortable with you, Devin," she said.

He laughed and leaned back to gaze at her. It was so wonderful the way he loved to look at her. She'd seen that in his eyes last night, but she feared he had been uneasy regarding her nonhuman parts. Now there was nothing to keep him from enjoying her fully, and the light of anticipation was bright in his eyes.

She knew what he wanted and she was thrilled to be able to provide it.

But the legs were ungainly as she tried to move them to provide the access he needed. New muscles reacted in ways she was uncertain about; new skin buzzed with unfamiliar stimuli. It was wonderful and disappointing. She wanted to be so perfect for him.

"Devin," she invited, shifting her hand from his skin to her own. She touched herself in the hollow of the new human body. "Is this as it should be for you?"

She found herself warm there. Life in the lake was not generally warm, but this new human addition to herself was warm. Devin would like that. She slid her fingers past the tuft of hair and investigated further. The warmth became heat, and she pulled her hand back in surprise as more of the tingling jolts radiated from her touch.

"What is it?" he said, questioning her sudden movement.

"I felt ... strange," she said. It was impossible to put into words what she had felt. Not pain, but not any sort of pleasure she'd encountered before. At least, not entirely. She had felt something similar in the water with Devin last night.

"It was like last night, how you made me feel then. But different now," she continued.

"Different? How so?"

She smiled. He seemed so much to want to understand. "Last night I felt you, how you felt. Today, it is me."

He did understand. "So you don't slip into this pretty little body every day, I take it?"

"No. This is…special."

She knew he wanted more explanation, but hoped he wouldn't ask for it. She was afraid if she told him it was only for a short time that he would be upset, that the idea of it would cause him greater pain.

It was clear his obsession for her was very strong. Raea had been right. Aliya could see it in Devin's eyes, feel it in his touch. Even out of the water that carried thoughts and vibrations so clearly to her, she could still read his mind. He was consumed by his desire for her and could think of nothing but wanting to be with her. His obsession was complete. If she tried to warn him of the consequences now, he would simply not hear it. In fact, he might become even more determined not to let her go.

Which was just as well. She didn't want to think of the dangers, the Old Revenge seeking him out. By the Deep, she couldn't think of that just now. She was human and her body felt everything as a human's did, perhaps even more so, since it was so new. Devin wanted her, but she wanted him just as badly. Nothing would interrupt her time with him. Here in the air, with the setting sun warming her naked human flesh and Devin watching her with dark, smoldering eyes, she felt her obsession grow just as powerful as his. Twenty-four hours with him would never be close to enough to satisfy her.

She pushed herself to sitting. It was a lot harder out of the water, but the muscles in these new legs were strong. Acclimating herself to her new abilities, she folded the long legs and drew her knees up toward her chin. She had from now until sunset tomorrow to put this body to good use. Well, no need to dawdle.

Shifting to lean forward, she could see the whole thing: legs, feet, knees, and—just barely—that mysterious dark, wet center at the crux of it all. The opening for Devin's appendage. She couldn't help but smile and enjoy this strange new feeling of power.

"Amazing, isn't it?" she asked him after a long moment.

He was quiet, at a loss. Finally he found his voice. "Yeah. Amazing."

She scooted toward him and reached to touch the silky soft hair that haloed his chest. She never expected dry to feel so enticing. Her fingers trailed over him, across his chest muscles and around the little circles of nipple he had there. He was a powerful man; solid and tight, but so soft and pleasant to touch. Such a combination of conflict. Were all humans like this, or only Devin? It didn't matter. She would never care for any other this way.

Chapter Nine

"Come on," he said, taking her hands in his. "Let's try out that new body of yours."

To her amazement he pushed up onto his feet. He was so tall! He still held her hands as she sat there on the boat, but he seemed a giant looming over her. In the water they had felt so much more equal. She had a heartbeat of fear looking up at him, but his smile dispelled it.

Devin would never use his size to harm her. She was safe. With one deep breath, she put her weight into his hands and planted her new feet on the floor.

And then he pulled her up. She was standing! It was as if she'd risen up into the sky. She was surrounded by air, with just the bottoms of her feet touching the boat. The water was far, far below.

But Devin was holding her. That made it all right. Devin wouldn't let her crumple back to the hard wood of the boat. She leaned into him and forced a smile.

"Remarkable," she said when she could.

"Don't get out much, huh?" he said.

"I've never been out; not like this."

He was watching her face, studying her. His hands were warm where they made contact with her skin. There was no water between them, nothing but sun-warmed skin against skin. She shifted position and thrilled at the lightning sensations as his body hair grazed her.

He noticed her excitement and it seemed to spark his own. Leaning against him, she shifted again to feel the increasing bulk of his hardening appendage. He noticed that, too.

"You've got a one-track mind," he said.

I just don't want to waste any precious minutes with you, Devin, she wanted to cry out.

But she wouldn't say that. She wanted him to believe they could go on forever, if that's what he wanted. It's what she wanted.

"I want to be with you," she said. "Really with you."

"Can you walk?" he asked.

She was confused. *Walk?* They were on a boat. Where should he want her to walk?

"I, um, I don't know," she said honestly.

"I'll help you," he said and began leading her toward a doorway that appeared to lead to an opening down inside the boat.

She found her legs did indeed know how to walk, graceless though it was. She was glad for Devin's sturdy body beside her when they got to the opening, though. The flat surface of the deck gave way to nothing. She halted.

"These are stairs," he said as she hesitated. "Take just one step at a time. Hold on to me."

Hold on to him? That would be easy. But negotiating this passage...How did humans keep track of all these gangling body parts? And what sort of invention were these stairs? She was afraid she'd fall and embarrass them both.

Why was he bringing her in here? He seemed to want her, she

was certain of it. Things had been just fine there on the deck, outside in the pink glow of the setting sun. Why didn't he just hold her and touch her and let her give him pleasure? Why all this talking and moving about?

Humans were so hard to understand sometimes.

Still, she knew she could trust him. She took a deep breath and allowed him to lead, making it down into a very human room at the bottom of the wooden walkway called stairs. It felt quite alien and exotic. Larger than expected, too. Funny, she'd never realized there was so much inside these things. All she'd ever really considered was the outside of a boat, the part that kept the water out.

From the look of things, though, humans appreciated the inside. And it seemed they brought much of their lives from the land out here onto their boats. Furniture, utensils, all sorts of gadgets of varying sizes, shapes, and textures littered the place. Did they need all of this for surviving here on the water, or did they always need these things, even on the dry? She could only guess at the purpose for most of it.

All she knew was it was very distracting. She wanted to be wrapping her new body around Devin, feeling him against her, in her. It seemed far too crowded inside this dry room for that.

"Let me get you something to drink," he was saying as he followed closely behind her.

"Drink?" she asked.

"You know, a drink. Juice, pop, beer…bottled water?"

It was unintelligible to her and she shrugged. He stared at her like she'd lost her mind. Well, that wasn't part of this wonderful wish she'd made!

"You don't *drink*? Anything?"

"I'll do whatever you want me to, but I'm afraid I don't know what this drink is."

He ran his hand through his hair. She liked his hair, such an unusual color. Dark, like the wood from an old ship, but full of sparks of color when the light hit it. She stepped closer to him so she could touch it.

"You really do come from another world." He sighed.

She pulled her hand back before she'd made contact with his hair. What was that in his eyes now? Was he disappointed in her? No! She didn't want that. She was human now; she couldn't disappoint him.

"I'll drink for you, Devin," she said quickly. "Please, just show me how. I want to make you happy."

He made a warm growling sound and wrapped her in his arms. She liked that. The shirt he had on was open and she pressed her body as close to his wonderful, firm chest as possible. The way he smiled was anything but disappointed.

"You don't have to drink for me," he said with almost a laugh. "I guess living in water you don't really have to do that."

When he saw her confusion he explained, his breath warm against her ear. "It's like eating, but it's liquid. We have to drink fluids to keep our bodies hydrated."

"Oh! *That's* drinking? I never thought of that. Yes, you would be very dry inside, wouldn't you?"

His body shook with laughter and she knew it was at her expense, but she didn't mind. As long as he would just keep holding her against him this way.

"And it's something we do to be polite. When we have company, we always offer a drink. I guess it was force of habit."

She leaned back just enough to look at him. "And you were being polite for me. That's very sweet, Devin. But I don't need a drink. Maybe later. Probably later."

He was studying her again, like he just couldn't figure her out.

Well, she certainly felt the same about him. He still wanted her, so why wasn't he kissing her again? There must be more, something about this human politeness that she was missing.

"Is it wrong for me not to want your drink, Devin?" she asked finally. "I want to be polite for you, too."

"Jeez, Aliya. Coming onto my boat naked and staring at me like that is just about as polite as it gets, I would say."

"You like my being naked? I wasn't sure. You keep looking at me with a strange expression, and I see you are wearing clothes on your legs."

"It's the polite thing to do, but yeah. I like your being naked."

"I'm glad."

"I just…damn it. I just don't know what to do with you, Aliya."

"You don't? I'm not like the other females you've brought here?"

"Uh, no. Not by a long shot."

Well, that didn't make her happy. "I'm not? What's wrong? I was told I'd be human, really human in every way!"

She was going to kill her fairy friend for making her wrong.

But he just laughed and held her tighter. "No, don't worry. You look just fine to me. All I meant was you're such a different kind of person from the women I usually…well, you know. You're special, Aliya. And I like that. A lot."

"I like you, too, Devin." She snuggled closer to him. "Is there more politeness we need to do, or can you join with me now?"

When she met his eyes he didn't seem to know what to say. That was good. Conversation wasn't what either of them really wanted, she could tell.

In the dry it was harder to read Devin's thoughts, but she was becoming attuned to them. With her body resting closely against his she could feel his heartbeat as well as the emotions that surged inside him. His desire was strong, and went beyond the very physical response that was so very obvious. Aliya tingled with her own response.

She was learning this new body and what all the sensations and reactions meant. Much of what she felt was foreign and still unexplainable, but one thing was certain; this body wanted to join with Devin. Badly. And soon.

She slid against him, feeling his hardened appendage through his clothing. He let out a deep breath and heat radiated from his body.

It wasn't necessary to think anymore. Aliya ran her hands over his chest, across his shoulders. She wanted to feel him, the strong arms and the solid flesh of his body. He seemed to have no objection, so she set to work on the clothing covering his lower portions. They wouldn't slide off as easily as she hoped, and he laughed again, putting his hands over hers to help.

"We have to undo the zipper first," he said and showed her what he was talking about.

He undid a sort of fastener, then helped her to slide a small metal contraption down. The whole concept of clothing fascinated her—always had. Now the idea of getting this particular human out of his clothing held even greater allure.

At last her fingers made contact with the heat of his skin. Ah, his appendage was free. She cupped her hand around it in an almost desperate caress. Would he come inside her at last?

He breathed again, loudly, and leaned into her hand. She grasped him firmly, pulling him toward her. It was much more difficult without the water to buoy them, but she had to get him inside. She stood on tiptoe, trying to reach.

His arms tightened around her.

"Aliya," he said, but she wasn't sure if it was aloud this time or if she had become more aware of his thoughts.

He brought his lips to hers and kissed her. Deeply. She surrendered to them and let his tongue brush inside her mouth. That, too, was a devastating sensation. Her knees felt weak and she had to rely on his arms to hold her upright.

His kiss was long, and drew deep inside her until she was sure he was searching her soul for whatever secrets she still held. She followed his lead and glided her tongue along his, ignoring everything but the warm vibration that began at her lips and spread through her whole body, down to gather in a trembling heat between her legs.

She huddled closer into him, holding tight and guiding his appendage toward that heat. The wanting was too much. Nothing mattered but getting Devin inside her.

"Come on," he said, breaking off the kiss almost abruptly.

He was backing her toward the wall, and she was glad for something to lean on. He would hold her there and plunge himself into her. She strained to hold herself up higher, thrusting her throbbing center toward him. Any second now she would feel it…

But the wall behind her gave way. Devin had reached around her and released some sort of latch that caused it to swing open. It was not a wall but a door, paneled with wood like the rest of this boat. Behind it was another small room.

She staggered back but Devin held her. She wanted to ask what was happening, but his lips had taken over hers again and the waves of sensation this brought were washing over her. She barely noticed when her backward steps were halted by a long, low object behind her.

Instantly Devin had her up in his arms. Her feet were off the floor and he was holding her. His kiss never stopped, even as he was lowering her down to lie on something soft. Her body sank back into fabric, which was smooth like an oyster shell, but soft and comfortable. It molded around her body and it smelled like Devin.

"Satin sheets," he said as she rubbed the fabric between her fingers.

She nodded, as if his words held meaning for her.

He smiled. "Now just lie back and relax."

She did. Right away she knew this position was more accommodating for joining. Devin was over her, stretching his tall body out beside her. The smooth fabric against her body allowed her to wriggle her body to the perfect place. She felt his appendage pressed against her at just the right spot. All she would have to do was push herself toward him and…

He bent forward and pulled one of her nipples into his mouth. Her nerves responded with a flash of sensation like a storm over the water. She trembled and tingled with electricity that only grew stronger as his hands roamed over her body. Every part of her was alive to him; the slightest move of his hand across her belly, the gentle demands of his mouth on her breast.

Then he was touching her where she most wanted to be touched. It was so wonderful, so overwhelming, that she cried out. She never wanted him to stop touching her. She wanted more.

She arched her back to get closer to the wonderful pressure of his hand. He obliged, letting her move against him until two fingers dipped inside her. She breathed out her delight. If only it were more…she had to have more of him.

"You're so ready for me," he said, leaving her nipple to whisper into her ear.

"Please, Devin, I need you!"

She was begging but didn't care. She'd do anything to get him to fill her, to stop this spiraling tumble into desire that was almost painful.

He shifted position and for a moment she was afraid he was leaving. Her fingers dug into his skin, clinging for dear life. She pushed against the soft platform beneath her to bring herself closer to him.

"Devin...please..."

But he just moved over her again, this time directly in position so that she could feel his hardness against her.

"Shh, I'm not going anywhere," he said gently.

She knew he would not leave her aching this way, but the burning inside her was so strong she could barely think straight. Her senses felt heightened, her skin prickled everywhere, and the hot juncture between her brand-new legs throbbed for something she knew only he could provide her.

"Come inside me, Devin," she pleaded.

"Don't worry." He smiled and kissed her lips again. "I'll take care of you, Aliya. But you haven't done this before and it might..."

She didn't wait to hear what he had to say. Using those wonderful legs she pushed herself up toward him. She felt his appendage, hot and solid. She shuddered with a thrill as she felt him press against her. It was what she needed more than breath itself.

Holding him urgently, she wrapped her legs around him. His appendage was huge; at least that was her impression. It would fill her entirely and finally give her what she wanted so very badly. Why was he not helping her? Her fingers raked his back, forcing him to join with her.

"Devin, I need you now."

"Oh God, Aliya," he said. His resistance was gone—at last—and he drove himself into her.

She gasped for air. It was beyond her imagining. Her body was overcome by a brilliant white flash of sensation: pain, pleasure, longing, desire, joy. Devin was inside her.

Legs tight around him, she gripped him with every muscle she possessed. How could she ever let him go? How could she ever live apart from him again?

But any thought of the future was lost as Devin moved. Slowly, he pulled back. Her nerves flamed at the sensation. Before she could beg him not to leave, though, he thrust forward again. She moaned.

"Aliya." He breathed over her. "Is this all right?"

"It's perfect," she said, letting her eyes drift shut to concentrate all her energy on feeling.

"You're so tight, so wet…," he said, but went back to silence as he continued the gentle motion of thrusts and tantalizing retreats.

Aliya rocked with him. Any initial discomfort was gone and forgotten as Devin became the entire universe for her. She met his pace, feeling herself hover in a place halfway between today and eternity. Colors swirled behind her eyelids.

Gradually she was aware of a change in their tempo. Her pulse was speeding up, and Devin's motions matched it. His thrusts became more insistent, plunging farther and farther into her, connecting with parts of her she could never have imagined.

Something was welling up inside her, too. She felt it building, growing. As Devin's breathing became more labored she found herself holding more and more tightly to him. Was she even breathing at all? She didn't know.

He was fairly pounding at her now, faster and faster. She was unable to control her body and simply clung to him and waited. Something was happening; she was being washed away by a tidal wave and had no desire to save herself. She wanted the wave. She'd let it crash over her with all its force and drive her downward until she was left to float helpless in its wake.

And there it came, just as big and violent as she knew it would be. Her body reacted, arching and writhing under Devin's continuing onslaught.

She was loud. "Devin...oh! By the Depth of the Deep, don't stop ever!"

But then the wave hit him, too. She felt it, both in the physical spasms that wracked him and in the wild emotions and images that coursed through his thoughts. They surged together, her cries echoing with his fierce growl. At last, he collapsed down on top of her. Finally she understood the human fixation on this all-consuming act, the sounds she'd heard when Devin had been with his many partners, the urgency she'd sensed in their vibrations.

This time his fixation had been on *her*, the sounds had been her moans of passion, and the urgency had been of their own making. It was wonderful. Amazing. Everything she could have hoped for. And she wanted to do it again.

Chapter Ten

Kyne the Summer Fairy fought it as long as he could, but finally he gave in. Even the air around him smelled like passion. He had to follow it, and he did. His wings flared in the breeze and he flew.

The scent and the sensing led him back out over the lake. Somewhere out there, lovers were entwined in that horrible, wonderful thing humans did. Their joining, mating, sex…whatever they liked to call it. Making love, even. That had a nice ring, but Kyne couldn't quite believe it fully described what went on.

What humans did was primitive and carnal—a thing of earth and earth creatures. Creatures of the Air only ever spoke of it with distain and raised eyebrows. It was clearly nothing a fairy should be interested in.

By the Skies, how he'd tried not to be.

But he was. His body craved it; his mind dwelled on it. When he was near humans doing it, strange vibrations resonated in the air and he felt it. Then he reacted.

Kyne hated himself for his weakness. He threw a hundred accusations and taunts at himself. Damn this burning in his blood, his imperfect fairy body that betrayed him like this.

Yet here he was, helpless to keep from seeking out the vicarious release he got from nearness to the humans. He would find them, then soak up those strange and alien feelings that would surround him in their vicinity. It was the only way he had found to get some relief from this desire that continued to build up inside him.

He only hated to think what would happen when even this proved not enough. He knew beyond all doubt that eventually the foreign urgings would grow too strong to be satisfied by simply being near the humans and their passion. Someday his body and his mind would finally ruin him in the eyes of Fairykind.

He didn't like the idea of being exiled, but there was a worse worry. How far would he let things go before the others would realize his problem? And who would he drag down with him?

One pink Wish Fairy was immediately in his mind. Again.

No, he'd never do that to Raea. She deserved better. He wouldn't think of her that way...except that he *did* think of her that way. He could imagine everything quite plainly, as a matter of fact: Raea with her elegant pink wings fluttering over him, moving closer, reaching for him...

By the Clouds, he wasn't going to let himself think about that. It was wrong and he was better than that. He may be half human, but he was half fairy, as well. Fairies—not humans—had been the ones who took his mother in after what that human brute had done to her. They'd welcomed her back under their protection despite her condition, and they'd helped raise him and teach him the Ways.

He was a fairy first and foremost, no matter what tainted blood ran in his veins.

So why did he tremble as the air brought senses of passion to him? By the Skies, he felt it stronger than ever tonight. He closed his eyes and homed in on the source.

There, off to the north of him, he felt the humans. Their passion was strong. He followed it, flapping with all his strength only to pull up to a stop when he saw the boat.

He recognized it. It was the same boat he'd visited last night, drawn there by the same man. One of Raea's wish recipients.

Damn, was she here tonight? He scanned the horizon, the skies above him. No sign of Raea. Thank the Clouds.

He tried to push her from his mind but couldn't. Reveling in the passions he could feel emanating from the boat, it was impossible not to think of Raea. And oh, so sweet.

He dipped lower in the air, closer to the boat. Inside, he could hear the humans now. There were moans of pleasure, murmurs of contentment, and the sounds of bodies moving against each other. It sounded like ecstasy.

There was no excuse for him to be this close to the human vessel, but he moved in ever nearer. He touched it. Tentatively, he hovered beside a window. Did he dare? He shouldn't. But he had to.

He peeked.

The humans were well occupied and didn't notice him, so he stayed, watching in awe. The man was tall and well formed, with dark hair and suntanned skin. He was definitely the same man who had been on this boat last night. The female was slighter, but not like any other human Kyne could ever recall seeing.

She was especially fair. Her hair was almost translucent, and her skin was as pale as if it had never been touched by the sun before. But it was being touched now.

The man ran his hands over her as she made throaty sounds, encouraging him for more. They kissed, they clung to each other, and the man's body drew back, then pushed forward as he entered the woman. She raked his back with her fingernails.

It was beautiful.

Kyne gave in and allowed himself a moment's fantasy. How would it be to have a female come to him that way, willing and open? She would let him touch her, taste her, drive himself into her the way this human male did to this female. It would not be disgusting or criminal. It would be wonderful, and so very, very satisfying.

He faltered, his wings forgetting their rhythm. Damn it all, he knew better than to get so carried away. His body ached, the evidence of his damnable human parentage growing stiff at his groin. And he had no one to spend himself on as the man inside the boat did.

It was stupid to put himself in this position, to follow the leading of passion. He drew in a deep breath, but the air was so full of the lovemaking it made him dizzy. He shouldn't have come here. He should have stayed away—far, far away.

"You're amazing," he heard the man say, his voice thick and lazy.

Kyne tried desperately to calm his pulse and regain control of his wings, but he couldn't help overhear the couple inside the boat.

"You make me feel things I never thought possible," the woman said.

Her voice was like a sigh that floated in the air and hung over the water's surface. It was an odd voice for a human. Where had Kyne heard this sort of voice before?

"And you make me feel things I never thought possible again," the man said. "How did I get so lucky to pluck you out of the water like that?"

"You must have been wishing for it," the woman said, then laughed.

It was just meaningless banter, Kyne supposed, but he couldn't help wonder at the woman's words. The man's next statement was just as intriguing.

"Hell yeah, I was wishing for you all day. I swear, Aliya, after last night I was obsessed with finding you again."

"I know," was all the woman said before she changed the subject. "But now you've found me, Devin. Let's not waste any of our time together."

The man murmured something softly and she giggled. Kyne forced himself not to look, but he was sure they were touching intimately again. His body ached. What he wouldn't give for someone to touch him that way.

"And to think," the man said after a heavy silence, "an hour ago you'd never done this before."

"You've been an excellent teacher," she said.

The woman had been inexperienced. A virgin? And was it a coincidence she'd spoken offhandedly of wishes? Could be. Then again, this man was known to Raea. Kyne suddenly had a feeling he knew a bit of what was going on here.

This was Raea's little virgin already. Had she really won their bet so quickly? Well, obviously this was a man who would have taken the bait easily enough. But how on earth did Raea find the woman and get her involved with him so fast? Kyne needed to get to the bottom of this. Whatever was going on here, something simply did not feel quite right. What had Raea done?

The couple was laughing and whispering endearments. Hard to believe, but Kyne could feel the electricity crackling through the air as their emotions began to escalate toward yet another physical encounter. Did these humans possess some strange telepathy? Or was the passion simply so strong that Kyne was beginning to develop his own? He swallowed back his forbidden emotions and physical response.

"Slow down, honey," the man said with a chuckle. "We've got all the time in the world, don't we?"

She didn't answer. Kyne knew he'd better get away from there while he could, but he hovered, listening just a moment more.

The man was persisting. "Come on, tell me. There isn't some kind of time limit on this, is there?"

"We've got time," the woman said at last. "All the time we'll need."

"Well, all right then. I sure would hate to lose you so soon."

"I'm here for a while," she said, then added sadly, *"Twenty-four hours."*

The man didn't respond. In fact, it seemed he hadn't even heard her last words. Kyne frowned. Actually, he hadn't really heard her speak those words, either. He'd simply been aware of them. It was as if she'd merely thought those words, yet he'd heard them. He was not used to communicating this way, but something about it seemed vaguely familiar...

And then there was another sigh. The woman's sigh swallowed him, wrapping him in her joy and, at the same time, an unspeakable sadness. How could Kyne be so attuned to her thoughts? Everyone knew humans weren't telepathic, and fairies weren't, either. Aside from certain animal species, the only creatures he'd ever encountered with that ability were the mermaids, and obviously this wasn't...

Or was it? By the Skies and all the creatures of the Air, had Raea cheated?

Kyne chanced a quick peek back into the room. The man lay with his arms wrapped around the woman, and she was curled beside him. Her long, nearly white hair tangled around them.

That smooth, pale skin…those green eyes…the way the man was watching her with fascination and awe…her almost tangible thoughts…everything about her could have easily passed for mermaid. She *was* a mermaid. There could be no other explanation.

Somehow Raea had put legs on a mermaid and given her to this human. A mermaid—how devious! Their wager had been about humans and the human drive for sex. It had nothing to do with Veiled creatures. To involve this innocent mermaid was the height of deceit.

Worse yet, it was a vile and cruel thing to do. That poor woman—mermaid—would be shunned by all of her kind if anyone found out about this! How could Raea do this?

Well, if he was trying to get control over his flaming loins, this certainly helped. Anger was rapidly overtaking any feelings of desire he'd been fighting. Anger? No, that was too mild. Blind fury was more like it.

Damnation! He had more than a few choice words to say to Raea. He'd just have to wait a while. If he found her right now, he'd likely wrap his hands around her little pink throat and choke her to death.

Unless she might mention she was interested in some other sort of physical activity…

No! He had to quit thinking about that.

* * *

Raea waited until it was good and dark to go to the boat. Naturally she wanted to give the little lovebirds some time to themselves, plus it really wouldn't do to have anyone see her. Not that anyone would have a clue Aliya was a mermaid.

No, she'd done a fine job of giving that girl legs, and all the other human workings, too. By the Skies, she really was a talented Wish Fairy. Too bad she wouldn't get to show off her handiwork to anyone.

She'd accomplished her goal easily. Aliya made a very pleasant-looking human, and from what Raea saw when she peeked into the cabin of that boat, Devin had more than approved. It was just after midnight, and the couple was sleeping soundly. They were naked, wrapped in each other's arms with sheets tangled and strewn around them. Quite a scene to get the blood pumping, if one were into that sort of display.

It did nothing for her, of course. She could view the whole human sexual encounter completely detached. Her only interest in this was the simple pride in having won Kyne's bet so swiftly. Surely that was the only reason for her great interest in this case and the odd stirring inside her as she peered over the lovers.

Yes, this feeling was nothing more than pride in her accomplishment. She could hardly wait to see the look of defeat on Kyne's face when she told him about it. Hmm, then again, just what was she going to tell him? And what if he questioned her? How was she going to prove to him that she'd won? They hadn't decided on that. Well, she supposed she'd just have to bring him out here and show him. All he'd need was one look at Aliya's smiling, satisfied face and he'd know Raea had won.

That's what she'd do. She'd bring him here and they'd peek in the windows together. He could see for himself the weary satisfaction on the faces of the lovers. He'd hear their contented sighs, notice how they wrapped their sweaty human limbs around each other, see them turn in their sleep and caress each other. Skin was on skin, bodies ground into each other, nipples grew taut, moans and groans and sighs filled the air...

She was suddenly dizzy. Perhaps it might not be a good idea to bring Kyne out here with her. He might question her motives again, not that she had anything to hide. Well, she did, of course, but not what he suspected. He was annoyingly suspicious.

What if he became suspicious of other things, as well? He might figure out Aliya's secret. True, Kyne wasn't exactly the brightest star in the firmament. He was half human, after all, and couldn't be expected to figure things out. She was sure her secret was safe. He'd peep in the window and see nothing more than a sweet, innocent young woman in the arms of her new lover and he'd be forced to agree that she'd won. She'd probably even make him apologize for those horrible accusations he'd made about her questionable preferences when it came to granting wishes. Finally he'd admit she had nothing to be ashamed of.

Now things in the Forbidden Realm would go on just as they had, and no one would be breathing down Raea's neck about which wishes she granted and how much time she spent around humans. Not that she spent too much time with them. It was her job, after all.

Yes, she would go find Kyne. He needed to know about this and she needed to gloat. It wasn't like this was something she could go brag about to just any fairy. But Kyne would understand.

And he'd be impressed. She'd proven her point in record time. He'd have to acknowledge she was more than efficient at what she did. His golden eyes might even fill with respect when he looked at her. She liked his eyes. There was something just a bit different about the heated amber of Kyne's eyes…

Not that Raea was unduly fascinated by them, or any other part of him. Really. Kyne was different. So what? Everyone had unique traits and characteristics. She herself had one wingtip that was slightly more rounded than the others. It was just the way things were. She was not going to get caught up in rumor or speculation. Whatever color Kyne's eyes might appear, he was nothing more than just another fairy to her.

All she cared about was seeing the disappointment of failure in his eyes when she told him how easily she'd won the bet. He'd try to deny his frustration, of course. His eyes would get smoky and he'd order her to prove it. She'd just laugh at him and lead him out here, to the lake. Then she'd smile and point to the couple on the boat, wrapped around each other, moaning and sighing and touching in intimate places.

Places where fairies never touched each other. Places that were usually ignored. Places that Raea never even thought about, except here lately, around Kyne. But that was just healthy curiosity.

Everyone probably wondered about Kyne from time to time. It was only natural, considering the rumors that swirled around him. How could she not wonder? Was he half human? If so, it would stand to reason that he might have certain noticeable human attributes. It was perfectly understandable, then, that she might occasionally steal a quick glance at Kyne, at that area of his anatomy. A couple times she even thought she noticed…

But that was ridiculous. If Kyne really did have these human attributes—*well-developed* human attributes—it wouldn't be a secret. The Fairy Council surely would know about such a thing. His fairy parent would have been chastised and Kyne would have been sent away somewhere. Half-breeds were never tolerated. Fairies had distanced themselves from this sort of mingling eons ago.

Despite the fact that fairies and humans had some similar basic physical attributes, in every way that counted they were different. Yes, infants were incubated in their mothers' wombs, just as humans were, but fairies sprang into being there by far different means. Fairies did *not* reproduce through carnal, human means.

The fervent Child Wish of two Committed Fairies was as different from human biological intercourse as night was from day. The results were different, too. A fairy was born only when truly wanted, on a specially chosen solstice and only to parents who were prepared to give him or her their very best. Fairies chose their partners specifically for these practical purposes, not for foolish human passions or romantic notions of love. Humans certainly did not approach procreation in any sensible manner. At least not a large percentage of them, as far as Raea could tell.

No, if Kyne was human in any of those respects it would never remain secret among Fairykind. He would be discovered and rejected. As such things should be. Everyone knew what danger it could be. Millennia of peace and harmony among their kind would be upended.

It had taken generation after generation of fairies living carefully passionless lives to evolve beyond the carnality of their past. Fairies, of course, *could* engage in carnal joining activities. It was physically possible. Ages ago fairies had been no better than humans, ruled by desire and enslaved by the whims of their own bodies. But that desire led to discord and passion bred resentments. Fairies were led astray by their lust, falling prey to lascivious humans and jealousies within the Forbidden Realm. Creature turned against creature and war threatened to destroy all of them. The Fairy Council had been formed to oversee the construction of the Veil and to monitor its maintenance.

Frail humanity was relegated to the mundane world, while the magical world concerned itself with the pursuit of peace. Carnal desire became a thing of the past in the Forbidden Realm.

Things were so much better now that fairies had rejected their shameful past behaviors.

Still, though, they all knew what they could be capable of.

And that, of course, was why it was so forbidden. Fairies were free from that bondage but they still needed to be cautious. Giving in to those old ways could lead them back to the destructive behaviors of their past, those actions that made them no better than humans. That sort of thing was fine for base creatures and was useful as a way to control humans, but it was ruin for fairies. Just thinking of what it must be like—all that touching and moaning and writhing—was dangerous for them.

Her skin suddenly prickled. Was it cold out here over the lake again? It must be, though she usually was unaffected by cold. Very unusual.

Well, she'd simply wish herself well and get on with business. And right now, business was to find Kyne and give him the good news. Where would he be right now, in the middle of the night? Was he alone? If not, what was he doing?

Her skin got all prickly again as the image of those two lovers on the boat flooded into her brain. But something was different; the man was changed in her mind. He'd become Kyne, somehow.

Raea faltered in mid-flight. A strange sensation came over her, an odd quickening deep inside. In an instant she could picture all of Kyne's not-quite-fairy body. What this did to her she wasn't entirely sure she liked.

She enjoyed it, but definitely didn't like it.

Chapter Eleven

Aliya stepped out into the moonlight. She was getting better on these legs, though after all her activity they were feeling a bit shaky. But surely that was to be expected. She'd noticed in the past how tired Devin's partners seemed to be after a night's lovemaking.

That's what Devin called it. She liked how it sounded. Much more tender than just "coupling" or "joining," although both of those certainly fit. She knew now what it felt like to be completely joined to another being. Standing here on the deck of Devin's boat, she still felt as if she were beside him. He had become such a part of her she felt they could be separated by miles and miles of water and still be as one.

It was wonderful, and terrible. She loved him in a way that she'd never understood was possible. She knew he loved her. How on earth could either of them go back to their lives tomorrow? It would be like severing a part of themselves. It would be awful.

How could what Raea said about humans be true? How could a mere twenty-four hours of this bliss be enough to cure such a deep-rooted obsession? There was simply no way. Raea must have been wrong.

Not that she thought her fairy friend had lied or intentionally misled her. Raea simply had no understanding of how strong this desire was, or the depth of obsession it created. After all, how could she?

Then again, maybe not all humans were quite as passionate as Devin. Perhaps Raea had seen other humans overcome their obsession this way because in those cases the obsession was less developed. Perhaps in those cases twenty-four hours of passion might be enough. That would make sense, she supposed.

But it did not feel like enough. She could no longer be sure if the thoughts she was attributing to Devin were truly his, or if her new humanity was clouding her understanding. Perhaps she was the one with the deepening obsession and Devin was well on his way to being cured. Could that be it? Was there a chance he might be saved when this too-short time was over?

She hoped so. But then again, she did not. She wanted this longing, this deep, heated craving between them, to go on and on forever.

A gentle sound behind her alerted her to Devin's presence. She could feel him in the air, almost as surely as she could if they were in the water together. Obviously her new human senses had not fully taken over; deep down she was mermaid. She was simply learning to feel Devin's thoughts as subtle vibrations on the air instead of in water.

And she could feel them quite clearly right now. He wanted her. Again.

She turned to him, her body already responding to his desire. He had only to look at her and she felt herself sigh. The sensations began as his eyes swept her. He loved her body, and she was only too willing to offer it to him yet again.

He left the shadows of the doorway where he'd been watching.

It was dark and they were alone, so neither of them had bothered with clothing. In the moonlight his skin looked smooth and solid, like the polished rock along the bank where Aliya sometimes sunned herself in cool weather. But she knew when she touched him he would feel warm and very alive. The sparse hairs that covered his suntanned body would tickle her. Everything about Devin sent her reeling with pleasure.

"Hey," he said. "I woke up and you weren't there."

"I came out to look at the stars."

"Just so long as you're still here."

She smiled at him. "I'm here, Devin."

"But you're going to leave me soon, aren't you?"

She paused. How could she answer that question? She didn't want to answer. At least, not with the truth.

"Talk to me, Aliya," he said.

The pain was evident in his voice. She felt it in the air, saw it on his face. It was her pain, too. Just the thought of leaving him brought stinging tears to her eyes. She'd heard of such a thing, but certainly never thought to experience it for herself. She didn't like it.

"You'll have me long enough," she said and tried to smile. Maybe it was the truth, too.

She didn't dare let him ask any more questions. The answers could only be more painful. It was better to spend their time in more pleasurable activity. She moved to him, letting her skin rub against his. Yes, there were much more pleasurable activities than talking about leaving.

She leaned into him and kissed his lips, allowing her emotions to flow over him like warm water. He groaned and wrapped his arms around her, his kiss parting her lips to let her taste him fully. She drew his tongue into her mouth and felt the tingle that ran through her as he teased her with it.

The boat rocked gently on the waves and Aliya felt herself sway into Devin. He was hard against her when her hip pressed against his appendage—his cock, he had called it. She tiptoed and turned just slightly to feel him pressed against her right there at the juncture of her legs. A flame ignited at the core of her being and she thrust herself closer to him.

But the motion of the boat kept her unsteady on her feet, and even with Devin's arms locked around her Aliya could not support herself to take him in. It was delicious torture, his hard humanness brushing against her, but she unable to welcome him inside.

"You're so perfect, Aliya," Devin whispered, his kiss moving from her mouth to a sensitive spot near her ear. "I want you in every way possible."

She loved knowing he was pleased with her, but there was a stab of guilt, too. Perfect? No, that was an illusion. The parts of her Devin now knew best were only temporary. In mere hours all this would be gone. That was about as far from perfect as things could get.

"Come into me, Devin," she begged, desperation taking over.

He just laughed, a low, rumbling sound that sent waves of longing over her with force enough to buckle her unsteady knees.

"Not yet," he murmured. "First I'm going to convince you to stay with me forever, Aliya. That's what I want with you—forever."

She couldn't protest. He would recognize her lies when he heard them. Perhaps she owed it to him to be honest, but as his hands and his mouth explored her body with deliberate patience, her voice was lost inside her. All she could do was sigh.

He started at her neck. His breath was moist and his mouth was hot. Slowly he nibbled at her skin and trailed down to her shoulders. He cupped her breasts in his hands and she sagged against him as he carefully rolled one tightened nipple between his fingers.

Without warning he dipped his head to take that nipple into his mouth. His tongue lapped at it as he sucked gently. Aliya arched back, longing for more contact with his hard shaft at her throbbing core.

But he wasn't ready to give in to her yet. His tantalizing ministrations continued at her breasts, moving from one aroused nipple to the other. Her dampened skin prickled in the night air.

She leaned in toward him. He smelled good: a mixture of soap, male, and love. So very human, but irresistible to her. She cradled his head as he moved down to work his mouth over her belly. He was on his knees, worshipping before her. She laughed from sheer pleasure.

Then he was kissing the delicate mound just above her burning opening. Oh, she wished she'd asked more questions. How was it that her body was doing all this? The sensations, the motions, the heavy breathing... it was completely foreign to anything she'd ever experienced before, but yet it came so very naturally. Was it just her newly created human form that made her feel this way? Or was this really a part of her?

But as Devin knelt before her she stopped thinking and let her mind drift into blissful awareness. Devin slid his hands up and down over her back and thighs, letting them settle on her buttocks where he massaged her with a wild tenderness. Nothing mattered but that they were together here and now. She would let herself enjoy this.

There would be time for explanation later.

"Lean against the wall for me," he said.

She realized she'd backed up beside the cabin and was glad for this support. Her hands found a line of decorative woodwork and she gripped it as Devin pushed her legs apart and nuzzled in, burying his face in her and making her legs go weak.

The flood of excitement was more powerful than any she'd experienced so far as he found her throbbing core and dove in with his tongue. She willed her shaking legs to open farther for him, inviting his probing tongue deeper and deeper. Sensitive nerves, newly formed and still waking, felt each delicious stroke of his tongue. The whisper of beard on his face rubbed her and heightened the pleasure.

Just as she was about to tumble over the edge and lose herself in the fever of sensation, he backed away slightly. His hands slowed their roaming; his touch was gentle and calmed her raging passion. His tongue flicked against her and his lips laid tiny kisses around her heat.

"Come inside me, Devin. Please!"

"Not yet."

She barely heard his response, but sighed in relief as his fervent kisses increased their intensity. Now he was sucking on her there, and she was back to floating on a sea of insensible bliss. His tongue stroked inside her. She ran her fingers through his dark hair.

She pressed against the wall, barely conscious of it. Devin was drawing something from her, something wonderful and thrilling. She was very nearly shouting to the sky when, again, he pulled away from her.

She whimpered. He was running his hands over her legs in slow patterns now, and his kisses had moved from her steamy center to the insides of her thighs. She knew enough of their lovemaking to understand he was doing this intentionally, but couldn't make sense of it. Why didn't he continue? Why had he stopped just as she was coming to the point of succumbing to his efforts?

Earlier he had been so excited by her passion. He said watching her, hearing her cries, was the best part of it for him. Why now was he so carefully keeping her from reaching a climax? There were so many things she just did not know about being a human, but everything she felt in Devin's emotions was that he was every bit as aroused—and frustrated—as she.

He must have sensed her confusion. He was getting good at knowing her thoughts and emotions. Was that because of her mermaid abilities, or was that all a part of this human act?

"I want to be so good for you, Aliya," he said, gazing up at her. "I want to be better than everything else, so you'll stay."

She saw the love in his eyes and understood what he was saying. He knew she was going to leave, and he thought it was because she would choose it. Her heart broke for them both. Suddenly it wasn't so very difficult to lie.

"I'll stay, Devin. I'll stay forever."

He smiled at her, and pulled her closer to him. Again his face disappeared and he was working magic on her. She slumped against the wall and pressed her hands into his shoulders to hold herself upright. By the Seas, he was amazing.

She felt his taught muscles under her fingers. He was holding himself back for her pleasure. He was being as careful with her as if she were the most precious thing on earth. He was giving her his entire being and she gladly gave herself up to him.

The pressure mounting inside her was unbearable. Devin's tongue, his hands, his lips, his scent... it was all too much. At last she came, crying out in nonhuman utterance and calling Devin's name to the stars above. Her body was quaking and just before she crumbled into a pile of pleasured flesh, Devin stood and took her into his arms.

He lifted her feet off the floor and held her against the wall.

She draped her arms around him and kissed his neck, his ears, his chin. With a growl, he drove his hardened cock into her.

She cried out again, awed by the revived wave of desire and passion that washed over her once more. She thought she'd already risen to the heights of pleasure just seconds ago, but now he had her drowning again in his love. She gasped for air, every moment her ecstasy increasing and gaining strength. The power of it was terrifying, and wondrous.

She arched into him. He thrust once, then again, harder. He was breathing heavily, thrusting into her again and again. She felt herself spiraling out of control, but never wanted it to end.

Her face was buried against his chest; she was gasping out words but not caring what she said. She only knew she was encouraging him, begging him to make her his own. Forever.

And he did. Panting and shuddering, he finally reached his climax, taking her with him. They fell into each other, leaning against the wall, still joined and clinging for dear life.

"You are amazing, Aliya," he said when he could speak. "Like no one I've ever encountered."

"That was more than I ever could have wished for, Devin," she replied. She did wish, however, that she could confess that she was falling in love.

Chapter Twelve

Kyne hovered over the field of wildflowers he'd taken refuge in. He'd managed to avoid everyone all through the night, but now the dawning sun was just brushing fresh, rosy fingers over the horizon and he breathed in the heady scent of dewy nature. This is where he belonged, here alone, halfway between magic and earth. This is where he was safe.

He'd been so angry last night when he discovered the mermaid. Raea had gone way over the line and he'd been ready to throttle her for it. But the more that he searched for her and the more he recalled those human bodies intertwined, the more he realized he couldn't quite dare to approach Raea. Not in the state he was in. It seemed anger served only to fuel his forbidden passion. He'd had to give up and retreat off by himself, far away from humans and fairies.

But he knew where Raea was. This time of the morning she'd likely be back near the city, granting the first of the day's wishes and muddling in human affairs. Human affairs that allowed them to indulge their animal lust and desire. He knew what she was about. Thank the Skies he was safe here, too far away for those passions to affect him. If only he'd been able to leave his own thoughts so far behind.

But those had followed. The anger at Raea for dragging an innocent mermaid into it, anger at the human for mistaking that poor creature for one of his own, and anger at himself for being so damn turned on by it all. By the Air and the Skies and everything in them, he hated himself.

Even with Raea and the humans nowhere near him, he had suffered throughout the night. His body throbbed, ached, begged for release. At first he just ignored it, tried to focus on his anger and how he'd confront Raea once he'd calmed down. But thoughts of her just made things worse.

So he'd put his energy into his work, using the last of his rationed Fairy Dust to make things grow, to seed the clouds for a gentle summer rain later in the day, to tint the breeze with honeysuckle and warmth. But nothing helped.

Everywhere he looked he was reminded of the natural urges of earth things. Night creatures called out for one another. Grasses swayed in the damp air, their fronds swaying and rubbing against one another like lovers.

Even the moon, a silver shaft in its phase, dipped in and out of the passing clouds in a rhythm that was entirely too familiar. The whole world was a constant reminder of what Kyne craved but could not have.

No, he corrected himself, it was not that he *could* not have it. He could have it any time he wanted, could flit around, taking whatever he wanted from any creature he desired. Human, fairy…mermaid, apparently. He could plunge his too-human part into anything soft and open and female. It would be paradise.

All he'd have to do would be sacrifice everything he'd ever

known. To acknowledge that the human ways were stronger than the fairy ways. To declare himself weak.

And that he would never do. Never! Humans had proven themselves everything he detested. They were dull, cruel, selfish. They lived only for those carnal desires and cared nothing for what it did to others, like his mother. She'd been used and tossed aside. No human man had ever come looking for them, wondering what had come of the woman he'd seduced or the child that he'd sired.

No, Kyne would never embrace that side of himself. If he had to suffer through every day of his life, he would never give in. He'd rather die first.

And he practically wished he *could* die by the time his body finally gave in to frustrated exhaustion and let him sleep. But it was a restless, dream-filled sleep and now he was finally glad to be awake. Fairies needed very little sleep, after all. Plus, the tree he'd chosen to settle in hadn't been any too comfortable.

Now with the sun just coming up and another day dawning, he let himself hope that things would be better. The flowers were flourishing under his care, the bees buzzed in harmony, and a perfect summer was under way in this part of the world. He could take pride in that. He was a damn good Summer Fairy, if he did say so himself.

And he did say so, over and over again, assuring himself that this was the best life had to offer and that he was wholly satisfied with it.

He almost had himself convinced, too, when Raea flitted up and interrupted his mantra.

"So here you are," she said. Her voice was cheerful and perky, and her pink was even more pink than usual.

By the Skies, she looked good in the morning.

"Of course I'm here. I'm working. What are you doing here? There's no one making any wishes around here, that's for sure," he grumbled. "There's no revolting human sex going on, either."

She just rolled her lavender eyes and looked annoyed. And smug. He pretended to be very interested in a wilted milkweed in need of some tending. Infuriating fairy. She thought he had no clue what she'd been up to. Just how stupid did she think he was?

Then again, she hadn't expected him to be out spying on her lusty little mermaid. Hmm, that might be uncomfortable, trying to explain what he'd been doing out there in the middle of the night, eavesdropping on their tryst. He'd have to come up with some logical excuse. As soon as he could formulate logical thought.

Raea hovered in the air, not two feet away from him. Her wings stirred up the pollen in the air, filling Kyne's senses with summer smells and Fairy Dust. The combination played havoc on both of his halves, human and fairy. Damn it! How did she have this effect on him? Why couldn't he just be angry at her, instead of noticing how soft her skin looked in the warming dawn light?

And why could he not get this milkweed to stand up straight? It only served to draw attention to the certain particular object that ought to be drooping—but wasn't. Damn his human half!

"So, how's that summer stuff coming?" Raea asked with way too much cheerful indifference.

"It's just fine, thank you," he snarled. "Not as if you're actually interested."

"Well, I'd just hate to find out you've been hauled in for incompetence before I've even had a chance to beat you at our little wager."

"Oh? You're that sure you're going to win this?"

She tossed her wavy hair and gave him a smile that he would

have described as nothing short of flirty. *Flirty!* By the Skies, was Raea flirting with him? Great. That's all he needed. Fairies didn't flirt. He had to be imagining it.

But she fluttered closer to him and started circling. He was glad his feet were currently firmly on the ground. Flying would be decidedly difficult at this point. Raea's lovely rounded breasts, covered in her traditionally scanty costume of close-fitted dove feathers, were exactly at Kyne's eye level. And near enough for touching, if he were so inclined.

Which he was—quite intensely—but he managed to restrain himself. She was a cheater, a mermaid-user, a rule-breaker, and all sorts of other undesirable things. He didn't want her at all. Not in a million years.

Okay, he was lying. He wanted her badly and several million years probably wouldn't change that. He wouldn't mind testing that theory, however. A million years to satisfy his need for Raea...not a bad start.

"What's the matter, Kyne?" she said. No, it was more like purring. Damn her. "You look nervous. Are you afraid maybe you made an unwise wager with me?"

"I'm not afraid of you," he said.

He was terrified, in fact, as she came even closer. He could feel her breath now.

"Oh? So it wouldn't bother you if I said I'd already won the bet?"

He could feel the air between them crackling with excitement. Could she feel it, too? Did she know what a dangerous dance she was doing, flitting around him like a helpless hummingbird teasing a ravenous falcon?

"Have you?"

She smiled. It spread slowly over her face. This was not her

usual bright, open smile, but a sly grin filled with heat and anticipation and promise of something wonderful. If she had any
idea what it did to his already elevated body temperature—and
parts—she'd have flapped her little wings as fast as she could
back toward home.

But she didn't. She trusted her friend, so she stayed. It was torture for him.

"Even as we speak, one very happy former virgin is enjoying
the last hours of her wish come true," she said.

Images of the couple on the boat flooded Kyne. He swallowed
back desire.

"That's fast work, Raea."

"Naturally. I warned you it would be too easy."

And it would be only too easy to wrap his arms around her,
pin those dainty pink wings down, and hold her here. She was
small, a full inch shorter than he was. After all, he was a giant by
fairy standards. She wouldn't stand a chance against him. And
the way she was smiling all coy and fluttery at him, it seemed
perhaps she wouldn't put up much struggle, either.

"So the deed is done so soon, is it?" he asked, for something to
say. "And all the stipulations were met? You found a virgin, never
before touched by carnal pleasures?"

It was nearly painful for him to even form the words.

"I did. She was as innocent as the driven snow."

Kyne could only imagine. Mermaids had even less contact
with humans than fairies did, in general. That poor girl on the
boat could have had no idea what she was in for. She must have
been shocked, frightened even, as that man came to her in full
arousal. Kyne shuddered at the mental image that conjured.

And Raea had set her up for that. How could she do this
thing? Did Raea truly have no idea what went on? No, she'd seen

enough to know. She'd seen the power of a man's desire. She'd heard the cries of lovers in the midst of their ecstasy. She knew. Yet she'd still sent that mermaid into such a situation.

"The subject agreed to our terms?" he asked.

The slightest pause confirmed any doubts he may have had. Yes, Raea had cheated. The mermaid had not known the full truth. "Yes. I told you she would."

"So, this virgin knew what she was getting into and she's still happy about it this morning?" he asked.

"She's very happy."

By the Skies, he could make Raea very happy, too. She would enjoy what he could do for her. He could bring her to life deep down in those forbidden parts. He could make her know desire, heat, passion, and satisfaction. He could show her things she'd never imagined. He could love her in a way no other fairy ever could.

And she would join him willingly, he was sure of it. She'd give herself freely with abandon. They would enjoy each other to the fullest and no one would have to know about it. Ever.

"She was a willing participant?" he asked, his muscles tense from the struggle to keep his hands off her.

"She was more than eager to participate," Raea said.

Her wing brushed his chest as she drifted nearer to him, meeting his smoldering gaze unafraid. It was all the encouragement he needed.

A tiny gasp of surprise escaped her when he shot an arm out to catch her. In a heartbeat she was in his grasp, wrapped against him, her wings folded and useless. He knew his embrace was forceful, but he didn't want to run the risk of losing her.

His lips came down on hers, ensnaring her before she had a chance to realize what was happening. She tasted sweet and needy and pink. She tasted like he'd always known she would. She felt like what he'd been begging for all along. This was the rightest thing he'd ever done. All of the yearning and desire that he'd repressed for so long, the wants that he'd cursed year after year, wrapped themselves around him like a comfortable cloak. With Raea in his arms he was finally embracing the rolling tide of passion inside him. His skin, his fingers, his very essence, sizzled with anticipation.

She did not sizzle, though. He felt her body go taut. She was frozen in his arms, motionless and rigid against the onslaught of his kiss. His tongue probed for entrance, but her lips remained sealed. There was nothing yielding in her soft, curving body as he held her, touched her, desperately tried to drag passion from her.

It hit him like a thunderclap: Raea didn't return his ardor. She was shocked, stunned. She was disgusted. She didn't want him. She would never want him. He'd been wrong about her.

His pain at this realization was more than physical. All at once he realized what he'd just lost. Not merely the moments of physical pleasure he'd been so anxious for, but the trust and companionship of a valued friend. It was too awful to consider. He'd given in to his human side and it had cost him Raea.

"Oh God, Raea," he said, bringing his lips off hers.

But that tiny shift resulted in reaction in her body. Without warning, she was pressing herself against him. Her hands were no longer pinned to her sides, but instead slid up to his shoulders. He felt her nails rasp against his exposed skin. He drew in a jagged breath. What was happening?

Raea was responding to him, that's what was happening. He was almost afraid to trust his own senses, but when she buried her tiny hand in his thick golden hair, hope threatened to drown him. She pulled his face back toward hers and this time her lips claimed his.

It was better than his wildest dreams. She sighed, she melted into him, she pressed against his body. She opened her lips to him and allowed his tongue access. As he dipped it into her, she shuddered and there was no doubt what she was feeling.

Desire. Hot, steamy passion. He wanted her and she wanted him in return. His racing pulse pounded in his ears and he struggled not to crush her in his driving urge to take her fully. But he was determined to take things slowly. Sort of.

Raea didn't seem to share his conviction, however. She was exploring his chest with her fingers, tracing his teeth with her tongue, and snuggling up against him so tightly he knew she had to be aware of his very obvious erection. In fact, he was pretty sure she was intentionally rubbing against it.

Well, by the Skies, he hadn't been wrong after all. Maybe he hadn't lost Raea. Perhaps, instead, he'd gained paradise.

But before he could so much as release one shoulder strap of her feathery costume, his pink paradise jerked away from him. She broke off the kiss and pulled ruthlessly away, staggering back and nearly tripping over a clump of wild daisies.

"Holy Creator, what am I doing?!" she cried, a look of such horror and disgust on her face that Kyne was sure his heart had been ripped clean out of him.

Chapter Thirteen

W hat, by everything in the Air, are you doing to me?" Raea yelled.

She buzzed her wings furiously and got as much distance as she could between her and Kyne. But her body was shaking, unsteady and still reeling from all the incredible emotions and sensations surging through it. She knew she must look ridiculous, stumbling and swaying like she'd lost control of her own limbs.

Of course she had lost control. What had she been thinking? She was letting Kyne kiss her, touch her all over in the most inappropriate places! And she hadn't hated it, either.

Ugh, that's what made it so shameful. She'd been responding to him! Well, that was hardly her fault. He'd done that to her. He and those smoky human eyes and his despicable human lips and that…oh, Skies above, he'd been displaying that blatantly human male response! And she'd touched it!

Okay, she hadn't actually touched it. They'd both been fully clothed. But she knew it was there. Yes, it had certainly been there.

So Kyne did possess that attribute, after all. She'd always had suspicions about that. She'd stolen peeks down there before, when no one might notice, and she'd always imagined that...

By the Air and Sea and Land, what was she doing? Fantasizing about what secrets Kyne kept in his pants? How vulgar! Thank the Stars it was still a secret to her, too. Mostly. Even from where he was standing ten feet away from her she could still make out that clearly defined bulge. A very large bulge it seemed, too. More so, proportionally, than many of the humans she'd...

"If you're so disgusted by it, stop staring at it!" he said. He sounded big and grumpy and entirely too human.

Her gaze flashed up to his eyes. How mortifying! He'd caught her looking.

But his eyes weren't much safer for her. The fire she saw burning there almost frightened her. And it wasn't just the physical desire she read in them. Every other emotion blazed there: longing, fear, elation, pain, anger... and something wild and forbidden, too. Something that stoked the embers of an untamed desire in her own being.

Oh, this was very, very bad.

"Well, you can't very well say I started that!" she said.

"Does it really matter at this point who started it?"

"Of course it matters! I'd never do something like that if you hadn't seduced me!"

Curse that lopsided smile of his.

"I seduced you?" he drawled. "Seems to me you were doing a fair bit of fluttering those little pink wings and waving your breasts in my face."

"I was fluttering because I was flying. And I have never waved my breasts in all my life, Kyne. You are a beast and ought to be ashamed of yourself!"

"You're sounding awfully uptight for a fairy who just had her tongue stuffed halfway down my throat, Raea."

"Only because you made me! Ugh, I can't believe I let you... and the germs! By the Skies, Kyne, if I come down with some sort of cold because of this..."

"Shut up, Raea. You enjoyed it."

"You arrogant yellow flower pollinator! I didn't enjoy one single second of that revolting encounter."

She wasn't usually a liar, but she hoped in this case she was at least halfway convincing. If Kyne ever found out what had been going on inside her while he let his fingers do the walking all over the outside of her...

"You didn't enjoy it, huh?" he said, still nailing her with that grin and those simmering amber eyes. "Not even when I did this?"

She wasn't quick enough. He rose up into the air and wrapped a solid, sinewy arm around her waist. She pulled against him but all that accomplished was crumpling the one secondary wing that he'd pinned against her.

She sagged in defeat as his lips came down on hers again. What a sorry creature she was. He tasted like sunflowers and honey and she gave in to the temptation to feel that hot, boiling desire well up in her again. It was delectable.

"You cannot tell me this isn't enjoyable," he whispered into her ear.

He was right; she couldn't.

"Or this," he added, trailing gentle bites along her neck and sliding his hands down to massage her buttocks.

Again, he was right.

"And this," he said.

To her surprise he lifted her up a few inches higher. Her skin slid against his and it felt more than just enjoyable. It felt right.

And now she could feel his huge human legacy pressing against her just at the right spot. The very heart of her steaming need. Oh, so right! She could lean into him, let him hold her like this, and…

No, she couldn't. It went against everything she'd ever known, ever lived for. It was wrong.

"Stop." She barely breathed.

He jolted, as if stung by her voice.

"This is wrong," she said.

He let her pull away from him. She sank back to earth, smoothing out her wings and taking deep breaths to settle herself. She needed to regain control, remind him why they could most certainly not do this ever, ever again.

"It's wrong," she repeated finally.

She made herself look up at him. He had landed a couple feet from her. His breathing was as ragged and uneasy as hers, but somehow his eyes were completely calm. Too calm, she realized.

"So, this is wrong?" he said after an unbelievably uncomfortable pause.

She nodded.

"Wrong. Like what you did out on the lake last night?"

She struggled not to let him see the dawning concern washing over her. He knew something. But he couldn't, could he? Oh, no wonder he thought she would have no difficulty succumbing to his lust. He knew about Aliya.

"Why a mermaid, Raea?" he asked slowly, softly. "An innocent, helpless mermaid, of all creatures. And you threw her to that filthy human just to win a stupid bet. A damn, worthless bet! By the Air, you say what we've done here is wrong?"

"It's not like that," she said. It sounded like a weak, pitiful excuse. "It's what she wished for!"

Now his grin was gone, replaced by hard, cold disgust. "Oh, don't even pretend you believe that. I know mermaids; I know what they're like. You used her because it suited your purposes. There's nothing in your blessed code about granting wishes for mermaids."

"You're the one who wants to change that code, as I recall."

"I want to make it stronger, more focused on keeping us separate and safe from the lustful humans," he growled.

She took a step back. How could he say that? Everything about him seemed to cry out to the universe that he had fully embraced the very things the Veil was supposed to keep them separated from. How could he possibly expect her to believe that he was in favor of a more strenuous Great Code? Was he trying to trap her? She was so confused by all of this.

"What you've done is exactly what I've been fighting against," he said, his words clipped and his voice tense. "Can't you see how powerful passion can be? Didn't you feel it inside you, building in fury until you felt you must burst from it? Imagine what devastation that could bring if it's allowed to cross between our Realm and theirs, to allow our magic to mingle with human pettiness and greed, all fueled by the raging torrent of uncontrolled passion."

"But I...I merely bent the rules a tiny bit. I swear, I set it all up to go right back to the way everything was."

"It can never be the way it was. You crossed the line, Raea. You took advantage of your position and in your selfish conceit you've ruined a Veiled creature."

"I didn't ruin her. By tonight she'll be back to herself again and that human will be long gone. Everything will be just the same."

"It won't. She's been a human now, Raea. She's been with a

human—really, really *with* him. All night long, as a matter of fact. You can't change that."

"But it doesn't mean anything. By the Skies, Kyne, you know yourself how meaningless that physical activity is to humans."

His expression changed. What did she see in his eyes now? He was still angry, but that was fading. Now she was seeing the pain. But why should her words hurt him? What she'd said was true. Everyone knew it. All that sex humans were so interested in was just animal instinct. It really *was* meaningless to them.

"Is it, Raea?" he said softly.

Hadn't he said so himself? She was confused. Kyne had been the one all along condemning humans and their base behavior. He had more contempt for humans—and their sex drives—than most fairies. He wanted to rewrite the laws, even, to see that humans and fairies had even less interaction. He was disgusted by what humans did.

So why had he kissed her? What could it mean? If he didn't approve of desire, then why would he allow himself to touch her, to use her, to...Oh, a thought began forming.

He was trying to trap her! He hated humans and believed Veiled creatures should have nothing to do with them. For what she had done, he probably wanted to take her before the Fairy Council and have her investigated!

That must be it. He was using his human side to throw her off guard, to make her implicate herself in all sorts of terrible, forbidden things. He was punishing her.

And she'd almost fallen for it! No, she *had* fallen for it. Twice now he'd had her melting in his arms, giving in to things she knew she should despise. He'd been the one in control, unaffected by it. Even with his half-human body and those inherent urges he was still unmoved by what they'd done. He must be!

How else could he just stand there, glaring at her as if he'd just as soon have her ejected from the planet?

Well, she wasn't being taken in like that again. He was right; what she'd done to Aliya was wrong. She'd cheated on the bet and she'd involved her friend in things a mermaid shouldn't be involved in.

Of course Kyne wouldn't care about her explanation, and he'd never believe Aliya really *had* wished for it. But for all the Forbidden Realm, Raea was not going to let him stand before the council and mislead them about it, about *her*. No, she'd find a way to avoid that at all costs.

"All right," she said after a pause and a big, healthy deep breath. "You're right. I messed up this time."

He looked surprised. "I'm glad you can admit it."

"But it's not too late. I can fix it. This doesn't have to go any farther than it already has. What went on between us—you and me—was a mistake."

"It was illegal."

"As well I know, and we won't talk about it again. I've learned my lesson, thanks to you. What I did with Aliya, well, I can undo it. I'll turn her back into a mermaid, send him back to the shore, and give them both a big dose of Forgetful Dust."

"I thought that was a controlled substance."

"I've got clearance."

He nodded. "Impressive."

"I'm not a total slouch, Kyne. Despite what you obviously think of me."

"How can you know what I think of you?"

"I know you're just dying to drag me in to the council," she said. "And maybe I deserve it. But isn't the important thing that we keep the balance between the Forbidden Realm and the humans? I can do that. Give me until sunset, and I'll have it all worked out."

His eyes narrowed slightly. It looked like he was considering her words. Good. At least he hadn't already made up his mind to turn her in.

"Just one day, Kyne," she said. "You'll see. I'm really pretty good at what I do."

He smiled, and she knew she'd won. Or…maybe not.

"I never had any doubts about *that*, Raea. But be assured, as good as you think you are, *I* can be better."

Chapter Fourteen

And these are eggs," Devin explained, scraping the food he had just prepared out of the skillet onto Aliya's plate. "I scrambled them."

She eyed the fluffy pile dubiously. "Eggs? You mean the unborn offspring of fish?"

"No, these are eggs from chickens."

He watched her frown. Adorable. Naturally, she would have no idea what a chicken was. He smiled. God, it was fun having Aliya around. So many things to show her, to experience through her amazed, innocent eyes.

"A chicken is a bird. It lives on the land and can't fly."

Her shell-pink lips opened wide. "A bird that can't fly?"

"Yeah. A chicken."

"But, if it can't fly, how do you know it's a bird?"

He tried not to laugh. She was delightful.

"Because it has feathers and lays eggs," he explained.

She looked back at the food on her plate. "So this is bird's eggs. And you make it hot over fire?"

"We cook them. We cook most of our food."

"Why?"

Well, that was a good question. "We like it better that way, I guess," he said. "And some things just aren't healthy to eat raw."

His toaster popped and she jumped. "Is that more food you've cooked?"

"It's toast," he said, smearing a slab of butter on a piece. "Something called bread that's been heated up until the surface gets browned."

"Why?"

"Makes it crunchy. Here, try it."

She tried it, and liked it. "This is good! We have nothing to compare."

"Tell me what you usually eat for breakfast."

He settled in at the table across from her and listened in fascination as she described the mollusks, small fish, and various plant life her people made meals of. She looked wonderful, her long, nearly white hair tousled and tangled from their active night. He'd given her one of his shirts to put on so she wouldn't be cold, but it was almost more tantalizing to see her dressed that way than when she'd come on board completely naked yesterday evening.

He took his mind off her body and listened, amazed, to her tales of life underwater. She explained the art of recognizing a good snail from a bad snail. For eating, he supposed. Then she told about the annual algae festival where her mother always performed some sort of ritual involving letting air out of a container. For what purpose, he wasn't quite sure.

It was all so impossible and surreal, although Aliya was careful to describe things in ways he might understand. It was clearly very real to her. The love and contentment for her life underwater was evident as she spoke, a warm smile touching her perfect lips. He could sit here forever, listening and watching her expressions.

She had a rich life under this dark lake. She had friends, family, a job. How could he expect her to just walk away from it to come live in his town house on dry land? How on earth was she going to fit in with the life he knew?

The more Aliya talked, the more Devin felt his heart sinking. She'd promised him forever. He couldn't make her keep that promise. But how could he let her go?

"Devin? Are you not feeling well?" she said, interrupting her own telling of the Weekly In-Swim, when mermaids gathered to discuss the trends in commercial fishing and other human activities on the lake.

"I'm fine," he said. "Go on with your story. It's amazing."

"It is not." She laughed. "It's dull and I can tell your mind has wandered. What are you so worried about that it's made your beautiful warm eyes hold such concern?"

He took her hand and gave a squeeze. "How can you know me so well already? We've barely just met."

"It seems like a lifetime."

"No, not even close. There's still so much about you I don't know."

"Dear Devin, I've been rambling on for ages. What could you possibly still need to know about me?"

"Well, how about your last name?"

"Last name?"

"Sure," he said. "Where I come from, we usually have a first name—like Devin, for instance—and a last name that tells what family we're from."

She nodded brightly. "Yes, we do something similar. We are given a name, but are also called by our mother's name. I am Aliya of Coraline of Nelana."

"Nelana is where you're from? Is it far away, in the ocean?"

She shook her head with a giggle. "No, I'm not an ocean mermaid. They're quite different from us, I've heard. Bigger, wilder, less concerned about humans."

"Oh," he said. "So Nelana is here, in the lake?"

"No. Nelana was my grandmother, my mother's mother. But she has gone on now."

"Oh. I'm sorry to hear that she's gone. So you're named after your mother and your grandmother?"

"And the mothers before them. We are careful to keep the memories of our ancestors alive through the generations. If I may boast, my sisters and I are honored to be from a very distinguished line of lake mermaids. My grandmother is just one of several grandmaids in my lineage."

"Grandmaids?"

She looked down at her plate and blushed. "Women who have been privileged to birth more than one hundred mermaids."

He choked on his coffee. "One hundred! Holy shi... I mean, that's quite a privilege."

"A mermaid has to earn the right of motherhood," she explained, noticeably shy. "It is not granted frivolously."

"That's very intelligent," he said, hoping it sounded, well, intelligent. "Still, one hundred little mermaids swimming around..."

"It is spread out over years and years. We live a bit longer than you, and of course, not everyone births so many. Things like that are carefully managed. The whole community participates in the decision to produce a new life. I take it things do not work that way in your world."

"No, not so much. For us, each person makes his own decision whether to become a parent. At least, usually that's the way it goes."

"Are you a parent, Devin?"

"No. I am not."

"So you decided not to have children?" she asked.

It didn't sound like she was making any judgments about that, but just curious. He hoped so. If parenting was such an honor in her world she might have a hard time understanding how he and Judith could have put it off and put it off, thinking they had all the time in the world to get around to having kids.

They didn't.

"We decided to wait a while for that," he said.

"Oh," she said.

She didn't sound like she understood that answer any more than he understood that business about her grandmother having a hundred kids. Wow, there were a lot of things they were going to have to get used to about each other. Thanksgiving dinner with all of Aliya's relatives would be hell!

Then again, he figured they probably didn't have to worry about that. If she stayed with him as she promised, there would likely be no family get-togethers for Aliya anymore. Had she thought it all through? Could he let her give at all up?

"You must have a lot of people wondering where you are right now," he said, then wished he hadn't. He really, really didn't want to think of those cousins and siblings and relatives, those hundreds of reasons for her to leave him.

"They would not notice my absence for another few days," she said softly, "at the In-Swim. I'm not due to check in until then."

"But don't you call your mother every now and then, or something?"

She laughed again. "In times of need we are aware of each other, but it is not a consistent link. She will think nothing of it if she does not sense me for a few days. She knows my duty is to the Veil. It gives her honor when I uphold my responsibilities properly."

"And you're not worried what we are doing now might conflict with that?"

"Oh, it does indeed! That's why…why I will be careful not to let anyone know."

He could have sworn she'd been about to say something other than that, but she did not elaborate. Did he want to pry into her life? Yes, he did, but of course he wouldn't. He just had to trust that she would share with him when she was comfortable. Still, a few more casual questions couldn't really be prying, right?

"What about your sisters? You said you've got sisters so I figure you must be pretty close."

"Yes, many of us get together frequently."

"Many of you? Jeez, how many are there?"

"Only twenty-four, and a few of them have gone on to posts in other areas. My mother has been very devoted to her work, but she has not been honored as frequently as my grandmother was at her age. We are still very proud of her, though."

"I'm sure you are! Heck, my mother barely kept her sanity raising two of us. I can't imagine twenty-four. What does your father think of it all?"

Now she really looked confused.

"You know, your father? Your mother's husband, or whatever you call that arrangement down there?"

She looked up at him, puzzled. "But, you know I'm a mermaid."

"I'm not likely to forget that!" He chuckled. "But you've got to have a father somewhere, right? Can't have mermaids without mer-daddies."

"Mer-daddies?" This made her giggle. It was a charming sound, but he didn't quite like the feeling that he'd said something stupid.

"There are no mer-daddies," she assured him. "We are all female, of course."

All female? Well, that was interesting. How on earth, then, were they popping out little baby mermaids? No wonder the whole sex thing was such a new experience for Aliya!

But all female...well, that gave him something to think about. Images of wet, sleek mermaid bodies like Aliya's all heated up and writhing around one another flooded his mind. Man, baby-making in Aliya's world seemed pretty damned appealing. They ought to charge admission for something like that.

Then again, he was probably being a pig. Whatever these gals did with each other to spawn little mer-minnows was obviously special to Aliya. He was pretty sure it was out of line to be getting hot thinking about it like this.

But, damn, what he wouldn't give to be scuba diving that day!

"Devin?" Aliya was saying.

He pulled his mind out of the gutter and smiled innocently. "Yeah?"

"Did you say something?"

He hoped not, since it probably wouldn't have been exactly G-rated.

"No, I don't think so."

"Oh." She frowned, and chewed her lip. "I thought I heard... something."

Shit. He'd forgotten she was some kind of telepathic.

"Well, maybe I did. I don't know. I was just...well, I was trying to figure out how a bunch of females manage to keep on reproducing. Up here pretty much every species needs a pair. Male and female, you know."

"Oh. Yes, that would make sense. You are a natural species, after all."

"Natural species?"

"You—humans, that is—occur by nature. Like the fish, and the birds. Of course you will have a male and a female. I keep forgetting we are so very different."

"So how do you...um, I mean...well, how do you make more mermaids, then?"

"It's obvious, of course. We are half fish."

"Fish?"

Oh God, they did it with fish! Okay, that image wasn't quite as nice as the one before. He wasn't so sure he liked the idea of Aliya slithering around with a horny hammerhead. Fortunately, it appeared she was happy to give him something of an explanation.

"When a mermaid has reached full maturity and earned the honor, we have a ceremony. The Life Fish is sacrificed and the eggs are taken. The mermaid makes herself willing, and the eggs are placed in her hollow where they are incubated until birth, some months later. And then, if the mermaid survives, her essence combines with the eggs and she becomes a mother."

"If she survives! Good God, how dangerous is this?"

"There are always risks. My mother's sister died three seasons ago after her first Life Ceremony. But obviously many of us survive."

"Please tell me you haven't done this."

He knew he should be happy for any special honor she'd been given, but to be inseminated by fish eggs and risk death! He would never wish that on his Aliya.

"I have not been granted that honor," she said, with more blushing. "My body has not been ceremonially altered to accommodate the incubation process. That's why you found me unable to satisfy your needs when we attempted to couple underwater two nights ago."

"Well, I'm relieved to hear that. And, as I recall," he added with a grin, "you managed to satisfy my needs pretty darn well that night."

"As you have done for me many times since."

"We're damn good together, aren't we?" he said.

And he was determined there had to be a way they could keep on being good together. He'd make her so happy, she'd never miss that life she'd left behind. Whatever it took, he'd do it for her.

It looked like he'd have to start cooking differently, that was for sure. She'd barely touched her eggs. Damn. He was fresh out of snails and algae for her.

She noticed him frowning at her still-full plate.

"I'm sorry, Devin," she said. "I just am not hungry. Really, I don't think this new body needs to eat much."

"Well, when we get back to shore I'll take you shopping and we'll find something you'll like better."

She was studying her eggs again. "Shopping? Is that something you do on the dry?"

"It is. There are stores…buildings with all sorts of things to buy. We'll hit a grocery first thing and you can go crazy in the seafood section."

"Will there be many humans there?"

It was impossible not to notice how her voice broke.

"We won't do anything you don't want to do," he said gently. "If you're not ready to go back, we won't go. I can call the office and work from here for a few days. I won't take you away from here until you're ready, I promise."

She smiled and it nearly blinded him. How had he lived without her all this time?

"Thank you, Devin. I will go with you whenever you want to go. Just teach me what to do."

"Teach you, huh?" he said. "Yeah, there's a lot I'd like to teach you."

"I can't wait! Tell me everything I need to know to be the perfect human for you."

He laughed and stood up. "You're already that, Aliya. All you need to learn is the details."

She stood with him, matching his movements as he gathered the breakfast dishes and began moving them to the sink. "Details? What details are those?"

"Well, first off, you need to learn proper after-breakfast protocol."

"That sounds complicated!"

"Not at all. You just sit back and relax while I wash the dishes."

He took a cup and two spoons out of her hands and pointed her back to her chair. She laughed and simply reached for the plate he'd put the toast on and a stray fork. She carried them to the sink.

"Hey, you're breaking the rules!" he said, emptying her hands again. "Everyone knows after a night of incredible lovemaking, the man has to clean the kitchen when breakfast is done."

"It seems the men in your world are very misused," she said. "You wear yourselves out giving incredible pleasure in bed, then your women force you to work in the food preparation areas."

She was a treasure. Damn, he almost hated to take her back to his world. Humans were unworthy of Aliya.

"Couples who care about each other take turns," he said. The dishes began disappearing under warm water and soap bubbles in the sink. "Sometimes you let me take care of you, and sometimes you get to take care of me. Today, I take care of you."

She smiled at him, then her attention was caught by the foaming soap. "What is that? How do you make the water fill with air that way?"

He let her come up beside him and explained about soap and how it formed bubbles in running water. She was fascinated, tentatively reaching to touch the bubbles, then studying a glob of them carefully in her hand. He stood close, just watching her and enjoying the view.

She was unversed in such complicated things as buttons, so the shirt he'd loaned her was gaping at all the strategic places. As she studied how the light bounced off the soap bubbles, and how they sparkled and popped in her hands, he studied how her nipples were taut against the fabric of his shirt and it gathered at the small of her back where her wonderfully rounded bottom teased as she shifted and leaned over the sink.

He moved closer to her, feeling the wonderful warmth of her skin against his. She backed up to lean against him, holding the bubbles up to the sunlight filtering in through the galley window. She smelled good—warm woman, hot sex, and lemon dish soap. His groin hardened against her.

She felt him and made a breathy moan, moving slightly so his cock was pressing into her from behind. His reaction was overpowering. He wanted her every bit as badly as if he'd never had her. A growl escaped him as he reached around and slipped his hands inside her shirt. He found her nipples tight. She let out a sigh as he cupped her breasts and rolled those nipples between his finger and thumb.

She rested more of her weight against him, rising to her tiptoes and allowing his rigid cock to slide into the juncture between her legs. He thought he might come right then, but somehow managed to control himself. He needed to slow down. It wasn't fair to ambush her like this. Heck, she was probably more interested in the soap bubbles right now than boffing in the galley.

Then again, she was making those sweet little mermaid sounds and arching back into him. Yeah, she wasn't altogether indifferent to him, that was for sure. She moved even closer to him and leaned her elbows down on the sink.

Wow, her bottom was presented to him in a most delightful way! He ground against her, careful to go slow. She was hot and ready for him, he was glad to find. He could barely reach the swollen moistness, that delicate hot flesh he couldn't seem to get enough of, but he could reach enough to give her pleasure.

Reacting to his fervent probing, she bent farther to enhance his access. He took advantage and thrust himself into her. Oh, she was wonderful. Her hands grasped the windowsill above the sink and her nipples, still under his control, dipped into the foaming dish water. She moaned.

Letting the bubbles embrace her breasts, he slid his hands along her sides and down to her hips. He pushed the shirt up and watched their coupling in awe. He was far into her now, her round backside pressed up against him and sending flashes of heat and thrill through his whole body. She rocked with him, and he caressed her skin.

So soft, so yielding. She seemed in tune with his every move. She would let him do anything he wanted. And what he wanted, more than ever, was always.

"You're so wet," he breathed, pushing his way even farther inside her.

"Of course," she said, her voice as husky as his. "I'm a mermaid."

He laughed.

"And," she added, "you're really, really good."

He groaned. One hand skimmed around to touch her mound, applying gentle pressure just above where he was joining with her. His other hand went back to minister to her breast. The sink began to spill over, but neither of them cared.

He was thrusting against her with more force now, and she was making sounds of pleasure and encouragement. He held her to him for support and her knuckles whitened where she gripped the sill. Bubbles clung to her arms and where the shirt was wet it became transparent. He couldn't take his eyes off her; the shape of her body where her waist tapered and flared out at her hips, the texture of her silky, fresh skin on her lovely buttocks, the sight of his cock disappearing into her.

He rocked again and groaned as she shuddered and tensed around him. They came together, as he knew they would. It was always perfect with Aliya.

Perfect, except...there was something she wasn't telling him. He could feel it. Even as they stood together, her body still spasming around him and his knees barely stable enough to hold him up, he knew something was there between them. And it was bigger than either of them.

Damn, he couldn't lose her. Not now. Not ever!

"Mine," he whispered in her ear. "You're mine, and I love you."

"Devin," she murmured, letting him break their union and turn her to face him.

He kissed her and she melted into him. Maybe if they spent the rest of their lives together this way, joined in some physical fashion, they could hide from whatever unspoken force it was that appeared to be trying to separate them. Hell, it was worth a try.

He shut off the kitchen faucet, scooped her into his arms, and headed back to the bedroom.

Chapter Fifteen

Aliya rolled onto her side and watched the clouds drifting by outside the window. The sun was high in the middle of the sky now. Her stomach was beginning to ask for lunch. Yes, she supposed she should be hungry, after all the exertion of the last three hours.

Devin was like a starved man with a feast. He must know that their time together was nearly over. That fact hovered over them like a dark cloud. In just a matter of hours Raea would return and change her back to her true form. She would be a creature of the deep again, and Devin would go back to the dry. He would be over this obsession. He would forget her.

The clouds outside became blurry as tears welled in Aliya's eyes. Funny, she'd never had need of tears before. Odd that it would take living in the dry to make water collect in her eyes. But what she felt inside was even worse.

How could she live without Devin? How could she go back to any life she'd previously known? She couldn't. That life was past; Devin was her future now.

Something made her startle. What was that? A voice? No,

Devin was still sleeping soundly and there was no one nearby. But it seemed like...

Silently she slipped from the bed and padded out to the galley. There was still a puddle on the floor where the sink had run over, but other than that things were just as they should be. She could hear nothing outside but the gentle sounds of water and an occasional bird in the distance. Still, she could not discount the feeling they were not alone.

Cautiously she ducked up the stairs and scanned the deck. Empty. Silent. Peaceful. Not even another boat on the horizon. They were alone.

Hello?

She heard the voice clearly and jumped. But there was no one. No, she hadn't heard a voice. Her ears detected nothing. But she'd felt it. A timid, quiet voice calling her in the same manner her people called to one another through the water.

She peered over the side of the boat and into the water. Was someone searching for her? She hated to think what they would do if they found her here, like this.

"Who's there?" her mind called, reaching out toward the water. Communication was strained and awkward without the wetness surrounding her to carry the thoughts.

I don't know, the reply came back. But it was different from what she'd expected. Closer, even, than the water around them.

"Where are you?"

I like it here.

"Where? Where are you?" she asked aloud.

She glanced around the boat again and it was unnerving that there was nothing anywhere. Who was she talking to?

"Here. I'm right here."

She whirled, but this time the voice belonged to Devin. He'd come out onto the deck behind her and was smiling. She realized she was naked again and remembered how he'd explained that humans were used to seeing each other with clothing on. Good thing there hadn't been other boats nearby or she definitely would have drawn unwanted attention to herself.

But Devin never seemed to mind seeing her naked. The look on his face right now made it clear he very much appreciated her lack of clothing. The bulge in his shorts confirmed it, too. That made her smile. She was determined not to waste any of their precious time together.

"Did you hear a sound?" she asked him.

"A sound? I heard you come up here. Why? Did you hear something?"

She shook her head. "No, there's nothing."

He scanned the lake around them. "Are you sure?"

"Yes, I was imagining things."

Devin stepped out and put an arm around her. They stared off into the blue sky together. "You miss your home already, don't you?" he asked after a pause.

She considered his question before turning and meeting his eyes.

"No. I don't."

She spoke the truth. Every part of her meant it. She loved Devin and would be content even if she never again saw her family or friends of the deep. She dreaded Raea's return.

"Are you certain?" he asked.

Yes, she was. In fact, she would do anything to avoid Raea's return and the cursed Fairy Dust that would change her back into her old fish-self and ruin it all.

"I'm sure, Devin," she said, snuggling closer to him. "But I need you to do something for me."

"Anything."

It was a lot to ask. More than he could even understand right now. She shouldn't ask him. For his own good, he should be allowed to forget her. But she couldn't. Devin was her obsession now, just as she was his. She had to ask.

"Take me back to the dry."

"Take you back?"

"Yes. Now. Quickly."

He studied her face and she let him feel her thoughts. He had to understand how important it was. He had to take her where Raea couldn't find her and where she would never be changed into her old form again.

"And wish with all your heart that I may stay there. With you," she added. "Forever."

He pulled her close for a kiss. "Of course. That's easy."

Chapter Sixteen

The afternoon sun was hot. Raea could feel its rays against her skin, on the tiny scales of her wings, and it made her drowsy. It also made her remember the heat she'd felt this morning in the field, when Kyne had…but no way was she going to dwell on that!

What had happened between them was, as he'd said, illegal. It had been nothing more than his attempt at entrapping her, paying her back for what she'd done to Aliya. Well, it hadn't worked. She'd gotten him to promise to give her time to fix things, and fix them she would.

Just as soon as she found that damn boat.

Where was it? Where had Aliya and that hormonal human gone off to? She'd been hovering over this lake for hours now with no sign of them.

But she had to find them. It was almost time for Aliya's wish to wear off. Raea needed to find them and administer the Forgetful Dust before the man saw Aliya in her mermaid form again. For twenty-four hours his lust had been sated by a human. Forgetful Dust would wipe that away and his obsession would be cured.

If, however, the man knew that his lover was, in fact, a mermaid, the obsession would grow stronger and he'd remain in danger. The Old Revenge was too strong for Forgetful Dust. Raea could cure a human obsession, but not one after a Veiled creature. The man couldn't see Aliya's true form or they'd be right back where they started.

No, that wasn't true. They could possibly be *worse* than where they'd started. Aliya had been touched by a human. Forgetful Dust might erase the foul memories, but it would not change the fact. Whether she would remember it or not, passion would somehow leave its earthy mark on Aliya. Raea would not have believed this before, but now—thanks to Kyne—knew it for a fact.

All Kyne had done was kiss her, yet she felt as if her whole body was different. Her mind was straying in directions it had never gone before. Her skin was craving a touch she'd never imagined before. The rest of her seemed to be suddenly aware of something, too. She wanted Kyne—wanted him *that* way, that human way. The way Aliya and Devin had been satisfying their wanting all night long.

How on earth had she assumed this would never leave a lasting scar on Aliya? Human coupling was indeed much more than simple animal behavior. It truly meant something. And now that she had delivered Aliya to that man, her friend would suffer when she was forced to tear them apart. She should have listened to Kyne when he rambled on and on about the importance of the code and keeping themselves uninvolved in human life.

He knew. He, more than any other fairy, knew how painful this would be. By the Skies, he'd been right and she'd been wrong and now Aliya would suffer.

And Raea would be suffering right along with her. Let Kyne

take her before the council, let him tell all the other fairies about her unnatural taste for human sex, and still she'd be fighting these dreadful desires. For him. Damn and damn, but she wanted him and would just keep on wanting him. She'd be exiled from her people, and she'd be sitting out there on a cloud all alone somewhere remembering Kyne and the terrifying and wonderful taste he'd given her of pure, earthy desire. And dreaming about that bulge…

Oh, where was that damn boat? She had to find it. She couldn't just give up now and spend the rest of her life pining away like that. She *would* find Aliya, she *would* administer the Forgetful Dust and turn her back into a mermaid and she *would* make things right again. She had to. There was no other option.

So where would Aliya be? They couldn't have gone back to land. The sun would be setting soon and Aliya would turn into a mermaid again. Surely she wouldn't go to land for that, it would be suicide. Right?

Unless she was running away. By the Clouds, she wouldn't do that, would she? Didn't she realize it would be pointless? The wish had already been made and granted; Aliya would turn back into a mermaid at sunset whether she was on land or not. It wasn't an option!

Then again, maybe Raea hadn't exactly made the details clear. She'd been in such a hurry to win that bet, maybe she hadn't paid so much attention to explaining things. She'd been so sure she understood all this human interaction business it never dawned on her how important it was to Aliya—that the mermaid might actually want to remain human afterward.

Well. This was not good. They could be anywhere by now! How was she going to find them? She hadn't been on duty this afternoon, so wishes weren't being transmitted her way. How else was she going to detect their location if she couldn't hear Devin's wishes? By the time she started receiving again, it would be too late. The sun would be down and Aliya—wherever she was—would be a mermaid again.

And Raea would be in a heap of trouble. A sudden mermaid at the local McDonald's would certainly draw some attention. The council would bring charges of interference, and all of Raea's stupidity would become public knowledge. She would be punished, Aliya would be punished, Devin would be lost to the Old Revenge, and Kyne would get the thrill of turning her over to public censure. He and his interesting bulge would continue on happily, and Raea would be stuck in solitude wondering what could have been.

Things just couldn't get any worse.

Wait, she was wrong. They did get worse. Kyne showed up, bulge and all. And she couldn't help checking it out.

* * *

"Looking for your friend?" he asked.

Raea did not appear happy to see him. Well, he should have expected that after what he'd done earlier. Still, she might at least have the guts to look him in the eye.

"It isn't my friend, and…oh, you mean Aliya?"

"Of course. What other friend did you think I was talking about?"

Raea blushed a beautiful fuchsia. What was that all about? Maybe it wasn't blushing. She was probably flushed with anger.

Well, he couldn't blame her for still being upset with him. He'd been an animal. A very frustrated, unfulfilled animal. An animal who'd still jump on her any chance he could get. He was hopeless.

"I...I'm worried about Aliya," she said, ignoring his question. "I'm afraid she might have gone to land."

"What? But isn't she going to turn back into a mermaid? Won't that be a bit hazardous on land?"

Raea sighed. "Yes, it will. The deal was that she'd have until sunset today. That's just another hour or so. At least, I thought that's what the deal was. Maybe I didn't make it exactly clear to her."

"You mean, maybe you were a little too excited about winning that bet to consider how bad you could really mess this up."

"Shut up, Kyne. I swear, I think I like you better when you..." She closed her mouth quickly and darted off in another direction.

He followed. "You like me better when I what?"

"Nothing."

"Aw, come on. You like me better when I do what?" She didn't answer, so he replied for her. "When I hold on to you and put my body against you and..."

"Shut up! No. I do *not* like you better then."

"Oh? Then maybe it's when I kiss you, or when I..."

He'd gotten close enough for their wings to brush, but she sped up and moved away from him. "No, definitely not then."

"Huh. Well, then it must be when I—"

"It's when you're *gone*, damn it. I like you better when you're *gone*. So go away, Kyne."

Of course he didn't. He knew she was struggling with this just as much as he was. He was not alone in his wanting and that made it all the harder to...well, it just made it harder. It was stupid, unnatural, and illegal, but Raea wanted him the way he wanted her. Of course he wasn't going away.

On the other hand, if they didn't find that mermaid soon, Raea would be in a world of trouble and then no amount of wanting would ever count for anything. He'd lose her forever, before they'd really done anything even remotely worthy of being punished. If he was going to spend the rest of his life in frustrated solitude, he was damn well going to earn it.

"You need me, Raea," he said.

"No. I don't," she said sharply, pausing in flight to turn and face him. "I don't need you or your disgusting kisses or your bulging... thingy. Isn't my life messed up enough right now?"

"Yeah, it's pretty messed up. But you still really do need me."

"You started all this, if you recall. What more can I possibly need you for?"

"You need me because I know where the mermaid is."

She faltered mid-flutter. "What?"

"Yeah, I know where she is."

It felt good to get her attention.

"You do?" she asked, eager.

"I do."

"You saw them?"

"No, not exactly, but I know how to find them."

Now she was suspicious. "How?"

By the Skies, suspicion and distrust made her eyes alive with fire. Obviously she was warring with herself. Part of her wanted to believe him, part of her wanted to hate him, and part of her wanted to... well, he really hoped there was still an itty-bitty part of her that wanted to do exactly what he wanted to do. Badly.

But first, she was still waiting for him to answer her question. Well, they were never going to get on with things if they didn't take care of the mermaid issue. He had to get his mind back on business. For now.

"I can feel where she is," he said simply.

It wasn't a detailed explanation, and he hoped she'd let it go at that. He would rather not explain the details, or how he could feel where she was.

"You can *feel* where she is? What exactly does that mean?"

"She's a mermaid. They're telepathic."

"Yes, but *I* can't feel where she is. Their telepathy works only in the water, between mermaids, you moron."

"No, the water helps but that's not it. You can't feel her because you're a fairy."

"So are you. What does that have to do with anything?"

"Don't pretend you haven't heard the rumors about me. You, of anyone, must know the truth by now."

"The truth?"

He was going to have to tell her, wasn't he? There was no way around it. For the sake of making this right, of setting the balance, he'd have to be honest with Raea.

"It's true, what they say," he admitted with as much dignity as he could manage. "I'm half human."

She didn't cringe or pretend to be shocked. She simply nodded and shifted her eyes, toward anything but him.

"Yes, I suppose I figured that."

"It's my human half that can feel them, can sense them."

"Because humans are more telepathic than fairies?"

"No, because…"

By the Skies, he hated admitting this. He hated anything that forced him to acknowledge his human side. He hated that Raea would have to know the very worst of him this way.

"Why, Kyne? How can you know?"

"Because she's with the human."

She dipped lower, toward the water, scanning in earnest for the boat that was simply not there.

"But there's no sign of him. Did she take him down with her, underwater?"

"No, they're not here. They've gone to the docks, near the land."

"But that's miles and miles away. How on earth can you *feel* her that far?"

He could see Raea was still confused. She would drag this confession from him, wouldn't she? He took a deep breath and continued.

"Because she's with the human. I can feel it."

If they'd been standing on the ground she would have stomped her foot. As it was, she just glared at him and buzzed her wings furiously.

"You can't feel a human so far away. Humans aren't telepathic, Kyne."

"No, but mermaids are and she's with the human. I mean, she's *with* him. Right now. They're...doing it again."

"What?"

"Look, I can feel the passion, okay? When humans are... aroused...I can feel it."

"There's nobody else around here, aroused or otherwise," she said, then gave a meaningful glare. "Believe me."

He ignored the insult. "The mermaid's telepathy makes it stronger. I can feel them a longer distance away than usual. And believe me, she's *with* him right now. At the docks."

He couldn't help but notice her involuntary glance down at his most human attribute.

"You're sure?"

"Yes. The bulging *thingy* is not entirely on account of you."

She dragged her eyes up to his face. The fuchsia crept back into her cheeks. Apparently it had not been purely from anger before. That was just slightly encouraging.

"Okay, so where are they?" she asked.

"I'll show you. Come on."

"No, just tell me."

"I can't tell you. I won't know exactly what dock they're at until we get there."

"Oh, so you want to get closer so you can *feel* them better." She rolled her eyes.

"Exactly."

"Pervert."

"Pervert kisser."

"Shut up!"

He started off to lead the way and she followed grudgingly. He could hear her wings a nice, safe distance behind. He'd rather be following her so he could enjoy the view, but figured having Raea staring at his backside all the way to land wasn't such a bad thing. Might give her some interesting, unfairylike ideas.

"Told you that you needed me," he called back to her.

"I don't need you, Kyne. Just concentrate on finding Aliya."

She needed him, all right. By the Skies, he was determined to make sure it would be for far more than just locating a mermaid.

Chapter Seventeen

Devin's lovemaking had been heavenly. Aliya would never tire of being with him this way. Or any other way he could think of. Devin was a very creative human.

Their journey to the dry had not taken very long. She was surprised by how fast Devin could make his boat travel. It was invigorating to move through the air so quickly. They had arrived at what Devin called his marina, and she was surprised to find how many other humans kept boats there. Some of them even lived there, on their boats. She liked that idea. Maybe she could live here with Devin.

She had waited on board while Devin used ropes to secure the boat, and he had said they would leave, then to go to his home. But she had become confused about the clothing he'd given her to wear and he'd tried to help her dress and things got all out of control.

Once again they'd ended up in each other's arms and Devin had come inside her in that wonderful way of his. Time had slipped away and it was nearly sunset. Raea was probably out looking for her again.

That made her nervous. All afternoon she'd been on her guard. She'd had the unmistakable feeling they weren't alone; someone was nearby, just out of sight.

But how could that be? They'd left the open waters behind. There were no mermaids here in this crowded marina. She kept looking over her shoulder and scanning the skies, but there was no sign of Raea. So how could she explain this persistent presence surrounding them? What was it? Something to fear?

Am I safe?

She felt the voice transmitting again. It was the same quiet voice she'd detected earlier. Hardly even there, but undeniable all the same. And so very, very close.

"You're safe," she answered back. Whatever—or whoever—this was, something compelled her to reassure. She'd heard the fear in the tiny voice and it ripped at her soul. *"I promise, you're safe."*

I believe you.

The relief and the trust were evident. The tiny voice was at peace. Aliya herself was suddenly overwhelmed with emotion. It wasn't any emotion she could name, but more like a wash of many emotions all swamping her together: joy, anticipation, concern, fulfillment, fear, and a hundred other things she couldn't pick out of the mix.

One thing she did know, however. She knew where this mysterious and miraculous voice was coming from.

"What is it? You look a little worried," Devin said, rolling onto his side to watch her.

She snuggled against him, glad for the closeness and even more glad that this allowed her not to meet his eyes. Not just yet. She couldn't face him yet.

"We should be getting dressed again," she said.

"I like it better being undressed."

She had to agree. His body was so warm, so strong, so comfortable against hers. The light hairs on his skin prickled and tingled where she brushed against him. No, she just could not let this end.

"Make love to me again, Devin," she said, reaching to touch his hardened shaft.

But he took her hand in his and raised it to his lips. "No," he said softly. "First, tell me what's wrong. I know something's bothering you. I can feel it."

She couldn't answer. Of course he was right; he could feel her turmoil. But what could she say? She couldn't tell him. What would he think of her if she explained that all along she'd been lying to him? That at any moment Raea could show up and tear them apart forever?

That now there was more involved in this than just the two of them and their unexplainable passion. No, she couldn't tell him.

"Aliya, please. Whatever it is, we can make it right. Together."

She made herself meet his eyes. There was so much love there! He did love her. She could see it, feel it in the air around them. And she owed him the truth. If it changed how he felt about her, then so be it. She would let Raea find her and go back to the water.

"I have lied to you, Devin," she said finally.

He still held her hand. His body was still warm against hers. But she felt the cold well up in his heart. Already her words hurt him.

He waited for her to continue, but she couldn't. At last he said, "You're going to leave me, aren't you?"

She felt those tears again. Such an odd sensation. "I don't want to," she began. "But if she finds me, I'll have to."

"Who? If *who* finds you?"

"Her name is Raea. She's my friend."

"If she's your friend, why would she make you leave?"

"Because she has to. It's a part of the wish, you see."

Now she felt his confusion. How was she going to make him understand? Could he ever understand?

"I've been getting a lot of new information the last two days," he said with a smile. "I think you'd better start from the beginning and fill me in slowly."

She sighed. At least he was willing to listen. "Raea is a fairy."

She launched into an explanation about fairies and their duties regarding humans. His eyes grew wider, but he didn't argue or stop her in total disbelief. It was almost as if he were glad to finally understand how a mermaid could suddenly show up on his boat with human legs.

He nodded as she reminded him of their first encounter that night in the water. She told him how Raea had heard his many wishes the following day, how it was obvious he had come under the spell of the Old Revenge. He wasn't quite as receptive to that point as she would have hoped, but she understood he wanted to believe there was more to their mutual love than simple obsession.

When she told him of the bargain she'd struck with Raea, he became angry. She'd expected that. Maybe it was for the best. Perhaps it would be easier for him to let her go if he was angry.

"So this Raea knew how I felt about you, knew you cared about me, and still all she gave us was twenty-four hours? That doesn't sound like much of a friend, Aliya."

"But she didn't know, Devin," she defended. "I didn't know. We'd never been told that this sort of attraction could be anything more than just a temporary and unnatural temptation. She thought it would help you to get over me."

"Well, it hasn't."

"I know that now."

He paused. "And what about you?"

"About me?"

"There's something else you're not telling me."

"No. I told you everything about the wish."

"Did you?"

"Of course, Devin." She tried, but she just couldn't make herself look at him.

"No, I know you better than that, Aliya. There's more."

"But Devin, I just can't…"

He flopped onto his back and rubbed his eyes. No doubt he was exhausted from their lack of sleep. This must all be very hard on him. Maybe it would be better if she just let Raea find her and send her on home. As it was, she could only ever be a burden to Devin, especially now that…No, she'd better not even think about that or Devin might feel her emotions and know.

"What is it?" he asked, turning back to her.

She just shook her head. She couldn't even trust her own voice right now.

"Aliya," he prodded, "just tell me. Whatever it is, I'll understand. If you want to go back, that's okay."

Go back? Is that what he thought she wanted? Maybe he wasn't as aware of her thoughts as she assumed he was if he could believe she actually wanted to leave him. It would be the best thing for him, but it was far from what she wanted.

"I want your happiness above all, Devin," she said. That much was true.

"Then you'll stay with me," he said and reached to pull her close again.

"Yes."

Yes, she would stay. She'd find a way to avoid Raea. She'd stay human and be with Devin, and somehow she'd find a way to tell him the rest of it. He loved her, so he'd understand.

She melted into him, pushing all worries and fear from her mind. Raea wouldn't know to look for them here. For a while, at least, she'd still be out on the lake, searching there. By the time she realized they'd headed for shore, they could be well hidden among the humans. After all, fairies weren't telepathic or all-seeing. So long as neither of them started making any wishes, Raea would never be alerted to their location.

It seemed a good plan. And Aliya would make Devin so very happy he would never have to wish for anything again. She only hoped she could live up to such a promise.

Well, she knew how to start. Her body was already tingling with anticipation of just how happy she could make him.

* * *

Devin groaned under the onslaught of Aliya's attention. She'd certainly gained some confidence over the last twenty-four hours! The things that girl was doing to him—amazing. He'd given up trying to take over when she practically pinned him to the bed and parked her beautiful derriere right on his chest as she bent to run kisses all up and down his throbbing cock. Yep, he was perfectly content to lie there.

He'd thought he'd known everything there was to know about making love to her, but he'd been wrong. This was a whole new side of Aliya, and he was liking it. She was eating him up with a vengeance.

She'd started by kissing him on the lips. He had found such passion and connection in it that it surprised him when she'd moved on down to other body parts: his neck, his nipples, his navel, and now this. She knew what he liked.

And now she brought her mouth down to cover him. She took him all in, her teeth slightly grazing his sensitive skin. He sucked in a grinding breath, forcing himself to be calm and let the pleasure continue. And it did continue.

With her lips firmly around his rock-solid cock, her tongue flicked over the tip. It created a gentle suction and she made a contented little moan, tasting him fully. He struggled not to succumb to her motions. It was damn hard to resist what his body wanted so badly.

Her naked heat was pressed against him. He could feel her wetness against his skin. He wanted to touch her there, but he kept his fists firmly clenched in the bedding beside him. This was Aliya's ride. She'd let him know when she was done tormenting him and ready to take some pleasure for herself. He knew exactly how much she was enjoying this newfound power of hers and wasn't about to stop her. Yet. He knew what Aliya was doing was well beyond his ability to hold out for long.

"You taste good, Devin," she said, stopping for a breath. "What they say the sea is like. But sweet."

He couldn't quite think of words to express exactly how she made him feel. There was nothing to come close. Instead he just groaned softly and tried not to come in her face.

She must have been aware of his great effort. With a light laugh, she turned gracefully to face him. Her eyes were bright and her lips were swollen and red. That nearly white hair of hers trailed down over her shoulders and brushed across his face.

"I want you, too," she said, echoing his inward longing.

Without pause, she slid back just enough to bring herself down on him. His cock slid easily into her. God, she was so wet and still so tight. He held back the urge to thrust up into her, bringing them both to climax before they'd even begun.

But she anticipated him and rose up onto her knees. Just the very tip of him was still inside her, teased by her burning heat. She smiled at him sweetly.

Ever so slowly she lowered back down again, letting him fill her. He watched her face glow with enjoyment. Just watching her and knowing how she loved him was almost as good as actually doing it with her.

She teased him for a while, slowly riding up and down his throbbing shaft. She knew him well, it appeared. Every time he was nearly about to explode under her, she shifted her rhythm just enough to bring him back into control again. It went on and on for ages. Thank heaven.

Finally he was aware of a slight change in her. The steady motion of her rocking hips was getting to her. He watched her eyes drift shut and knew she was becoming lost in their pleasure. He rubbed her hips in gentle circles, urging her to give in to herself and let the climax take her.

She responded to his touch more than he could have imagined. Her nails dug into his shoulders as she worked her body against his. Again and again she backed off, only to bring herself crashing down onto him. He was deep, deep inside her and the sensation was rapidly overtaking him. He didn't fight it a bit.

His hands were still massaging her hips. She was so firm and womanly rounded there. Her skin was soft and velvety. His fingertips tingled where they contacted her. Her movements were fluid and demanding. He gave her everything he could.

With an animal growl he came. Spasms of pleasure shook him and he emptied into her with throbbing urgency. She was right there with him, crying out his name and wrapping her body around him. It was impossible this time could be more intense than all the others, but he was willing to swear that was true.

Aliya seemed more affected, as well. She was gasping for breath long after the wave of sensation had subsided. He stroked her back to calm her. His cock was still inside her, so he knew her own body was still reacting heavily to him. Her taut muscles contracted and held him tight.

"By the Creator, Devin," she rasped. "I feel it happening!"

He smiled. "It's not unusual. Some women are able to experience multiple…"

But he stopped as she jerked her body off him and rolled awkwardly away, grabbing for the bedsheet.

"Don't look at me!" she cried.

His mind was still numb from the sex. What was she going on about? He reached for her, trying to turn her back to face him. She only struggled harder with the bedding, burying her face in a pillow.

"What is it? Aliya, what's the matter?"

"No! No, no, no! By the Sweet Waters, please no!"

She was sobbing now, writhing in the twisted bedding. He was more than a little confused, but the pain in her voice was obvious. He grabbed her, pulling her close to him and pushing the pillow away. Her hair was tangled over her face and she thrashed back away from him.

"Aliya, talk to me!" he ordered.

He was feeling something like panic now as he looked into those glaring crystal blue eyes of hers. She looked wild and miserable.

"My God, Aliya, what's wrong?"

But she didn't answer. She just stared up at him and slowly her terror faded. Her body went limp. At last she blinked at him and tears welled up against her eyelashes.

"I'm so sorry, Devin," she murmured.

"What is it? What in God's name is…"

Then he stopped. He knew. He felt it.

In his efforts to hold her, he'd managed to slide one hand inside the sheets she'd quickly rolled herself in. Now he felt her, touched the skin at her thigh. It was satiny smooth and cool to the touch. The skin of a sea creature, not a woman.

Oh God. He knew why Aliya cried.

"I couldn't stop it!" she said. "I tried, but…"

"It's okay," he assured her, brushing her hair back and meeting her gaze.

"I thought if we came here, where Raea couldn't find us…"

"It's okay," he repeated.

Somehow he believed himself. For all the strangeness of their situation, he still held Aliya in his arms and he still loved her. Whatever she was, she was his. They'd find a way to make this okay.

"I'm so sorry," she said.

"Don't be. It's not your fault."

"I should never have let any of this happen."

"What? No, Aliya. These past twenty-four hours have been the most amazing time of my life. You reached inside and found a part of me no one ever touched before. I've felt things deeper than I could have imagined. No, I wouldn't wish our time away for anything."

"But it's gone! It's over now!"

"Not by a long shot. What we've meant to each other—what you still mean to me—will never be gone. Things are a little different than I expected, but you're still here, aren't you?"

She smiled a weak smile and touched his face. "I can't very much go anywhere like this. You'll have to carry me to the water."

"What? Throw you back? Not on your life!"

He'd meant that as a joke, but she didn't get it. Her eyes clouded over and a tear slipped down her cheek.

"But you'll have to, Devin."

"Have to? You mean, you can't live out of the water?"

"Not for long. It's so dry up here. There's so much air. And I feel heavy…it's hard to breathe."

"Oh, damn it, Aliya. I can't lose you now!"

"You have to, Devin. I can't stay with you. I need to be back in the lake. It's been so long already, and now there's…"

He frowned. She'd started to say something, then caught herself quickly and shut up. More secrets? What on earth could the girl possibly have to hide from him now?

"Now there's what?" he prodded.

She looked away from him. Her tail twitched nervously under the covers.

"Nothing."

Well, he didn't believe that for a minute.

"Come on, tell me. After all we've been through already, I'm pretty sure you can trust me not to freak out, whatever it is."

"I don't know."

"Come on. What's the big problem now, aside from the obvious?"

She gave him another thin smile. "This might be big enough to make you—what did you say?—freak out."

"Try me."

She took a deep breath and made a slight wheezing sound. It was too dry for her here, he could tell. Damn it.

"It's something I never expected. I promise, Devin, I never even dreamed it was possible!"

"Go on."

"It usually doesn't work this way, so perhaps now that I've changed back…perhaps it cannot even proceed."

Her eyes darkened again, but the tears were drying up. He knew she'd be shedding them if she could, though. Whatever this big dilemma was really had her torn up.

"I'll do whatever I can to help," he said, taking her hand to his lips. Her skin was cool and dry.

"I know you will, but for this there is nothing you can do."

"Then I'll just keep on loving you, no matter what."

She smiled and there was a little of her usual calmness and trust in it.

"You are a good man, Devin," she said. "Better than most humans. I am very proud to be carrying your child, even if only for a brief while."

"Well, I…wait, what?"

"I'm sorry, but I cannot know if I will be able to produce a child in this form. It's never done this way in our people, so I never even imagined it could happen."

He was in shock. Was she serious? Had he heard correctly? Aliya was pregnant? It couldn't be. Even if it could, she wouldn't know about it already. They'd been together exactly one day! She had to be just speaking hypothetically, right?

"I don't understand." He managed to gulp.

"I'm sorry. I've shocked you. I shouldn't have said anything about it."

"No…no, you should. Definitely you should! But I just don't see how…I mean, I know how that could happen and all, but I just don't…it's just that…" He made himself take a deep breath and gather a coherent thought. "You're saying you're pregnant?"

She nodded. "Please do not be angry. I promise, I will require nothing of you, and certainly you're not to blame…"

"I hope to God I am to blame!" he said quickly. "I don't want to think anyone else...but how can you know? It's too soon, I mean."

"The child speaks to me," she said simply.

"It does what?"

"Speaks to me. I can sense thoughts and emotion. At first I wasn't sure what it was, I thought I heard voices from outside, but now I understand. I was unaware it could be so soon, but the tiny life is well and truly there and I feel its presence."

"It's that whole telepathy thing?"

"Yes."

This was a lot to digest. His lover of twenty-four hours was a pregnant mermaid carrying his psychic baby? A lot harder to comprehend than the market analyses he was used to getting at the end of the day.

"And you're sure it's not just...a regular mermaid thing? I mean, you're sure this baby has something to do with me? I'm not, well, I'm not questioning you or doubting you, I'm just trying to understand."

God, he felt like a heel even saying that. As if Aliya would lie to him about this!

But she didn't seem offended. She smiled and laid one trembling hand against his cheek.

"I have not been deemed mature enough to be granted the honor of motherhood," she said. "Many of us go our entire life without a Life Fish ceremony."

Man, he was damn glad to hear that. No matter what her people thought was an honor, he could never be happy about Aliya going through that. It was dangerous, after all.

But dear God, how much more danger would a regular human pregnancy be for her? Jeez, she was half fish now. Her body was not made for birthing human babies. Damn it, but he could have endangered her life here!

"My God, Aliya." He sighed. "I should have used condoms."

"Is condoms one of your rituals?"

"No, not exactly. But it should be. If I'd used my brain instead of just my... well, it is protection against this sort of thing. You would not have ended up in this condition."

"So you are upset. I knew it would not be good news for you, Devin. I'm so very sorry."

He held her tightly. "I'm not upset, Aliya. Not at you, anyway. I just hate myself for not thinking of you. I don't want anything to happen that might hurt you."

"I'm all right," she said. "Like I told you, perhaps this child may not even be able to continue and we will not have anything more to... worry about."

She tried to sound calm and casual, but obviously the thought of losing her child, even at this early date, was misery for her. Devin had to admit he didn't much like that idea, either. If Aliya was carrying his child, even if it was only twenty-four hours along, he damn well wanted both of them to be just fine. But what on earth could he do about this? No obstetrician he knew of had any experience in this sort of thing.

She coughed. It was a dry, crackling sound. The sound of someone in trouble. Aliya needed water. Now. He had to get her back into the lake, and here in the middle of this crowded marina was not the place for it.

"I'm taking us out to open water. We've got to get you wet again."

"I like when you make me wet, Devin," she said softly.

At first he thought it was just his dirty mind that gave another meaning to her words, but then he caught that glint in her eye. She knew what she was saying. Even with all these crazy things going on around them, Aliya was still interested in the fun stuff. Definitely he was not going to lose this woman.

He pushed the sheets aside to stroke her fish skin. It was dry but still soft to his hands. She sighed under his touch. Even out of water, this area was obviously very sensitive for her. He spared just a moment to run his fingers over her and watch her relax.

"I like that," she said. "Keep touching me, Devin."

"But don't you think we need to get you out to the…"

"I'm not going to wither away just yet," she said. "This feels very nice."

He kept doing it, stroking slowly with the grain of her tiny scales. So soft, like velvet. He let his eyes take in her whole form: beautiful, perfect woman and lithe, exotic sea creature. Strange as it was, he still desired her.

"Do you hate to see me this way, Devin?" she asked quietly.

"I love you however you're shaped, Aliya," he said, bending to kiss her at the waist and then lower, where she became all fish.

She purred under his caress. He trailed kisses up her abdomen and then found a pink-tipped nipple to draw into his mouth. She tasted salty and wonderful.

His cock was hard again and he brushed it against her. The sensation was remarkable for both of them, judging by Aliya's pleasured sighs.

She took him into her hand, holding him and squeezing him as he suckled at that nipple. Damn it, but she was going to make him come again. He only wished he could return the favor.

Chapter Eighteen

They're this way," Kyne informed as he led Raea through the sunset-gold sky.

"Are you sure?" she asked.

"Yes," he said. He didn't want to have to explain further. He knew where to find the mermaid and her lover; it was painfully obvious they were at it again.

By the Skies, it was hard to fly. The passion those two emitted was thick and heavy, like honey. It filled his senses and weighed him down with longing. Yes, he knew exactly where they were.

"Really? There have got to be a million boats at that marina, and a dozen other marinas all up and down this shore. How do you know this is the right dock?"

"It is," he said, narrowing in on the boat.

"How can you be sure?"

"I just am, all right?"

Raea giggled. "You can't be serious. They are actually doing it *again*?"

"Yes," he admitted. "This human appears to have amazing… stamina."

"Obviously Aliya is not such a slouch, either. But…you can feel it?"

"Yes."

"Do you mean you can sense that it's going on, or that you can actually, you know, feel it?"

"Both."

He searched his emotions, his senses, to locate the boat. One quick glance at Raea let him know just what she thought of his unusual talent. She wrinkled her nose. In disgust, obviously.

"Do you like it?" she asked after a pause.

"Shut up, Raea."

"Well, I was only asking."

"There's the boat." He pointed.

The sun was perched just on the horizon, sending gold and pink rays through the thin clouds that smeared over the sky. Fortunately, this provided some cover for the fairies. They could blend in with this backdrop, invisible to anyone who might have taken time to let the enchantment of this brilliant sunset open their eyes. He felt fairly safe, though. Humans were so caught up in the mundane, they rarely noticed magic.

"All right, then, come on," Raea said, moving carefully past him. "There's no one around right now."

Kyne hesitated. Raea looked so damned good, hovering in the pink sky just in front of him. The rhythm of nearby passion pounded in his veins. Could Raea feel it, too? Her wings took on a steady beat, matching it. He wanted to touch her, to join in that rhythm.

It was getting harder and harder to ignore these base urges. What was it, his prolonged exposure to humans, or to Raea? He wasn't sure. One thing he did know, though, was that he couldn't take much more of it. Not without breaking.

"Come on, get over here. What are you waiting for?" she whispered toward him.

He gritted his teeth. If she had any clue what he was fighting against, she wouldn't be such a smart-ass. And she sure wouldn't want him any nearer to that unfettered passion. Or to her.

"I'm not sure we should go down there right now..."

She turned on him, her little pink hands balled into fists and propped primly on her hips. Her wings buzzed, and he knew she was trying to shame him. But it wasn't shame that was making his skin itch and his breath come in rough, ragged draws. It was pure, unadulterated lust. And it wasn't just because he was near the passionate couple.

It was because of Raea. She was studying him as if trying to figure it all out. He'd love to have given a very instructional lesson.

"Is all the sweating and moaning and carnal human activity so very troublesome to you?" she asked. "Well, only one thing to do. You've got to get down there and face your fears, Kyne."

"I'm not the one who ought to be afraid right now, Raea," he said calmly.

She was intelligent enough to hear the huskiness of his voice and notice what had to be burning in his eyes. She backed up a bit. Yeah, she'd better start realizing exactly what a delicate spot she'd gotten herself into.

By the Skies, those two on the boat were going to drive him into insanity! It took every ounce of his fairy blood to cool the fire inside as he felt their raging climax. It was especially strong this time. He wasn't sure how, but he managed to stay airborne. His vision blurred slightly, though, and he was vaguely aware of Raea putting more air between them. She could see what was happening to him, and was beginning to fear it. He could read this on her face.

Instead of hating himself for it, though, her vulnerability just served to make him grow hotter.

"It's almost sunset," Raea said quickly. "Aliya will be changing soon…"

The sudden shift in emotion made Kyne dizzy. He'd been fighting back the surge of passion that tried to sweep him into oblivion with the lovers below, but now what he felt emanating from them was something different. It slammed into him with tangible force and he shuddered. But his vision and his mind cleared instantly. The climax he'd been expecting—dreading, actually—had been averted. The lovers were suddenly interrupted by something well beyond their control.

"Too late," he informed her. "She's changed back."

Now Raea seemed to falter. "What? Oh no! Are you certain?"

"Positive. I felt it happen while they were, er, joining."

Raea cringed. "So is she…I mean, what will the human do now? What will he do to her?"

This simple question was like cold water thrown over Kyne. *What will he do to her?* The human brute had been lied to, deceived. There was no telling how he'd react when he suddenly found a mermaid in his bed.

By the Clouds and Stars, if he hurt that poor creature…

"Come on," he said, now in full control of his faculties. "Let's get down there."

"No, not yet," she whispered. "Let me put some Veiling Dust on you first."

He took a minute to let this sink in, then eyed her in surprise. "You have Veiling Dust?"

She shrugged, pulling a small pouch from her belt. "Yeah, a little. I requisitioned it for this job I did a while back where I had to be around humans but couldn't afford to be seen."

"Aren't you supposed to turn in any leftovers?"

"I only have a little," she repeated with a hiss.

"And you kept it for yourself? Just what sort of human interaction did you have in mind that might require Veiling Dust?"

She didn't bother to answer his question. "You of all people shouldn't be such a rule stickler."

He just shook his head. There'd be time to read her the riot act over this later. *If* he decided to bother with lecturing, and really that wasn't exactly the first thing that came to mind when he thought about what to do with Raea and her aptitude for disregarding rules.

"Stop it," he said, brushing away the sparkling powder she began to fling over his shoulders and wings.

"Hey, I just put it on you! They'll see you if you don't keep it on and wait for it to go into full effect."

"I'm not about to get picked up for using a controlled substance off-duty," he said and turned to brush off any of the residue. "And neither are you."

"Stop it!"

She fought him, but he managed to dust off the clinging powder. It was harder keeping his hands off her once the job was done, however. Her skin was so soft…even her wings felt good to him. He wanted to go on touching her, and it had nothing to do with getting rid of the Veiling Dust.

For a split second their eyes met. What other rules could he persuade her to break today? He could think of a few he'd be happy to suggest. But not now. Now he had a mermaid to think of and he needed to keep focus.

"You wasted some perfectly good Veiling Dust," she grumbled, looking hastily away from him.

"I would prefer to be visible right now."

"Oh? Because you think I like looking at you?"

He couldn't help but smile. She blushed, and he knew it was because she'd been painfully transparent. She *did* like looking at him, and now she'd as much as gone and admitted it.

He, however, had to keep his mind on the job. For both of their sakes.

"No," he answered coolly. "Because I want that damn human to know what he's up against if he has any dumb ideas about treating your friend down there badly."

Raea put her chin up in the air and smoothed her clothing down where he had been brushing her. He was happy to note that anywhere he'd touched her skin, she'd gone a deeper shade of pink.

"I don't think there's any reason for you to continue using vulgar human curses."

Had he been? He hadn't noticed. Damn.

"I just want to be sure that human understands me. Now, if you promise not to scream, I'd like to show you something."

"There's nothing you have that I want to see."

He knew she was lying, so he grinned. "Yeah? Just watch."

He reached into his pouch. He had plenty of Sizing Dust, though he doubted he'd need much for himself. He'd barely managed to keep control over his body while the lovers on that boat had been going at it full force. Now, however, he realized that was exactly what was needed.

The human would hardly be intimidated by two tiny fairies landing on his boat, but if these fairies were human size that would get his attention. It would feel damn good, too, considering how his body now ached after such a close call with those lovers. It was hard enough to maintain his fairy appearance when he was in full control of himself, but when arousal entered the picture...well, a nice dose of Sizing Dust would give him part of the release that he needed.

"Here," he said, tossing the Sizing Dust over himself. "This is what we need now."

He took a deep, full breath and let the dust settle over him. The tension in his muscles eased, his skin tingled, and he felt his essence swell inside him. Other parts, as well, but just for now that was not going to be a problem. He stretched his wings to their full width and let go the last little bit of constraint that held his body in check. At long last he had a good, legitimate reason to let his human blood flow unhindered.

His body grew to enormous proportions—*human* proportions. Raea's eyes blinked wide and she fluttered backward, moving away as he became a huge, winged human right in front of her eyes. It felt wonderful to finally present himself as he was. It was even more wonderful to recognize something more than simple surprise on Raea's delicate face.

She was not merely horrified by him, she was intrigued.

"You…you used Sizing Dust."

"And so should you. Do you need some?"

"I have my own, thank you, but—"

"Don't you think this will be more impressive for that human than my usual form?"

"Yes! By the Skies, Kyne, you are…I mean, the human will definitely take us more seriously if we are so large and imposing…with shoulders, and…"

She was nervous and fumbling around at her belt. He didn't let her notice him laughing at her. He hoped she didn't notice any of his other reactions to her, either.

Finally she pulled out another pouch and gathered a handful of dust from it. She threw it all over herself and then took a deep breath, waiting for something to happen. It took a moment, but then suddenly she was at his side, literally growing in stature to nearly match him. She looked touchable and holdable and bliss-fully sturdy. She, however, had needed twice the Sizing Dust he had used to achieve such proportions.

"That's a very good look on you," he said.

"Let's hope it serves the purpose," she replied. "We'll be certain that human takes us seriously here."

Their increased size was going to make them highly visible as the remnants of the Veiling Dust wore off. It was also making it harder to hover. Kyne let himself sink toward the boat. He landed with an unfairylike thud on the wooden deck. The small opening in the cabin behind him was undoubtedly the way he needed to go. Raea touched down silently next to him.

She huffed a bit. "Very well. What are we waiting for?"

"I'm not waiting for anything," he said, giving her a deep, searing look and then heading through the doorway.

He barely fit through the small opening. His flame-orange wings had to fold in to get through, and going down the tiny stairway was almost comical. Yeah, he hoped he intimidated that brute down there, abusing some sweet, innocent Veiled creature. He only hoped the poor mermaid wasn't emotionally scarred for life from this ordeal!

As he made his way through the interior and toward the room with the lovers, their passion still hung thick in the air, even from beyond the closed door. That surprised him. He would have expected it to have dissipated by now and not be so troublesome for him. In fact, he might have expected to feel some of the horror the mermaid must be feeling as her lover recoiled in disgust from her changed form. But he didn't feel any of that.

Instead, he felt...well, by the Skies, they were getting back at it again!

"What is it?" Raea whispered at his shoulder when he paused

at the door. But even she must have felt his growing tension. And other things.

He couldn't answer. He didn't quite believe what he was feeling. He flung the door open, and there they were. The two of them, human and mermaid, wrapped around each other and fully in the throes of passion. Again.

Holy hell, shit, damn, and fuck! His human half was every bit as shocked as his fairy half. The human really did care for the mermaid, and the passion and emotion surrounding them had Kyne grabbing the door frame to keep himself upright. Well, most of him needed help with that. One particular body part was upright just fine.

Chapter Nineteen

Raea peered around Kyne in amazement. The human was practically gnawing Aliya's nipple right off her left breast, and oh my! Aliya was yanking on the man's penis as if her life depended on it! It was shocking and disgusting, and immediately her own body flared into arousal.

Raea's own traitorous breasts cried out for some of the same attention Aliya was getting, and the most horrid image of Kyne's humanlike body parts burned into her brain. It was awful! And entirely distracting. By the Air and the Skies, she was far too close to Kyne now, pressed up against him, gawking at the lovers, imagining their feelings and craving them for herself.

She gasped, or perhaps moaned. Aliya heard it and looked up, then made some unintelligible exclamation. The human left Aliya's breast and turned to find them there. His eyes got wild and he uttered an oath. Quickly he scrambled to pull the bedclothes over himself and Aliya.

He sat up quickly, making an obvious attempt to keep his own body between the strangers in the doorway and Aliya in his bed. Everything about his expression and position was instantly defensive. Was he ready to battle them for the sake of his mermaid? It certainly appeared so. How terribly sweet! Perhaps Aliya was right; this human had some finer qualities than most.

She wasn't sure if Kyne noticed any finer qualities, though. He marched toward the man like some avenging angel, his fiery wings humming with anger and his eyes blazing. It was a sight that would have scared the feathers right off Raea if he'd caught her in a position like that, she was sure. But the human took it in stride.

"Who the hell are you?" he growled.

"I am Kyne of the Summer Fairies," Kyne replied, with a dramatic pause for effect. "And why, may I ask, are you laughing at me?"

The man *was* laughing. It was the oddest thing.

"Kind of a summer fairy?" the man repeated, incorrectly. "That's not exactly a phrase to strike terror into the hearts of men, you know."

Raea was not about to sit by and let this mere human insult Kyne! He was magnificent, as fairies went, and deserved some respect. She buzzed toward the bed.

"It's Kyne of the Summer Fairies, not 'kind of,' you moron," she said boldly. "And he's terrifying. Just look at him. He's huge!"

Kyne *was* huge, and he *was* terrifying. His fringe-tipped wings, his molten gold eyes, his deep heated colors, his body rippling with powerful muscles...any sensible human would easily mistake him for a War Fairy, although thankfully there weren't many of those around these days. But he'd make a fine one, if there were. So tall and so broad, with those powerful legs, and arms that could encircle her and hold her against him any time he wanted...He was unlike any fairy she'd ever seen. And she'd better stop thinking about him right now, that was for sure.

"Get away from the mermaid!" Kyne ordered.

"I will not," the man replied. "How did you find us, anyway?"

Kyne was caught off guard by that question. What a ridiculous thing for the human to ask. As if it had been difficult to find them, with what they'd been doing pretty much nonstop for the last twenty-four hours.

"Raea?" Aliya asked, peering around the man.

She looked uncomfortable up here on this dry boat, wrapped in that sheet, shifting awkwardly to prop herself up on an elbow. It was pitiful. Raea swallowed back the cheerful greeting she'd been planning to give. Seeing Aliya like this didn't exactly make it seem like a cheerful occasion.

This had been such a stupid idea. How had she not realized all the trouble she'd be causing by trying to pass a mermaid off as human? Truly stupid.

"I'm here, Aliya," she said finally, stepping closer to her friend. "Are you all right?"

"I'm a mermaid again, Raea," Aliya said, though it was more than a little obvious, in spite of the man's attempt to cover her with the sheet.

It was also more than a little obvious Aliya was crying. Aw, rainclouds. She'd never meant to make things worse for her infatuated friend. Now look at the poor girl, stuck on a boat in a body no human could live with.

But in spite of Aliya's facial expression of ultimate sorrow, the tears trickled out weakly. Leaning closer, Raea realized her friend's breathing was labored and raspy, too. All in all, Aliya seemed a bit... dry.

Kyne must have noticed it, too. He glowered at the human. "What have you done to her?"

The human shoved Kyne roughly. "Get the hell away from her!"

Kyne rose up and Raea cringed. Things were about to get violent.

"You filthy human!" Kyne snarled. "Keep your hands off me! Is this how you've treated an innocent mermaid? I ought to..."

He was reaching in his belt for a pouch of something Raea was certain they'd all regret. She was half surprised he'd even bothered with Fairy Dust, since it seemed clear he could best the human in pure physical strength and determination. Then again, that human seemed awfully determined to keep Kyne away from Aliya.

"Stop it!" Aliya cried.

Huh, who knew a mermaid could get so loud?

"Raea," Aliya went on when she was certain she had everyone's attention. And she did, actually. "Try to understand this. I'm not going back; I don't want to. I want to stay with Devin. I wish it, and so does he. So, please turn me back again, Raea. Can you? Please?"

Now this was unexpected. She'd assumed Aliya would be itching to get back into the water by the end of the day. By the Skies, it was obvious the girl *needed* to be back in the water now that she'd changed to her old self again. Yet she was asking to stay? Wishing? Unheard of.

"You need to be in the water, Aliya," Raea said carefully. "You don't look so good."

The human wasted no time in checking this out for himself. He touched Aliya gently on the forehead, then held her hand.

"She's right. God, Aliya, you're dry as a bone. We have to get you out of here."

"I'm not leaving you, Devin," Aliya assured him. "Raea can change me back."

"Well, I..."

How to explain she wasn't able do that? A temporary change for just twenty-four hours was one thing, but a permanent change? That would require more Fairy Dust than she had. Even if she could do it, someone would find out and report it.

For that matter, Kyne would be only too happy to report the whole incident to the council. Raea would be punished, and Aliya would be hunted down and returned to her form, then exiled from everyone. And the human...well, he would be a loss no one in the Forbidden Realm would regret. No one except Aliya, of course.

"Changing you back is a little more than I can do, Aliya," she said finally.

Aliya's face fell. But the tears were gone. Dried up.

"We've got to get her back in the water," Kyne said.

"Hell yeah," the man agreed. "I'm taking the boat out."

With one last, longing look at Aliya, he pushed past Kyne and grabbed up some clothes on his way out the door. Not that she meant to look, but Raea couldn't help herself. She would admit they hadn't met this human today under the best circumstances, but it was plain Kyne had inherited a lot more than just half-human traits. He was twice the man this man was. At least, that's the impression she got.

Aliya's agonized cry pulled her back to the matter at hand.

"Devin! Oh no, please, Devin, don't take me back to the water."

The man's footsteps faltered, but then kept going until they could be heard up on deck.

"He didn't waste much time abandoning you," Kyne snapped.

Aliya looked devastated.

"Shut up, Kyne," Raea said. What a nasty thing for him to tell the poor mermaid. Couldn't he see she honestly cared for the human? Oh, this was such a mess.

Kyne glanced at Aliya, then back at Raea. His eyes were almost hateful.

"I'll go watch him and make sure he takes this boat out. Wouldn't surprise me if he's just putting his clothes on and going home."

"You do that," Raea said.

He had the feelings and sensitivity of a north wind. No, not even that much. Winds were warm and caring compared to Kyne.

Kyne tromped out after the human and Raea went to sit on the bed beside Aliya. The mermaid grabbed her hand.

"He's not abandoning me," she said. It sounded like she actually believed it, too.

"No, he's just doing what's right for you," Raea said. She wasn't sure if either of them believed that, though. Aliya looked absolutely heartbroken.

"So you will not change me back? To human, I mean?"

"I can't. I shouldn't have even done this. It was a bad idea from the start."

"So, this really was only temporary?"

"You knew that."

"Yes, you told me that. I thought it was a good idea, at first. I thought I could do this thing with the human and then he would forget me and I would forget him, but once I was truly with him...well, I began to hope that somehow when you returned to change me back I could convince you not to."

"I didn't have to change you back," Raea explained as gently as she could. "Your time was up. It was all part of the wish right from the beginning."

"I see."

"I never should have changed you at all. I'm really, truly sorry, Aliya."

Through the sadness Aliya managed a thin smile.

"Don't be sorry, Raea. These last twenty-four hours have been more than I ever could have dreamed of. I still wish there could be more, of course, but I'll never ever be sorry for what we had."

"Really? No regrets?"

"Oh, of course I regret that it ended. I regret I can't stay."

"You think you could be happy giving up your whole life just to be with this human?"

"Definitely. I love him, and he loves me. Isn't there any way? Can't you please somehow make it happen?"

"No, I just can't. It takes too much. There'd be too many questions…we'd both be in trouble. There's no telling what the Fairy Council would do about it. To any of us."

She was hoping Aliya had heard the horror stories of humans mysteriously disappearing when they knew too much about the Forbidden Realm and all other means of keeping them silent had been exhausted. If Aliya really did love her human, surely she'd realize he'd be in as much trouble as they would be over this. Probably more.

Aliya was silent as she seemed to ponder this. They heard the sound of the boat's engines. After some hasty thumping around on deck, the boat began to slowly move. Raea didn't much care for the sensation of it, but Aliya seemed to barely notice. Her face showed she was deep in thought. What exactly she was trying to figure out, Raea had no idea. She thought she'd been pretty clear about the issue of changing her friend back.

Raea watched through the tiny window as the boat began to pull away from the dock. Finally Aliya spoke.

"Would it change your mind if I said there's something more you don't know?"

"No, I don't think so. But go ahead. I need to know just how much trouble I'm in."

Great, what now? Had the human been showing her around,

introducing her to his friends? Had he made pictures of her with his human technology and then shared them with the whole human population? Or worse, was he one of those dangerous scientist people who were always poking their noses into the Veil, looking for explanations? There seemed no end to the list of difficulties Raea started imagining.

But Aliya's confession hadn't even come close to making her list.

"I'm carrying his child."

Holy Cumulonimbus! A human/mermaid child? It simply could not possibly be true. Could it?

"You're not serious?"

Aliya blushed and smiled. Oh, hailstones. She was serious.

"But how in creation can you be sure? I turned you human only yesterday!"

"I'm a mermaid," she said, as if that explained everything. "I can feel the child's thoughts. He's tiny and barely there, but he is there."

"He?"

Aliya blushed again. "Yes, I believe it is a male child."

No, no, no. This could not be happening. Aliya wasn't supposed to get pregnant from this! What were they supposed to do now? Even if they just threw her back in the water and left, someone was bound to find out what had happened. Mermaids didn't just end up pregnant without everyone in their clan knowing about it—that whole Life Ceremony, and all.

And even then, they didn't give birth to male half-human babies! No, this was about the worst thing that could happen. It was awful! There was no way out of this one. She'd blown it big-time.

"Oh, Aliya…," she said, covering her face with her hands.

"Please don't be sad, Raea. I want to thank you. This only happened because of you."

Wonderful. Wouldn't the council love to hear Aliya say that? This was a disaster. Could Aliya truly be *glad* for it? Had what passed between her and the man been so powerful that even such a disastrous ending still made it worth it for her? Unbelievable.

It made an empty spot in Raea's soul ache for something... something she could not name. She tried to tell herself she was just hungry for dinner. That was only partially true. She was hungry, indeed, but it had nothing to do with her dinner.

Chapter Twenty

Get the hell out of my way," Devin barked. The damn fairy man was standing on the ropes.

God, if anyone on the dock saw this...well, what difference did that make? Once he got Aliya out into the open water where she'd be okay again, he was going to threaten one of the fairy people with serious bodily harm if they didn't turn him into some kind of merman, too. No way in hell was he going to just dump Aliya out there and leave her. He was staying, if he had to anchor his boat out here and live on it for the rest of his life.

He shoved the orange fairy back against the wall and went about getting the boat ready to go. If anything happened to Aliya because of all this, well, a couple fairies were going to be wondering what happened to their wings. And a few other body parts. What a mess.

"What are you doing?" the fairy asked.

"I'm taking the boat out so we can get Aliya back in the water. Now shut up."

"Can't get rid of her fast enough, now that you know what she is, can you?"

If Devin hadn't been so focused on getting out to open water for Aliya's sake he would have taken a long enough break to punch the fairy's lights out.

Not that the fairy, despite his laughable name and ridiculous title, didn't look formidable. He was a lot bigger than Devin would have expected a fairy to be. Definitely no Tinker Bell. And pretty ripped for a fairy.

"I'm not getting rid of her," he said with clenched teeth. "Since you and your pink partner there don't seem to be inclined to help us any, I've got to get her out where it's safe and get her back in the water before she shrivels up in there. Damn. I hate this."

"Didn't count on any of this while you were making free use of her body, did you?"

"Shut the fuck up, you magical mutant."

The fairy just laughed at him. "You have no idea!" he said. "So, how much did she tell you about us?"

"*You* never came up in conversation."

The fairy laughed again. It wasn't a happy sound. "I can believe that, considering you were too busy taking your pleasure from her for the last twenty-four hours to waste much time conversing."

"What do you know about it?"

It was a rhetorical question and he was more than a little annoyed when the fairy went ahead and answered.

"You'd be surprised what I know about it. I stopped in to watch a couple times, but since it was just the same old scene time and again—you climbing on her, sweating, making uncivilized noises—I got bored and left."

Devin was guiding the boat through the channel and couldn't afford to leave the controls long enough to slug the pervert. He would have liked to, though.

"Sounds to me like you've got some kind of problem, fairy boy."

"Yes, but I can't toss mine into the water and simply go home. You should consider yourself a lucky man."

"I do. I have Aliya."

Just a little farther and he could anchor the boat and go give that damn fairy a piece of his mind. And a fist or two.

"No, you *had* Aliya," the fairy said. "Now she's a mermaid again and you don't have to worry about her anymore."

"You think I can just leave her? Is that what I'm supposed to do? Well, I won't. I love her, not that it's any of your damn business."

They were away from other boats now, only a few of them close enough to see well. The sun was low, just the tiniest hint of it still peeking over the horizon. Soon it would be dark and they would be far from anyone else. No one would see Devin beating the snot out of some guy in a fairy suit.

Would a fairy fight back? This one probably would. Oh well. A few bruises would be worth it if Devin landed a blow or two, after the way the guy talked about Aliya. Had he really been here watching them last night? Disgusting.

But the fairy was a brave man. He stepped out of the shadows and came closer while Devin silently fumed.

"You say you won't leave Aliya? And how exactly do you plan to stay with her?"

"I said it's none of your damn business. Unless, of course, you might be persuaded to change me into a merman, or whatever. It might be handy to actually be able to breathe underwater if I plan to live there."

"Change you into a merman? There is no such thing."

"I know that! She explained it to me. We did talk. Quite a bit, for your information."

"Then you know mermaids are only female."

"Yes. And they get named after their mothers and their grand-mothers and they do that thing with the fish eggs. I was quite interested in Aliya's life."

"And you want us to change you into one of them."

"Yes."

"A mermaid? A female?"

Well, this wasn't something he'd thought of before. Could the fairy do that? Could he let Devin stay with Aliya as a mermaid? That would take a little getting used to. Running Sandstrom Industries with flippers might be a little difficult. And driving a car? Hell, clearly there were a few things he'd simply have to give up in favor of a drastically new life. And, hell, just how much of him from the waist down would be different? Would he really be giving all *that* up, too?

Could he?

The fairy laughed. "I thought so. Staying with your lover isn't so appealing when you know you won't be able to have your car-nal way with her six times a day."

"You've got a thing against people, don't you?" Devin asked.

Damn this stupid fairy. What did he know about truly caring for someone, really feeling love so powerful you realize you could give up everything for them? By God, he could give it all up. And he would.

"And my answer is yes," Devin continued. "Yes, I want you to change me into a mermaid, and yes, I *could* live with Aliya that way."

The fairy practically laughed at him. "You could not."

"I could. She needs me! When the child comes…"

Oops. He hadn't meant to say that.

"When the *what* comes?"

"Nothing. I suppose those butterfly wings work, don't they? Why don't you fly yourself to hell. Or farther."

"You said *child*! By the Skies, is there to be a child?"

"It's none of your damn business! Now get out of here. If you care so much, go see how Aliya's doing. She wasn't looking too good."

"You wore her out."

"Shut up, you orange bastard!"

He was furious, but the fairy didn't seem to care. He just flapped those ridiculous wings and frowned.

"So Aliya is with child, and I assume it is from you. That will not be an easy thing for a mermaid, you know."

"I know. That's why she needs me. So, that's what I want. When we get out to the open, I'll anchor the boat. We'll get Aliya into the water first to make sure she's all right, then you and your girlfriend can turn me into a mermaid. I'll be able to take care of her."

The fairy stared at him. They was unnerving, those golden eyes. So human, but so obviously not.

"You would do that?"

It was killing him to know he would never again be able to feel Aliya roll under him in waves of glorious passion, to feel the heat of her core as he drove himself into her, but by God if it meant saving her life, it would be worth it.

"Yes. I would do that."

"And there is to be a child?"

"Yes. My child."

The fairy considered this. For a long time, as a matter of fact. Why was this such a hard thing for him to comprehend? Who knew. Obviously the guy was not normal; peeping on other people's love making, expecting him to just abandon Aliya out here, being amazingly rude. Devin didn't know what other fairies were like, but if this guy was an example of them, he was darn glad they usually kept to themselves.

"Go check on Aliya," Devin said. It was killing him that this boat couldn't go any faster. He sure hoped she could hold out long enough to get just a little bit farther out into the lake.

"You say you love her," the fairy said.

"Yeah, I said that." Huh, love must be an unusual concept for fairies, to guess by the confused look on the guy's face. "And I'm worried about her. Please go check on her and tell her we'll be in a safe spot in just a few more minutes."

"Yeah. Okay. I will."

Oddly enough, the fairy agreed. He left the deck without any complaint and headed down into the cabin. Good. Now maybe Devin could concentrate on getting them out there and anchored. Jeez, Aliya must be incredibly uncomfortable by now. Would this whole transformation harm her in her condition? And what about the child? Damn.

He'd only just found out about the little thing and already his gut twisted at the thought of losing her. He thought that whole part of him had been permanently dormant, set aside when he and Judith decided to pursue their business before family, then lost forever when Judith was gone. He thought he didn't want it, didn't need it. He'd been one hundred percent wrong.

It took all of this for him to finally realize that those dreams he used to chase after weren't really his. *This* is what he wanted, someone to care for and sacrifice for—not money or power or prestige. He'd had those and they'd left him numb. As long as Judith was alive she'd convinced him it all had some meaning, but it didn't. Without someone to share himself with, he was empty. Nothing in his life mattered now except Aliya and their child. Without them, he really would just cease to exist.

Chapter Twenty-One

Kyne heard the soft voices in the bedroom before he got there. Good. That meant Aliya was still all right. He knocked softly on the door frame before going in.

Raea looked up and smiled. She was running a wet cloth across Aliya's forehead. The bedsheets were damp, too. Good idea.

"The human is concerned for Aliya's health," he said.

"I'm fine," she said.

"I've been keeping her skin wet, and that seems to help," Raca explained. "But she needs to be back in the lake soon."

Kyne nodded. "The human says just a few more minutes now. And it's growing dark, so we can be sure no other humans will see."

"That's good," Raea said and smiled at Aliya. "We'll have you back home, safe and sound, in no time."

"Fine," Aliya said. She didn't sound quite as enthusiastic about going home as she should have. "And how is Devin?"

"The human?" Kyne asked, caught off guard. Why should she be worried about the human? He wasn't out of his element, struggling to stay alive.

"He expected me to stay with him forever," Aliya said. "I'm breaking my promise. He's probably upset."

"Shhh, don't get yourself all worked up again," Raea advised. She was right, too. No sense getting the mermaid nicely hydrated only to have her cry it all back out again.

"He is upset," Kyne said, amending his statement before Aliya could tear up. "But he's determined not to leave you. He says he loves you."

"He does," Aliya said simply. She glanced up at Raea. "It isn't just a case of the Old Revenge, or a simple obsession. It's not like that at all! Devin loves me, and I love him."

Raea didn't seem to know what to say to that. Kyne would have expected her to brush Aliya's comments aside and assure her that this would all go away and they'd be better after a couple days. But she didn't. Maybe she was finally getting the idea that this was serious and everything wouldn't all be better. Maybe she knew about the child Aliya was carrying.

"He told me about the child," Kyne said. He watched Aliya's face. She didn't seem concerned that he knew. She just smiled.

"It was quite a shock to him, you can understand," she said.

"He wants to go with you."

This did get a dramatic response from Aliya. She sat up, her eyes growing wide with concern. "No! He's got to stay on the boat. Please, you won't let him try to do anything foolish, will you?"

"He wants us to turn him into a mermaid."

Now this got a dramatic response from Raea.

"A mermaid? As in, a mermaid? He does know what that means, doesn't he?"

"Yes, but he's determined that Aliya needs him. And he is concerned for the child. He wants to be with them."

"But, Kyne...a mermaid?"

Aliya was just smiling sweetly at the thought. "Oh, only Devin could even suggest such a thing. But, of course, you can't change him."

"No, of course not," Raea agreed.

"Why not?" Kyne asked.

Raea gave him a look that was supposed to silence him, but he ignored it.

"After all, you were able to turn her into a human. Surely you could do that backward for him. And it would be a lot easier to do it that way than to take Aliya out of the lake."

"No, it wouldn't, Kyne," Raea said firmly. "How can you even suggest this? You know all the problems that would cause! We can't just go around creating Veiled creatures. What's going on? What did that human say to make you forget everything like this?"

"He is willing to give up everything to be with Aliya! Even so much as becoming a female."

Raea frowned. "It's not like being female is any great hardship, you know."

But the mermaid smiled tenderly. "Oh, Devin. How sweet. Kyne, you've got to tell him it wouldn't work. We'll just have to make some other arrangements. He can come out here on the boat sometimes and we can…visit."

"Why wouldn't it work?" Kyne asked.

Devin had come up with the only possible solution to the problem. He'd been willing to give up everything…including the sex. His concern for Aliya was real and honest. He did love her, and he wanted to be there for his child. Kyne could have never expected such a thing from a human. It went against everything he knew to be true of them. Still, he couldn't doubt the sincerity he'd heard in Devin's voice. Why wouldn't this work?

"You know we can't do it," Raea said. "Even if we wanted to. It would take too much. That's more than just a simple wish, Kyne. No, it's impossible."

"It is not!" Kyne insisted. "He wants to be with her, to care for his child! We've got to help them. They should be together, Raea."

Raea narrowed her eyes at him. "Is this about Devin and Aliya, or about your mother, Kyne?" she asked.

That left him speechless. He hadn't even thought about that, but of course the correlation was undeniable. Aliya was very much in the position his own mother had been in. With one difference: Aliya's human cared.

"If there's any way they can be together, Raea, we've got to help them. That child is going to need all the support she can get."

Raea just raised one eyebrow and gave a half smile. *"He,"* she said. "Aliya says the child is a male. Telepathy, you know."

"A male mermaid?"

"Yeah."

Kyne glanced down at Aliya. She smiled sheepishly. "I could be wrong," she said. "The child is still so very tiny..."

Of course she wasn't wrong. Her telepathic bond with the child would be infallible.

"By the Skies...a male mermaid." Kyne sighed.

He just had to find a way to convince Raea to change Devin into a mermaid. Once that child was born, Devin might be the only other mermaid besides Aliya to care for him. No telling how the rest of Aliya's clan would react to such an oddity. And Kyne knew all about being the family oddity.

Devin's footsteps clomped down the stairway and toward them. Kyne stepped aside to let him enter the small bedroom. His eyes were dark and they settled only on Aliya.

"How're you doing?" he asked.

"I'm fine," Aliya said, smiling brightly. "Raea has brought me water, and it's very refreshing."

"Well, we're safely away from everyone out here and it's getting dark. I'm pretty sure we can get you in the water now."

"That would be nice," she said. "I'm just so sorry to have to put everyone to all this trouble."

"Hush," Devin said.

He sat beside Aliya and stroked her long hair. Kyne tried not to be aware of the tender way they looked at each other, but it was too obvious. This human cared deeply for Aliya. He didn't care that she was a mermaid or that so many things separated them. He loved her.

At once it was tragic, and at the same time it filled Kyne with a contentment he'd never felt before. Maybe humans weren't all bad. Maybe there was good in them. Maybe that meant he himself wasn't quite as bad as he knew down deep inside that he was.

Devin continued his soothing words to his lover. "Now, let me carry you up top. I'll lower you into the water and you'll be good as new."

"Better than new," Aliya said, smiling bravely. "I've been with you now, Devin."

"And once we've got you back in the water," Kyne said, "Raea and I are going to change Devin into a mermaid. Then he will be with you and can help you with…whatever you need."

It was a bold step, but he hoped he could force Raea's hand on this. Raea glared at him. Aliya shook her head quickly. Devin smiled.

"That's right. Now, I know it'll take a little adjusting to… Hell, that's an understatement. It'll take a *lot* of adjusting to. But we'll be all right. We'll make it work, Aliya."

"Oh, Devin…" She sighed. "You'd really do that for me, wouldn't you?"

"Of course I would. I love you."

But Raea interrupted. "No! No, we can't do this." She paced the small room, and her wings buzzed with anxiety. "It won't work. You'll never be happy that way, Devin. Humans aren't made for living with Veiled creatures. And if anyone finds out! Oh, you have no idea how much trouble…"

"Stop worrying about yourself, Raea," Kyne interrupted. "This is a lot more important than just keeping yourself out of an inquiry. There's going to be a child now, and…"

"And what sort of life will that child have, Kyne?" Raea asked. "We don't even know what the child will be, more human or mermaid. Be realistic! What if this child is more human? How will he live underwater? What will he do with two mermaid parents? No, if you're really concerned about this child, then you need to think about that. Devin needs to stay the way he is…just in case."

Devin frowned and looked to Aliya. "She has a point, unfortunately. We don't know much about this child, do we? Can you tell if we're expecting a little mermaid, or a two-legged human who's going to need to breathe air?"

"Or maybe some combination of both," Raea added, unhelpfully.

Aliya was noticeably upset. "No, I don't know! The child is too young, too new in the world. What if he…oh, but if he can't live underwater what will we do? Devin, we would lose him! I know he is aware of me, so he must have some of the mermaid communication abilities, but what if…oh, I just don't know!"

"So what are we going to do?" Kyne demanded, glaring at Raea. "Just send Aliya off on her own to figure it all out for herself?"

"No! We're not doing that," Devin replied.

"I guess you could build a place for her to live at your house…"

Kyne suggested to the man. "Although that would take time that we don't have right now."

"I'm not putting the woman I love in a fish tank!" Devin growled. "God, this is insane."

"Then what?" Kyne asked. "Raea? What are we going to do?"

"I'm thinking," she replied grumpily. "There's got to be something."

"You got everyone into this mess," Kyne reminded her.

"Shut up. I'm thinking."

"Not very fast, I've noticed."

"I could think a lot faster if you would shut up!"

"If I shut up then there'd be nobody making any suggestions."

"You're not making suggestions," Raea shot at him. "You're harassing me."

"I'm harassing you? No, in the field this morning I was harassing you. You seemed to like that then, if I recall, though."

"There was absolutely nothing likable about that."

"Nothing?"

"Absolutely nothing."

"Oh, yeah? Not even when I…"

"Shut up! I can't think when you keep talking about…that."

It was perversely satisfying to know his stolen kisses where a source of great distraction to Raea. Then he noticed the way Aliya was watching their interaction and realized Raea was right; he'd better shut up. All they needed to make this situation worse was for word to get out of Kyne's unnatural desires amid all this.

Besides, he needed to use all his energy to come up with a way to help Aliya and her oddly devoted human.

"I think we need to ask Aliya for her opinion on all this," the human was saying.

That sounded remarkably intelligent. They were all so concerned about helping Aliya, maybe they ought to find out just exactly what she really wanted them to do for her. Kyne figured he already knew, however. Hadn't she made it perfectly clear what she wanted them to do? And Raea had refused.

But Raea got excited. "That's exactly what we should do! Let Aliya decide!"

"I already told you what I wanted, and you said it couldn't be done," Aliya reminded her.

"No, I can't make him a mermaid, and I can't change you into a human permanently, but I can grant a wish," Raea said.

"What are you talking about?" Kyne asked. "Making her human *is* her wish."

Raea was still pacing and fanning her wings, deep in thought.

"That's too big for me, Kyne. You know the Great Code. But a smaller wish, well, I could do that. Aliya will just have to make the right wish."

Devin looked less than impressed, and Aliya just seemed confused.

"And just what kind of wish would that be?" Kyne asked. "Seems like the two main options are already off the table."

Raea shrugged. "I don't know. Just let me think…"

"She's drying out here," Devin said. "How can I help her?"

"You made me human for twenty-four hours, Raea," Aliya said, her voice barely above a whisper. "Can't you do that again?"

"You need to be human for longer than that," Raea said. "There must be a way."

"I don't suppose we could take it before the Fairy Council?" Kyne asked, knowing the answer.

Raea just rolled her eyes at that one. "What do you think they'd do with a request like that? No way I could fake enough paperwork to get the approval for extra Fairy Dust to cover such a thing."

"Maybe a partial change for one of them?" Kyne offered.

"But how does that solve things?" Devin asked. "Won't we end up exactly where we are now?"

Raea pursed her lips and considered things. "Not exactly. It's all in how the wish is worded, of course."

But Devin didn't seem encouraged. "Either you can make her human or you can't. What difference does wording make?"

Raea shrugged again. "Bureaucracy and all that. Surely humans have such things? Now give me a moment and let me think on this. I've granted some, er, creative wishes before. I'm sure we can figure something out now."

Kyne snorted. He wondered just how creative those wishes had been. For certain, Raea toyed with boundaries and rules whenever she could. He tried not to think of other things he'd love for her to toy with.

"So that's what you do?" Devin asked. "You go around granting wishes? It doesn't make sense. I get the impression you fairies aren't especially fond of humans in the first place."

Kyne had to let out another snort at that understatement.

"We do it for the Forbidden Realm, of course," Raea said. "We have to keep you silly humans preoccupied with your lives so you don't start getting involved in ours."

"Only sometimes Raea gets confused on what exactly that means," Kyne added.

She sneered at him. "Shut up, Kyne, and let me get to work."

"But how can we work it?" Aliya asked. "What do I wish for, Raea? To be human for how long? I don't even know when the child will be born—no one's done this before."

"We don't want to be too specific," Raea explained. "Wishes tend to get hung up on extraneous detail."

"My child is not an extraneous detail," Aliya declared. "I have to be there for him, whatever his needs turn out to be. Oh, if only we knew what the season for birthing a half-human child was."

Her words hung in the air. This was not merely about granting a wish, it was about sustaining a life. A life no one had seen before or could even guess at its needs. How long before the child would be born? As she had said, who knew the season for birthing this rare individual?

The season. Kyne shot a glance at Raea the very moment her eyes had gone wide and she looked up at him. Could she have realized what this meant? She must. She gave him a smile. By the Skies, she really did need him to help fix this.

"The season for birthing, Kyne," she said softly.

"A season is never specific," he replied.

"Then she should wish for a season, shouldn't she?" Raea asked. "Can you help us with that?"

He patted the pouch at his side. He carried Nurturing Dust, Sustaining Dust, Growth and Maturity Dust...all the things needed to maintain living things through the season, however vague that might be.

But Devin was still confused. "What are you saying? Do you know what to do?"

"I think so," Raea said, but chewed on her lip as she considered. "If Kyne and I work together on this, we might just be able to do it."

"So will I be a mermaid, or will she be a human?" the man asked.

"But we just don't know," Aliya protested. "Which would be best for the child? What will he need as he grows? What if this body can't carry a half-human child?"

"Or vice versa?" Devin said. "How can we even guess what sort of wish we should make?"

"That's why you should wish for a season," Raea explained. "Aliya should wish for what's needed for the season of the child."

Devin didn't seem quite convinced, but Aliya nodded her head. She seemed to understand. Raea grasped her pale hands. Kyne was already rummaging through his pouch, selecting the—hopefully right—measures of dust.

"You understand what this means?" Raea asked her worried friend.

Aliya nodded again. "I do."

"Well, I don't," Devin said. "What the hell are you going to do to us?"

"We don't really know," Raea said, turning to him. "We'll combine Aliya's wish with Kyne's Seasonal Dust. The wish will be granted, but we can't really know what it will look like."

"You can't really know? What kind of magical people are you if you can't know about this? Honestly, Aliya, we can't do this without knowing how—"

"We have to, Devin," the mermaid said. "We don't have a choice. Our child is at stake here."

"But what if…what if you end up back in the lake and I'm stuck here?"

"If that's what our child needs, then that's how the wish will go. Perhaps it will take a mermaid to birth him, but a human to raise him."

"Then we'll be apart!"

Aliya found moisture for tears again. "I know. But for our child, Devin…"

"Yes. I know. Of course we'll do that," he said, then gave a long, heartrending sigh. "All right. Let's make the wish then, before you cry yourself dry again."

Kyne had to give the human credit. It could not be easy to

walk into this wish, knowing the outcome could be so far from what he wanted. But obviously this human—this man—was a creature of decent character. He was ready to give up the thing he wanted most for an uncertain future, all for the sake of his lover and unborn child. A child who would be, to everyone else, a mistake.

Aliya nodded, and sat up very primly, concentrating on her thoughts and emotions.

"Make your wish carefully," Raea advised. "It can only be one wish, not two or three lumped together. It must be clear, but not confining. Let it be full of love for your child and hope for the future."

"It will be," Aliya assured them, but she sounded a bit doubtful.

Devin came to her side and sat next to her. He held her hands firmly, caressing them and smiling.

"Don't worry. I love you, Aliya. However this turns out, we'll make it work. For us and for our child."

She smiled at him and leaned into his shoulder. He wrapped an arm around her for support. It appeared that she needed it.

"I love you, too, Devin. I'll wish very hard."

She cleared her dry throat and took a deep breath. The room was quiet. Everyone waited. At last she spoke carefully.

"I wish my child to have the parent he needs for the season he needs it."

Raea looked up at Kyne. He gave her as confident a smile as he could muster. It was a good wish, he could tell. Raea would be able to grant it. His input would help. They'd simply have to wait to see how it turned out.

With practiced skill, Raea pulled out her delicate pouch of Wish Dust and measured a small amount into the palm of her hand. Kyne already had his dust in his hand. She turned to him, palm up, so he added his dust to hers. Their fingers touched and he felt the tingle, the ache, the longing that always came with his nearness to Raea. She lowered her lashes and turned away.

Giving her attention back to Aliya, she held out the handful of dust. Pink lips together, Raea leaned over her hand and blew on the dust. It erupted into the air, then scattered over Aliya, raining down in a glimmering shower of magic. Dramatic, indeed. Raea certainly had her own flair. Her lips remained puckered even as the dust began to settle. Kyne watched her, forgetting all about Aliya's wish and making up a couple of his own.

The fading light through the window caught on the floating dust, filling the air with sparks of energy and magic. Aliya's eyes followed the glittering particles as they circulated around her in gentle currents, then slowly absorbed into her skin and disappeared. No one spoke. Devin sat beside his enchanted lover, surrounded by dust, and watched with wide eyes, desperately clinging to her. They each held their breath.

How would it go? Would she become human again? Some kind of hybrid, perhaps, like her child? The waves outside lapped against the boat and a gull cried somewhere off in the distance. The glow from the dust was gone now and the wish had been granted.

But nothing had happened.

Chapter Twenty-Two

Kyne watched Aliya's face fall. With all of Raea's theatrics, they'd no doubt expected something brilliant to happen. Had it? Or had the wish failed? It was a risky sort of wish, at best. Had Raea known it might not work?

"I didn't change!" Aliya said at last.

"I don't understand," Raea said. "I granted your wish. You saw the dust settle in. I don't know why nothing happened."

"Oh God," Devin began. "Maybe it did. Maybe this *is* what the child needs."

Aliya seemed horrified at the thought. "Oh no! Devin, I'm so sorry. I really thought we would end up together. I thought that's what the child would need—both of us, together."

"Apparently not," Kyne said. "It must need to be born in the water, and then raised on the land."

He had to admit he was somewhat disappointed for them. As earthly and as human as it was, he'd been hoping for a happy ending, one where Aliya and her human were happy. Together.

"I'm so sorry," Raea said to them, her pink wings drooping. "It was a good wish. Apparently this is simply the way it needs to be. For the child."

"It's all right," Devin said, sitting beside Aliya on the bed and caressing her hand. "We can still be together. I've got a boat. I'll spend every minute I can out here. We'll pick a meeting spot and you'll find me, won't you, Aliya?"

"Of course I will, Devin. And you can swim with me. At times. We'll make this work, won't we?"

Devin didn't even hesitate. His voice was reassuring and calm when he answered. "Of course we will."

The two lovers were clinging to each other. How could they not turn on Raea, beg her to do more? Clearly they had both fully expected some other outcome, some solution that would keep them together rather than pull them apart. How could they be so calm?

Kyne glanced over at Raea. Her forehead was furrowed, her eyes full of anguish. She'd obviously wanted to see things work out differently, too. She'd done her job well—there was nothing more she could have done for them. Apparently this was the way things would have to be.

The human slowly caressed his sad little mermaid. Kyne stared at them, captivated. Despite the sorrow that radiated from the mermaid by telepathy, Kyne felt something more circle in the air around him. Even as they grieved what they had both wanted so badly, there was hope emanating from them. It didn't make sense, but Kyne could feel it as surely as he could breathe air.

It seemed even without the ability to ever fulfill carnal lust, these two beings still had reason to hope. They still looked forward to their future. It was beyond comprehension. Maybe humans were not all the base, selfish creatures Kyne had always believed.

By the Skies, maybe that meant there was hope for *him*, after all.

* * *

Devin stroked Aliya's beautiful, fair hair. God, but he loved this woman. The last thing he wanted was to ever be separated from her, but he needed to get her back into the water. Now.

"I'll be there whenever you need me," he assured her. "In any way that I can, and…"

He stopped himself. Whoa. He was suddenly dizzy. It was hard to catch his breath and his voice sounded strange. The room shifted around him and for just a moment he thought he would be sick.

The warriorlike fairy took a stride in his direction, but Devin held up his hand to stop him. Something was happening. His skin felt prickly and strange. He tried to swallow but there was a tightness in his throat. What in the hell…? He slowly put his hand to his neck, then jerked it away quickly.

"Oh my God!" he cried. "Look at this!"

Aliya blinked nervous eyes and sat up, straining to look at him. Suddenly she put her hands up to her face and gave a squeal.

"Devin, you've got gills!"

It was insane. Just at the side of his neck, right below his ears, Devin had indeed developed three little slits that felt exactly like gills. He touched them gingerly, holding back the crazy impulse to sneeze. What on earth was happening here? Aliya didn't have gills, at least not gills like this that Devin had ever noticed on her. She seemed to have some kind of auxiliary lung system inside, which must have been how she breathed and had breathed for him. How in the hell had he suddenly sprouted gills?

He held up his hands in front of him and Aliya gasped at them. Thin membranes had grown between his fingers. How odd! Mermaids didn't have that either.

"What's happening to me?" he asked, glaring up at Raea.

"Looks like you're developing whatever features you might need to spend time underwater," she replied.

He had to admit, it appeared she was right. He still had his legs—and everything else down there, a quick check told him— but he'd be damned if he wasn't evolving into some kind of hybrid water creature. Apparently this is what their child truly needed. The wish had worked, after all. He stared at his newly webbed hands and laughed.

"Well, Aliya, looks like I'll definitely be able to swim with you."

Aliya, however, was a little more careful with her excitement. "But…you said you needed to stay at your job. Can you still do that like this? Will the other humans allow it?"

His first instinct was to say to hell with his career and any other humans, but he realized Aliya was just being practical. How would he support his new family? Running his company was the only thing that he knew. Would it be best to walk away from that, or would it be better to try to continue?

He frowned at the confusing notion, trying to picture how he'd hide all this from his employees and everyone he knew. As he pondered, though, another change happened. Right before his eyes, his hands went back to normal. He felt the gills merge back into skin. After just a few seconds of transformation, he seemed perfectly human again.

He could feel everyone's eyes on him.

"Oh, shit. I think I just made that all happen," he said.

"You made yourself human again?" Aliya asked.

"Yeah, I was just thinking about how I was going to have to show up in a turtleneck and gloves for my next Monday morning board meeting, and it all just went away. No gills, no webbing… it's all perfectly normal again."

"Can you make it come back? I mean…can you control the changes?"

He shrugged. What the hell, maybe he could. Wouldn't that be a fun party trick? He shut his eyes and concentrated on whatever he figured a person might concentrate on if they were trying to turn into a fish. Amazingly, his skin started itching and tingling and all of a sudden he felt the prick of air rushing over his gills. They were back. The finger webbing, too. He stared at his hands and laughed.

"What do you know? I *can* control this. I thought about needing those gills if I was ever going swimming with you, Aliya, and here they are again. It's the damnedest thing."

Now Raea spoke up behind him. "By the Air and the Skies, the wish did work! You see? It was a wish for the seasons of need."

"You mean, it worked on Devin instead of me?" Aliya asked.

"Exactly," the fairy said, her airy wings fluttering excitedly and making the curtains rustle from the breeze. "As Devin contemplates what is needed to provide for his family, his body takes on those attributes."

Now Aliya was smiling and nodding as if it made perfect sense to her. "So our child needs his father to be sometimes in the water and sometimes on land. Devin can do that?"

"It seems that way," Raea said. "I've never seen anything like it."

"It's perfect!" Devin exclaimed, pulling Aliya closer to him. "Come on, let's get you into the water right now. I can join you."

But Aliya didn't seem quite as excited about that as he thought she might be. Instead of throwing herself into his arms and letting him carry her out to the water, she stared at him, batting her huge, questioning eyes. He could feel that her thoughts were conflicted.

"But Devin," she protested. "I'm still a mermaid. I'm sorry, but you cannot join me like that. I can't do that for you anymore."

Ah, so that was her worry. Devin reached out for her, touching her gently.

"Aliya, any way I can be near you will be good enough for me," he said and brushed her face in a way he hoped expressed the depth of his love.

She smiled sadly, but then suddenly she gasped. All at once she was squirming against the bedding that still covered her body. Something was wrong; she was in pain! Damn, but she'd been out of the water too long. She needed his help! Devin lunged forward and pulled back the covers. Instead of a writhing, dry mermaid, he found a woman. She had legs once more where moments ago she'd had fins.

"I'm human again!" she exclaimed.

Devin could hardly believe it. She was human again? How did that happen? He wrapped his arms around her and pulled her tight.

"I guess it works for me, too!" she said, pressing herself against him. "I thought about how I needed to be human so that we could be happy, and suddenly my legs came back."

"Transitioning Dust," the pink fairy said quietly, turning to her companion. "You used Transitioning Dust, didn't you?"

The male fairy nodded. "Seasons are all about transition. Of course it's a primary ingredient in everything I do. But I didn't imagine that... by the Skies, Raea, did you plan for this?"

She shook her head, bouncing with excitement. "No, I honestly didn't know it would work out this way. But look at them, how happy they are!"

Devin had to admit she was right. The wish had worked out even better than expected. He was happy, and he could feel nothing but joy coming from Aliya.

The male fairy—Kyne, or whatever the hell his name was—didn't seem quite as enthusiastic in his approval.

"I thought the wish was for the needs of the child. So far it seems these changes are more for the benefit of the parents."

Aliya had the perfect answer for that. "This *is* for the needs of the child. He needs us to be together. Don't you see, Kyne? Devin and I will have more love for him if we share love for each other...emotional love *and* physical love."

The fairy grumbled a noncommittal consent and was forced to agree that this arrangement would, indeed, prove highly beneficial for the child. The female fairy shook her head in amazement.

"Never once did I imagine the wish working out this way. I don't think any of us realized the full power of human passions."

"Well, I do," Aliya said, stretching out her long human legs and rising from the bed. She smiled at her magical friends. "Thank you both so very much!"

She reached out for Raea to give her a warm hug of gratitude. The bedsheets slipped away, exposing every inch of her fully human form. Devin was powerless to avert his greedy gaze. The damned male fairy seemed to take note of her, too, and Devin wondered if he would need to kick some fairy ass pretty soon.

Instead he grabbed up the discarded bedding and wrapped it carefully around Aliya. He gave Kyne a warning glare that said he did not need to be telepathic to know just exactly what thoughts were running through the fairy's dirty little mind. Kyne nodded and took a step back. Apparently no magical ass kicking would be needed just now.

All he needed in the world right now was to lose these two fairies and get on with his life. With Aliya, the woman who made him whole and complete in ways he hadn't even known that he was lacking. Knowing that she wasn't going to die—and that she was even more magical than ever now that she had human body parts again—was urging his own body parts to want to make a little of their human sort of magic. Just as soon as they were alone, there were a few more wishes he'd be making come true today.

* * *

Aliya held the bedsheet tightly around herself and gave her final thank-yous to the fairies. She knew Devin was eager to have them gone, and it made him happy to see that she was keeping her new body covered when they were around. Apparently he wanted her all for himself, and she saw no reason whatsoever to argue with that.

Raea promised to check in and offer any assistance needed as they began their new life together. Kyne seemed concerned about what that would actually entail, but Raea convinced him that they should go now. It was up to Aliya and Devin to decide for themselves what direction their lives would take after this. Obviously both of them were going to be making a lot of changes.

They had a lot to consider. Aliya would have to confide in her mother, that much was certain. She could trust Coraline to help them keep their secret as long as possible. She would advise them wisely. Life would most likely not be easy for Aliya and Devin after this day, but whatever lay in store, she could take comfort in knowing that they would be together.

"Come on, Kyne," Raea said as she nearly pushed his human-size form out the door and onto the deck of the boat. "They've got a lot to talk about, and so do we. We're going to have to come up with some plausible excuse for using up so much of our dust, and for spending half of the day at the lake."

Kyne mumbled unpleasant things under his breath, but he left. Not before Aliya got an unusually strong wave of vibrations from him. By the Depths, even here in the air wearing her human form she had no trouble sensing the thoughts behind Kyne's gruff exterior. She'd never felt another magical creature so brimming with passions. The forbidden type. Did Raea know about this, she wondered?

"Just remember, I'll help you in any way that I can," Raea said, pausing in the doorway and smiling as if she were actually looking forward to involving herself in intrigue and conspiracy.

Perhaps she was. Aliya took a step forward and spoke so the males nearby couldn't hear.

"Thank you, my friend. And I want you to remember the same; I'll help you in any way that I can. The council will surely disapprove of you and Kyne, after all."

Raea frowned. "You mean...they'll disapprove of us helping you and that human."

"No, I mean they'll disapprove of you and Kyne engaging in carnal activities."

The fairy fanned her wings rapidly and glowed a bright pink. "But I...we haven't...that is...What do you know about that?"

Aliya decided not to inflict any more burden on her friend today. She stopped herself from elaborating fully on just exactly how transparent her friend's curiosity and Kyne's lust was.

"I know nothing about it, only that I can feel the passion flowing between you. I know he is not all he seems...and you're more than a little curious."

"But I would never go against the Great Code! I mean, well, I suppose we all know that's not entirely true, after today, but...I would never do that kind of thing with Kyne!"

Devin was coming up behind Aliya so she knew the conversation had to end. She simply gave Raea a knowing smile and nodded. "Of course. But let me just say, never is a very long time, Raea. And trust me...*that kind of thing* feels really, really good."

Chapter Twenty-Three

Devin put his hands on Aliya's shoulders. Her skin felt warm and moist. Thank God, she was healthy again. Their wish had granted them the hope of a future—both of them together. No: the *three* of them together. His head was still spinning as he grappled to comprehend this wonderful new reality. *The three of them*; a whole family soon.

Hell, this was more than just a wish. It was a dream come true.

He stood close to his lover, leaning in to breathe her scent and run his fingers through her long, cascading hair. Her firm little ass rubbed against him, bringing life into his groin. His cock roused at her closeness and he slid his hands over her body to reassure himself those legs were still there. And the wonderful, hot juncture between them.

They were blissfully alone, watching the fairies take off and disappear up into the evening sky. Odd creatures, those fairies. They'd seemed every bit as large and solid as the average human, yet they'd vanished from view so quickly, fading into the air around them as if they had never even been. He had so much to learn about this strange, magical world his Aliya came from.

For now, though, he'd much rather focus his attention on learning how else he could please her. She'd done more than she could ever know for him and he was determined to return the favor. Preferably in bed.

"I love how you touch me," Aliya murmured, leaning against him.

"Good, because I plan to do a lot of it."

"And…you truly don't mind that your life is suddenly very different than it was?"

"No. I can't explain it, but somehow all these changes just… well, they feel right. I know they shouldn't. Hell, I know your people have rules that say this is very wrong and I'd probably get locked away by my own people if I started bragging about how I fell in love with a mermaid, but whatever we have here, Aliya, it's exactly what I want."

She seemed content at first with his words, but even as he spoke them he knew they were not quite accurate. Not that he had any regrets, but he had to admit he'd not spoken the full truth of his emotions. What he and Aliya had now—their love, their passion, their child—well, in fact it *wasn't* exactly what he wanted.

And of course now that he'd admitted it to himself, she knew of it, too. He could feel her body react as her mind soaked in his thoughts. How long would it take to get used to spending his life with someone telepathic? He would never have secrets from her, he ought to know that by now.

"But it's not what you want," she cried, twisting in his arms to face him with worry-filled eyes. "Oh, Devin, you are lying to me now!"

"No…I'm not lying. I swear, Aliya. It's just that…"

"What is it? Please tell me."

"I don't know if you'll understand."

"I'll try, Devin. You know I will. Please tell me—I'm confused by your thoughts. You're happy, yet you aren't."

"I'm happy. Very happy; trust me on that. I love you, Aliya. I always will."

"But what am I feeling from you, then?"

He took her by the hands and wished she would just let him change the subject. She came from such a different world— her way of life was so foreign to him. Her people lived solitary lives, from what he could gather, and they had odd customs like implanting fish eggs and marking moon phases. He could only imagine human society would seem equally strange to her.

How involved in his world was she willing to get? Could he take her to his home, make love to her on dry land? Or was this human body she appeared in now only for use on occasion when they might steal away from their lives and meet here, halfway between worlds? If that was their future, he would accept it and be grateful, but the truth was…he wanted more.

"You want *more*," she said, laying her hand on his face and studying him closely. "I don't know what that is."

"It's not important," he said. "All that matters is that I love you, Aliya, and I am honored to be bringing a child into this world with you."

"But there is something you won't say. I can feel it in you, Devin."

"Is that all you can feel in me right now?"

"Don't try to distract me," she said, rubbing her body against his in a way that was more than a little diverting. "You need to explain what you are feeling. Please, Devin. Trust me with yourself."

"I do trust you, Aliya. You must know that if you can read any of my thoughts. I just…I want you to be happy with me."

"Of course I am. How can you doubt it?"

"I don't doubt it right now. We're safe, we're together...of course we can be happy right now. But what about when you go back to your life and I go back to mine? Will you be happy then?"

"I will be happy to know that we'll find a way to be together again soon. As we are now."

She was sliding against him and the sheet she'd been wrapped in fell away. Her skin felt too good against his. He was throbbing to be inside her again and she clearly was not opposed to that idea.

"Whenever we want to," she said, rising onto her tiptoes to whisper into his ear, "we can be together this way."

God, but it was difficult to concentrate on conversation. Her hands were running over his back, her fingernails grazing the taut skin on his ass. To hell with it. If she worried about what he was thinking, they could talk about it later. He'd nearly lost her today and he was ready to give up on life. But he hadn't lost her. Right now she was in his arms, blood pounded through his veins, and he needed her.

He kicked the crumpled sheet out of the way and scooped her into his arms. Her toes wriggled in the air as she squealed. The cabin was tight, but he maneuvered them back to the bunk and he dropped her into the softness there. She laughed when she pulled him down onto the bed with her.

Her breasts bounced with their movement so he took them into his hands. She was so firm and fresh. Her nipples puckered tightly as he rolled them in his fingers. Her laughter changed to sighs, the air hissing through her lips as her body arched under his. His cock was already straining to possess her. He tugged at the shorts he'd hastily slipped on earlier. His fingers fumbled in their desperation to get him closer to Aliya, so she reached out to help. At last he was free and he could glide his body beside hers, skin against skin and heat against heat.

"It seems like I get harder and harder every time I get close to you," he said.

She stroked his cock and bit her lip thoughtfully. "I believe you are right. You're solid as rock right now, Devin. What do you wish me to do?"

"No more wishes," he said as he stroked her in return, feeling her swell in moist anticipation of what was to come. "I have everything I could imagine."

She rewarded him with a teasing moan as he slid slowly inside her. He wanted to draw his actions out longer, but his emotions were raw from thinking he'd never have her again. His need was raging out of control and there was no hope of going slowly now. There'd be time for that later. For now, he needed to lose himself in the waves of their regained passion.

"You make me forget who I am," she murmured, rocking with his increasing thrusts. "You're my whole world when we are like this, Devin."

"And you're mine," he said. "I love you, Aliya. I need you like this. Forever."

"You will have me, whenever you want me."

Whenever you want me. In an instant images washed over him, flooding his mind with thoughts of Aliya. She was in his bed, in his car, walking up a tree-lined path with him, riding the elevator up to his leather-and-glass-bedecked office. Any part of his daily life he could imagine, Aliya was there. Those were all the times, all the places he would want her.

When he said *forever*, he truly meant it.

Not just when he could break away to come out on this boat. Not just when she could give her mermaid folk some excuse for her absence, not just when he could find a safe place to hide her and their hybrid offspring when he would come. He wanted Aliya the way any human man wanted the woman he loved. He wanted to build a life with her every day and everywhere.

It was like cold water in his face when reality dawned that this might not be the way she saw *forever.*

"What is it, Devin?" she cooed. "I feel your mind pulling back from me, even as I hold your body close."

It was true. He could already feel himself steeling his heart against the inevitable. She would know how he felt, how he wanted her in every human way, and she would reject that. How could she not? It would be as if he were asking her to be something she was not. He'd been through this before and knew how it would end.

If he wanted Aliya at all, he must be content with only part of her. He and Judith had made that work. He could do that again. Damn it, though, he just didn't want to.

"What are your thoughts, Devin?" she asked, the passion in her eyes fading enough that he could see honest concern.

He wasn't going to lie to her. Not now, not when they were so close and they'd already lost each other once today.

"I love you, Aliya. I will always love you, not just *whenever.*"

"I know, I can feel that so strongly in you. But why do you... why are you pulling away?"

There was no question what she meant by that. Even as his body pressed close to her, his impatient cock enveloped by the soft, wet folds of her heated body, his vulnerable psyche pulled away.

"Because I'm worried for our future."

"You are afraid we won't be like this in the future?"

"I promise I have plans for us to be like this a whole lot in the future. It's just..."

"Just what?"

"I don't want our life together to be something we hide. I don't want to sneak around as if we have something to be ashamed of."

"Are you ashamed of us?"

"No! That's exactly the point. You feel so good, I want your arms and your legs wrapped around me every day of my life. I want to make love and come inside you always, not just when we can sneak off to make it happen."

"You want to go out and do this in public?"

Her voice and the bright gleam in her eyes told him she might not be entirely opposed to that idea. His cock jumped and he couldn't speak; he only pushed himself deeper into her and thrilled at the sensations. By God, she did want him every bit as powerfully as he wanted her.

"No," he said finally. "I mean, yes, but that's not what I'm talking about. I want you in my life, Aliya. What we have here is magical, but I want you in the boring, everyday parts of my life, too."

Now she was beginning to understand. Maybe his words had been enough, or maybe his thoughts were clearing to let her see inside him. He watched her chew on the idea, turn it over inside her head.

"You want me to go on the land with you."

"Yes, I do, Aliya. I don't know how you feel about that, but—"

"I would love to, Devin. If you truly want me there."

"*Want* you there? I think we've pretty well established I want you every damn where."

"And the way the wish turned out, it seems that is what will be best for the child, too. We are suited to be part of each others' lives now, Devin."

"Yes, we are. I just wasn't sure how much of my life you might want."

"All of it, Devin. How much of mine do you want?"

His mind was open to her now. He could feel the sunshine of her thoughts, her emotions, as she reached inside to probe him there. She wasn't afraid to know him and he wasn't afraid to let her. All she would find inside his mind was love and a whole lot of desire.

"We will find a way to make this work, Devin. We can be what you want."

Embracing this moment of full honesty, he spoke the words he'd never been brave enough to say. Judith had never wanted to hear them, but he knew without hesitation that Aliya would. She really was his greatest wish come true.

"I want us to be a family. I don't know what it is to be a magical creature with twenty-four sisters who were birthed ceremonially for the sole purpose of serving the community, but I do know what it's like to live with people who love you and sacrifice themselves for the good of the family. That's what I want for us, Aliya. I live for you and you live for me and we both live for our child."

"It sounds wonderful."

"It does, doesn't it?"

"Then that is what we will be. We'll be a family like that."

She said it so easily and she meant it so fully. "Love" was too petty a word to describe what he felt for her at this moment. He pulled her tight and drove into her, sliding slowly and deliberately to connect all her most sensitive places. She moaned with pleasure for him.

"I need only one more thing from you to be perfectly happy," he spoke into her ear.

"Anything, Devin."

"Marry me."

He held his breath and had to pause in his eager lovemaking. Her answer made all the difference in the world. She would either grant him complete joy, or explain that there were simply some things they could not do. To bind herself in such a dry, human way might be asking too much. She came from a world where no one bound her by anything, where she was completely free and where humans were feared as oppressors. The last thing he wanted was to make her think he was asking to take her freedom away.

"It's really nothing more than a human tradition," he explained quickly. "A legal matter, and I agree it might sound confining and restrictive, but I promise that's not what I'm asking. If you aren't comfortable with it, of course I understand, but—"

"I will marry you, Devin."

"What?"

"It is the greatest thing you could ask of me; I can feel that in you and I am honored. It makes me so happy that you would want to be bound to me in that way!"

"It won't be easy, figuring out how to balance our lives," he said, feeling like he owed her complete honesty at this point. "And who knows what changes we'll have to make to do what's best for our child."

"We'll find a way. We have each other, Devin, and we have our wish. Surely knowing that makes you feel good."

"I feel good, all right," he said, thrusting slowly inside her, determined to hang on to some shred of control.

She moaned, wrapping her arms and legs even more tightly around him. The heat was intense. He tried to keep focused on giving her pleasure, but it wasn't long before his own pleasure built up to wild proportions. He was gliding in and out of her as if he'd never had her before, as if he might never have her again. The surge of passion drove him halfway to madness.

She called out his name, her fingers gripping his skin. That only urged him to drive harder, longer, deeper into her. It seemed he would keep up the pace for the rest of the night, but all at once the torrent of climax hit him. He throbbed and pulsated into her, the heat from his body burning off the cold droplets of sweat that had collected over his shoulders. His skin tingled in the air and he pulled her tight, cradling her for warmth as she began the throes of her own raging climax.

She clawed at him, groaned, and uttered oaths to the waters around them. This was the most intense lovemaking he'd ever experienced in his life and he knew it was because of her. Because he loved her completely and because she also loved him. Lust and desire seemed petty compared to this, what their love had accomplished.

There was no doubt in his mind that this kind of power could overcome anything that lay in store for them.

"Together," she whispered, sharing his thoughts.

"Yes, Aliya, together. Wet or dry or hot or cold, whatever we do it will be together."

He watched her face. She smiled, her eyes sparkling and her skin glowing with the flush of their passion.

"I have a feeling we'll be doing it a lot," she said. "You know how much I like being wet."

Chapter Twenty-Four

Kyne waited on the deck of the boat for Raea. She stayed behind for some quiet words with Aliya, but he needed to be out of that room with all of its raging passions and breathe in some fresh air. Not that it helped much. Such close proximity to those half-drooling lovers had triggered every lustful response he had in him. It was going to take every ounce of his feeble self-control just to be able to fly once they were done here.

Finally Raea emerged from the cabin. She was smiling her most enchanting smile and glowing even pinker than usual. Her eyes wouldn't meet his and she drew in a deep breath, her feathered bodice pulled tight at her breasts. He tried to look away, but he couldn't. Her satiny skin glistened in the last rays of amber sunset. She would feel so good against him, those breasts in his hands…

By the Skies, he needed to get away. There was too much emotion, too much desire, too much wayward lust in the vicinity. He could barely breathe.

"I'm glad things worked out for them," she said.

"So far," he mumbled.

"We'll have to keep it from the council, of course, but I'm sure they'll find a way. There's time before the child is born to make plans. I'm sure they'll figure out what to do."

Kyne nodded and moved away from her. "I hope so. The last thing I want is to get dragged further into this."

He could feel her glaring at him, but he stared out over the water. Her wings buzzed and he knew she was upset.

"Really? After all of this, seeing them so happy and knowing they even have a child on the way, all you can think of is saving your own hide? Do you really love the Fairy Council that much that all you want is to make them happy? Can't you care at all what happens to these two?"

She'd moved close enough to him now that he could feel her body heat against his wings. He could feel Aliya and the human, too. They hadn't even waited for the fairies to be off of this boat before they were back in that bed, groping and pushing and sucking and... by the Air, he needed to leave.

But hell, where could he go? There would never be escape from this raging hot need, the pulsating ache he could never dare soothe. He didn't bother with further pleasantries before turning his back on Raea and surging up into the chilled, lonely night air.

He tried not to be happy about it, but he knew she was following him. If he could just get them away from that boat... away from the lust and the sighing and all those things Kyne knew he didn't dare think about... maybe he could trust himself to have a conversation with Raea. The harder he flew and the farther away he got from the boat the more he knew the undeniable truth.

His body was hard and desperate for Raea and it wasn't simply because of that human. It was because he wanted Raea, and the minute he could get her alone, he intended to have her. For her own sake, he sped up to try to leave her behind.

He wasn't at all sorry that she was such a fast flier.

* * *

"By the Air, why are you in such a hurry?" Raea called, panting from working so hard to catch up to him, the jerk. He knew she was back here.

"Stop following me," he said, not bothering to slow down or to look at her.

"You don't own the sky. I can fly wherever I want."

"Well, you'd better start wanting to fly somewhere else."

"And if I don't, what will you do?"

They were over the shoreline now. Below them waves broke over a rocky beach. A tree-lined ridge made a dark horizon against the deepening blue of the night sky. Kyne hovered to a halt and whirled on her. She had to pull up hard to keep from crashing into him and for just a moment she was afraid. His eyes blazed with fire. But he took a deep breath and turned away, flapping off at a more leisurely pace in another direction.

"There are some agricultural plots that I'm scheduled for tending."

"So you're just going to ignore me?"

He seemed to be trying very hard to pretend he didn't even hear her. She followed, knowing he would hate that. But they had unfinished business and she was not going to leave things this way.

"We need to decide what we'll tell the council."

"I'm sure I'll think of something."

"Don't you think we ought to figure this out together? I could help you explain about the dust, and—"

"I don't need your help."

He said it as if the idea disgusted him. Was that it, did she disgust him now? She'd dragged him into helping a human, so now he couldn't stand to so much as look at her anymore. Well, that was fine. If he didn't want to be friendly with her, she could live with that. She didn't need a friend like him, anyway, with his lustful ways and dangerous background. She had plenty of other friends she'd much rather spend time with. Kyne wasn't the only fairy on the cloud.

He was the only one with such broad shoulders and those golden eyes, of course, but that wasn't any big deal. Fairies weren't so shallow as to put much stock in one another's appearance. Kyne could go on being golden and huge and gorgeous. It meant nothing to her.

All she cared about was keeping herself and her friends out of trouble.

"So, I guess you've changed your mind about humans now," she said after another few minutes of silence and tiresome following.

"No. I haven't. Why should I?"

"Well, it was a little obvious you didn't really mind helping out back there, not once you realized Devin was more about honestly caring for Aliya than just…you know. You discovered humans have souls."

"Of course they have souls. No one ever said they didn't. They just generally choose to ignore their souls, which makes them all the worse for it."

"Devin didn't ignore his."

"He's unusual. And you can't tell me these were ordinary circumstances."

"Well, maybe not, but he could have gotten away from his responsibilities easily enough if he'd wanted to."

"Who's to say he won't do that next week, or next month?"

"Why do you hate humans so much?" she asked.

As expected, *that* got his attention. He stopped again and faced her.

"You should know the answer to that."

"Well, I don't. It seems like you should have more reason than any of us to understand humans, to relate to them."

"I understand them, all right. I understand completely. I know all about their weaknesses, their animal impulses. You think I can relate to that? You're right. I can. And I hate it."

"You hate humans, or you hate yourself?"

"I hate *them*. My mother was nearly destroyed because one of *them* couldn't keep his filthy hands to himself. By the Skies, Raea, I have to live with that every day of my life. And you have to ask why I hate humans?"

"So your mother wasn't...she wasn't a willing partner with your father?"

"Of course not. She'd never willingly break the code that way. The human who fathered me used her and then abandoned her. I always hoped that wasn't normal human behavior, that they aren't all led by their lust and their passions."

Her heart ached for him. She could hear the raw pain in his voice as he laughed at himself before going on.

"Why do you think I made that damn bet in the first place, Raea? I wanted proof there was hope for someone like me. But there isn't. Humans *are* ruled by their desires and they use them to get what they want. That's why you can never trust them."

"But you aren't like that, Kyne. I trust you."

"You shouldn't."

He was hovering very close now, his eyes burning her with their intensity. In an instant she believed he was right. She shouldn't trust him. She shouldn't even be here with him right now. Not because he was half human, but because that half of him didn't disgust her.

"You aren't like the human who fathered you," she assured him. "You're not capable of such cruelty, Kyne."

"You'd be surprised what I'm capable of."

She almost didn't hear him, his voice was so low. She had a pretty good idea what he meant by it, though. He was capable of all manner of forbidden things. The real question right now, she realized, was what was *she* capable of?

"It's time for us to go our own ways, Raea," he announced as he dropped down to rest on a rocky outcropping just above the shore. "We've got a lot to do to get things back to normal."

"Things will never be normal again, Kyne. I think you know that."

"You should go now, Raea."

She sank down onto the rock beside him. "I don't want to go now. I want to stay here, with you."

He moved quickly and caught her off guard. His hands fastened on her arms and pulled her to face him. She winced. Her skin was on fire where he touched her. She blinked into his blazing eyes, not sure what to say, what to do. Slowly, his grasp on her slackened, but the connection did not break. His thumb brushed softly over her arm, his hand trailing upward, making a path of tingling heat over her shoulder. She couldn't move away; his touch was making her dizzy with sensation.

"You should be worried right now, Raea. Be very worried."

"You don't scare me," she said and tried to sound like she meant it.

"You don't think I have reason to scare you?"

"I understand you're mad at me. Things got kind of messed up and I had to drag you in where you didn't want to go. I'm sorry."

"You think *that's* what this is about?"

His golden eyes searched hers, then his gaze shifted to take in her hair and her shoulders and her clothes. She felt it as clearly as if it had been a caress. She tried to gather her thoughts enough to answer his question.

"Um...isn't it? I know what we did was wrong."

"Hell yes, it was wrong," he said, still running his fingers over her skin, his gaze over her body. "Everything about it was wrong."

She tried to catch her breath but the air refused to cooperate. "And you don't like wrong."

"No, Raea. I *do* like wrong. I like it very much, I'm afraid."

Slowly his eyes shifted back to her face. She'd been busy studying his lips, but now she met his gaze. It set her on fire inside. She knew exactly how to respond.

"I'm afraid I like wrong, too."

His lips parted, but he didn't speak. He was perfectly still, perfectly quiet. She matched his stare, his breathing, his slow, steady wing beats. He was waiting for her to pull away from him; she knew that. She wasn't going anywhere, though. It was obvious what they both wanted.

"I want to be wrong some more, Kyne," she said.

It was almost like begging. She didn't care. Too much had happened to her today, she needed to understand all of it. If she had to, she was prepared to beg now.

He didn't make her stoop to that, thankfully. His hands slid around her, pinning her wings gently and pulling her close. She wrapped herself around him and felt the strong, churning muscles where his wings attached at the shoulder blades. He was fully magic, all fairy. So strong, yet so earthy. And so capable of doing what she wanted beyond all reason.

He kissed her. She slid against him, opening her lips to his searching tongue. Kyne's kisses tasted like summer. Like honey and the scent of ripening wheat. Like the heat from the sun on a day with no breeze. Like everything she could ever hope for and then some.

She pressed her body against his length. His chest was solid, his abdomen tight with muscles, his thighs firm and sturdy. He was growing hard against her, too. She could feel his manhood almost as if there was nothing between them. As if his leather clothes and her feathered attire had faded away.

She wanted to feel more of him, all of him. She wanted that now and nothing else around them mattered. She needed him and was eager to comply as he laid her back against the rock they sat on.

Smoothed from eons of waves washing over, the gray rock shone white in the moonlight. It was still warm from the day's sun. Kyne was stretched out next to her and pressing her close. She could give up this fight against what was forbidden and concentrate on what they both wanted. It would be heaven.

Kyne was covering her, wrapping her inescapably in his arms and his wings. She let sensation rule her body. Sensation and Kyne. His hands were all over her now. His breath was labored. He kissed her almost violently, stroking, probing with his tongue, urging her to give herself to him.

She gasped, hating the air she needed to breathe. It was a hindrance to kissing him. Yes, air was not her friend right now. There was too much of it between them. She wanted to merge, wanted her whole body to be one with Kyne. Nothing between them. Flesh joining flesh.

This thing they were caught up in had nothing of the air to it. This was pure earth. Flesh, dust, human. Foreign and forbidden to her, to them both. But undeniable.

And then, she felt him. His manhood against her skin. He was pressed against her where her feathered tunic had been pushed aside. There was no barrier. They could join.

She arched toward him, eager for the union.

"No," he breathed in her ear. "We don't know what this will do to us. We can't…"

He was trying to push her away, but she fought him.

"Please," she said, her fingers tightening on his clothing. "I need this. I need you."

"But what if…"

"It's too late for that. Too late to worry. I need you, Kyne."

Her hands found their way inside his tunic. Ah, he was so warm to her touch. And there was a light cover of hair on him, his chest, his abdomen, lower. She'd never known a fairy with body hair. It was fascinating. She dug her fingers into it and pulled herself closer to him.

He groaned and kissed her as if he were devouring his last meal. She pulled at his clothing, and he pulled at hers, until somehow they were free of the restraints that separated them. Naked. She touched him everywhere.

He felt so good to her. She traced the taut muscles on his back, the sculpted curve of his butt. Oh, she loved how he felt against her body. She wiggled closer still, until he was pressing his hardened shaft solidly against the apex of her being. It thrilled and terrified her all at the same time.

"I want you so bad," he murmured and she recognized the strain in his voice.

"It's all right," she whispered. "I want you, too."

He slid his warm hands over her body, brushing between them until his fingers found her tingling nipples. He gave gentle pressure there, testing them, dipping to taste them. She writhed with inexplicable pleasure. How could this just keep getting better? It was almost as if they were dragging themselves up a never-ending mountain, compelled by some force and desperate to reach the pinnacle. She had no idea what awaited them there, but she needed it desperately.

She needed *him* desperately. Something was building up inside her and she somehow knew only Kyne could release it, bring her the satisfaction she thought she might die without. Was he feeling it, too?

She thought so. His breathing sounded rugged, hoarse. He trailed kisses over her skin, but she could feel his control fading fast. His movements were becoming labored, his kisses more demanding. He wanted release as franticly as she did.

"Kyne," she said and her voice was almost inaudible. "Come inside me, Kyne."

He moaned against her. "Oh God, Raea. I want to, but it's wrong."

"Yes, so very wrong. But I want it. With you."

And she felt the last inkling of his calm disappear. He growled and grasped her hands firmly in his, pinning them against the smooth rock up over her head. She drew in a surprised breath, but her heart beat in anticipation. He was not fighting her now. He was beyond worrying about codes and society and the Fairy Council. He was giving her what she needed and she loved him with every breath for it.

He moved over her and his weight prevented her from moving. She had a brief flash of panic, then the moment took over and she realized her fantasies were about to be fulfilled. His engorged human penis was throbbing against her tender flesh.

She opened up to him. *Yes, yes, yes!* She wanted to cry out, but the air and the words would not come. Silently, then, she thrust herself up to meet him.

With an animal groan he pushed into her. She gasped for breath that dragged slowly into her lungs. He was huge. He was hot. He was so very, very human. He was exactly what she wanted.

"I've dreamed of this, Raea," he breathed. "I've wanted you so badly. Are you sure this is what you want?"

"By the Creator." She finally managed to gasp. "It's perfect, Kyne. So perfect."

Her words seemed to reassure him. He kissed her heartily on the lips. She was overwhelmed by sensation and failed to notice at first when he began withdrawing his manhood from her tender core. What? He was done with her? But she was far from done with him!

"My Raea…," he said, then thrust firmly back into her.

She felt every inch of him. So hot, so hard, so demanding. He withdrew slightly again, only to come crashing back into her. She moaned.

"Perfect, yes," he said. "Everything I've ever wanted."

She responded by clinging all the tighter to him. She wrapped her legs around him and concentrated on matching his rhythm. He was so powerful, so strong. She felt safe like she never had before, as if they were the only souls on earth and nothing mattered but drawing him farther and farther into her quivering body.

His thrusts intensified and she was rocked against him the way she'd seen humans do when they coupled. She held on for dear life. It was as if she'd left her own body and was carried far away from anything she'd ever known to a place that was all light, all pleasure. And Kyne was her entire universe.

"I'm sorry, Raea," he said between rasping breaths. "I can't stop. I need to have you."

"No, don't stop. This is right… this is heaven."

And he obeyed her. The thrusts continued as she felt herself raised higher and higher, as if to the peak of a very tall mountain. She called out his name and he answered with kisses and filled her completely, her body and soul. Surely she would die from the emotions and sensations. And she didn't care.

Suddenly they were tumbling, leaping from the pinnacle of that mountain. Raea felt something let go inside her. It was the release she'd needed all along, but it was overpowering, intense. She buried her face against his shoulder and whimpered.

"Kyne, I'm falling! Oh, by the Stars, Kyne, don't let me go…"

"You're safe," he said, and was gripping her tightly. "I've got you, Raea."

With a final thrust and a loud roar ripped from his very spirit, she felt his release. He was pouring himself inside her, and she was helpless against the gale force of ultimate pleasure that racked her body. She shuddered against him and cried his name to the skies.

Slowly she became aware of the world around her again. She was surprised when her eyes slipped open to notice they had never actually left the rock. She could have sworn they'd been floating on clouds. Kyne's body was warm and heavy against her, pinning her to earth with his manhood still softly pulsing inside her. She felt a peace she'd never felt before.

Exhausted, he finally slid over to lean on his elbow, cradling her against himself.

"I knew it would be good with you, Raea," he said. "But I never dreamed it could be like that."

"Amazing," she agreed, nuzzling against him.

"You were right when you said nothing would ever be normal again. How can it be? Everything is different."

She reached out and stroked his golden skin.

"Everything is better."

He kissed her forehead. "And I will make sure you always believe that."

"Oh?" she asked, feeling limp and drained and completely happy. "Just how do you plan to make that happen?"

"Maybe I'll make a wish," he suggested.

She laughed. "As I recall, you don't get a wish until you've won a certain bet."

He kissed her neck. "And as I recall, the bet's over. You cheated."

"Maybe, but you did give me a whole week to complete the task. I can still prove my point in the allotted time."

"I think you've already proved it quite thoroughly," he said, running a finger from her throat, over her breast, and down to the slick area between her legs. "Humans are a sordid lot."

She sighed under his touch. "So, does that mean I won after all?"

"Hardly. In this wager, I'm clearly the one who got the prize."

"That's corny, even for you, Kyne," she said. "You really are incredibly human, you know."

"Not so much," he said and nibbled her ear lobe. "Humans generally require several long minutes between pleasure sessions."

She glided a hand across his thigh to take his manhood into her grasp. Solid and ready for action. She grinned.

In so many ways, Kyne was human. In all the important ways, he was more than that. In the most important way of all he was *hers*. No code and no law could ever change that.

The future might hold some difficult decisions, but that didn't matter tonight. Tonight was for wishing and, fairy or not, she would grant all of Kyne's without haste. And a few of her own while they were at it.

"I wish you weren't so far away from me," she murmured.

Like magic, his body was covering hers again, his warmth filling her soul and his forbidden humanness filling her being. She was willing to bet they'd be doing this a lot from now on. A whole lot.

Chapter Twenty-Five

The water was cool over Aliya's body. Her muscles flexed and relaxed, reacquainting themselves with her old, familiar form. It wasn't that she didn't like her human body—she loved it, actually. But she loved her usual form, too. She dived down under the water and let herself glide easily through it.

Devin was sleeping, back on the boat. Exhausted from their antics. She had slept, too, but woke before him. The sky on the eastern horizon was just beginning to show glimmers of dawn. Misty rays spread upward from the lake, fingers that brushed the wispy clouds with pinks and golds, all softly diffused by the chill of early morning.

She broke back through the surface to admire the sky. She'd never paid much mind to it before, considering air just another part of the dry that meant very little to her life. Now the whole world was opened up to her. She would be a creature of the land with Devin. He would take her into his world and make her his wife.

It was exciting, and frightening. Devin would help her make the transition, though. She would learn his ways and her new life would be more than she could have ever dreamed of here in the lake.

A sound at the boat caught her attention and she turned. She felt Devin's presence before she saw him there, leaving the warm cabin to stand and watch over her on the deck. They were far from the shore and the water was calmer than usual today. He stood peacefully there, his naked skin glistening with moisture from the cool air. The light was just bright enough that she could see him smile.

"I hope you don't mind that I left you," she said.

"As long as you intended to come back," he replied.

"Of course. I just thought I might come for a swim, but now that you're awake, I will come back on board."

"No," he said, stretching his waking limbs and shaking his head. "I'll come where you are."

She was going to warn him that the water was probably too cold for a human so early in the day, but he dove off the side of the boat and split the water expertly just a few feet away from her. She bobbed in the wake he made, laughing that he had splashed her. She waited for him to resurface so she could splash him, but there was no sign of him.

Just as she began to get worried, something brushed past her fins. She startled, then dropped down under the surface. Her eyes detected his movement, but she relied on her senses to locate him. He had gone down fairly deep, under the boat. Immediately she reached out her thoughts, hoping he wasn't in trouble.

But then he shot past her, moving as fast as any fish and every bit as agile. She felt his laughter and realized his mind was as open to her as any mermaid she knew. She felt his surprise, but the lightness and love that filled his mind, too.

"I can hear you down here," he said, though there was no speaking.

"You have reached my mind," she explained. "I had no idea you would be able to do that."

"I seem to be damn good at swimming, too," he replied. "These gills work like a charm."

"And you are not too cold?"

"It's refreshing, but I'm okay. How about you? Any negative effects of spending another night as a human?"

"I'm fine," she assured him.

He moved up next to her now, pulling her into his arms and stroking the length of her with his hands. She pressed against him, sliding in the cool water and wrapping her body around his. She could feel him respond.

"Yes, you are fine," he teased, taking her breasts into his hands.

She knew he could feel her response, too. It seemed no matter how many times she gave herself to pleasure in Devin's arms, she would never quite have enough of him.

"I hope not," he said. "Because I'm never going to have enough of you."

"We'll have to go back to the boat for that," she reminded him.

But he wasn't ready to leave.

"Not just yet. I want you to show me your world, Aliya. Let me be here with you, get to know you in your home."

"My home is with you, Devin. I thought you wanted me to live with you on land?"

"I want you to be my wife," he explained, pulling her up close to him and rising just enough so that there was light to look into her face. "You will be my wife in the water as well as on the land. And I want you to feel at home in both."

"But you want to know about my world?"

"I love you, Aliya. I want to know everything about you, whether we're wet or we're dry or we sprout wings and start to fly."

"Oh, I hope we don't do that. How confusing would that be!"

"But we'd find a way to make that work if we had to, wouldn't we?"

"Yes, of course we would. And I cannot wait to learn about your world. If you are happy there, Devin, then that will be my home."

"There's a cheesy old human saying: home is where the heart is," he said, and she didn't think it sounded cheesy at all. "My heart is right here with you, Aliya."

"Then welcome to our home, Devin, because my heart is wherever you are and you are right here."

He held her tighter and she melted against him. There was no need to think about air or about breathing. They both just did what came naturally and let their bodies drift in the darkness, touching each other inside and out. They spoke their vows silently, bound together by a kiss that ignited flames no wind and no wave could ever extinguish.

Please turn the page for a preview of the next novella in the
Forbidden Realm series,

By the Magic of Starlight

Available Fall 2014

Chapter One

It might have been the phase of the moon, or maybe it was the heady, sweet scent of summertime in the air. She really wasn't sure what caused it, only that her body was helpless against it. That warm, electric wave of forbidden desire was washing over her again and she could do nothing to make it stop. She'd been forced to leave tonight's gathering place and seek the chilled solitude of the Great Lake.

She headed for the darkest, loneliest stretch of shoreline she could find. At least here she could burn for things not allowed and no one would know about it.

"Hello, Raea. I'm glad you found me."

Raea's body instantly reacted to Kyne's warm, deep voice. It was in perfect contrast to the cool blue moonlight and the calming, wet air coming up off the lake. Fairies were generally unaffected by mundane physical things such as air temperature, but lately Raea had noticed herself becoming more and more aware of her physical surroundings. She was more aware of all sorts of physical things.

"I wasn't looking for you, Kyne," she said, her eyes searching the shadowed landscape around her until his form became visible.

He sat on the low, sandy ridge that flanked the rocky shore of the lake. The cool light of the moon toned down the fiery oranges and gold in his coloring, yet the very sight of him made her insides grow hot. No, she hadn't been looking for him intentionally, but it was all she could do to hide the fact that she was awfully glad to have found him.

"You seemed to be looking for something," he drawled in that self-assured tone that drove her half crazy. "And I'm definitely something."

Oh, but his cockiness grated. Especially because he had good reason to feel so overly confident. Kyne wasn't like other fairies. He had something… special. She just wished she could somehow stop wanting it.

But now here they were. Together. Stillness surrounded them, sweetened by a light breeze and the distant call of birds as they darted about, looking for a place to settle in for the night. Languid waves lapped at the shoreline, making a watery rhythm against the age-rounded stones strewn everywhere. It was peaceful, and very, very empty. They were entirely alone.

"It's good to see you, Kyne," she said, pretending it was easy for her to stare out at the lake, to ignore his golden coloring, his unfairylike broad shoulders, his strong, well-formed wings. "I've been very busy lately, and—"

"You've been avoiding me," he said, not allowing her to complete the lie. "And to be honest, I've been avoiding you."

She shouldn't have been disappointed in his words, but she was. "If you'd rather not be around me, why don't you flap on back to the gathering place where you're supposed to be?"

"Why don't *you*?"

Oh, he was infuriating. She knew better than to enter into foolish banter with him, but somehow she just never could help herself when it came to Kyne. She always did the wrong thing with him.

"Because I want to be alone," she replied.

He pointed out the obvious. "But you're not alone. You're with me."

"Not intentionally."

"Then why aren't you leaving?"

"I think I will."

"No you won't. You're going to stay here."

"And why would I do that?"

"Because you don't really want to be alone, Raea. And truthfully, I don't either."

She refused to agree with him. She couldn't let him know what she felt, what his presence was doing to her. She'd fallen prey to these feelings before and she didn't dare allow it to happen again. No matter how badly she wanted it—had been wanting it since that one single time that she'd let herself forget her breeding, her station, the very foundation of her existence here behind the Veil in the Forbidden Realm. She'd let passion take her over and it had been wonderful. Amazing. Magical.

But she could never let it happen again.

It should have never even happened once. What they had done was...well, it was forbidden. It was dangerous. It could unravel the carefully constructed Veil that for millennia had kept their world safe and protected from humans. Giving in to that passion was foolish and reckless. It was very nearly the worst crime a fairy could have committed.

And yet here she was, sensing Kyne as he left his perch on the knoll to come toward her. She could practically feel his eyes on her, roaming over her pink form with all the hunger and tenderness of a lover's touch. She wanted that touch so badly her body felt weak, as if starved for the very thing that might keep her alive.

"I've missed you, Raea," he said softly.

"You saw me two days ago at the end-of-week gathering."

"That's not enough."

"It has to be, Kyne."

"It isn't. We can't go on this way," he said, his voice ragged from fighting back the very same emotions she felt herself crumbling under. "I can't, at least."

"But we have to," she said and finally turned to face him. "It's just the way things are, Kyne. You live your life and I'll live mine and we can never let any of it overlap."

"Is that really what you want?"

"You know as well as I do that our *wants* don't matter. They're *wrong*. Very wrong."

"They don't feel wrong."

By the Skies, he was practically touching her. She could feel the heat from his warm, summer body. She was becoming mesmerized by his deep amber eyes. She was falling into the swell of desire that always threatened to take her over when Kyne was near. She was allowing herself to be seduced.

"We should never have allowed ourselves to feel those things in the first place. It's dangerous; it's foolish. It's how the…" She stopped herself before she said more than she ought.

Too late, though. He understood what she'd been thinking.

"That's how the humans live?"

"Yes, it is. But we aren't like them, Kyne. We just can't be."

"You mean *you* can't," he corrected, and rightfully so. "I can't very well help being like them."

"You're half fairy; focus on that. You don't have to give in to your human side. Come on, Kyne. You know what could happen, how important this is."

"Is it, Raea? Is it really as dangerous as the council keeps telling us? Is the Veil so fragile that a little bit of forbidden passion might tear it down forever? I don't believe it."

"Passion is human, Kyne. That's what will tear down the Veil."

"It's not human! By the Clouds, Raea, you felt it, too, I know you did. How is that since you've no human blood?"

"But you do! It's because of you, Kyne. I felt what I felt only because of you, never for anyone else."

That had been the wrong thing to say. She could feel the heat radiate off him, could see his wings beat faster and a flame ignite behind his eyes. She could sense the passion rise up within him. Clearly he liked hearing that he made her feel things no one ever had. And now she was feeling those things again. Her own heart beat faster, blood pounding through her body. Infuriating fairy! She could not let herself get caught up in this again.

"The world did not end because of what you felt, did it, Raea?" he asked softly.

"Stop it, Kyne. You know it can't be."

"I know it can, and I know you want it to be. Just as badly as I do."

"No! If we get caught you'll be...No, I can't let that happen. There's too much at stake. If you can't control yourself, I can. And I'm saying no."

But he was still close to her, his essence still affecting her ability to think straight. His body was changing, too, losing some of its delicate fairy elements and appearing larger, solid, more human. The passion roared inside her, knowing just what wonders he could do with those human attributes he possessed. It took everything she had not to flutter into his arms and let his humanity sweep her away.

"I could make you say yes," he whispered, one golden hand reaching out to touch her, to caress her cheek so very gently.

Her eyelids drooped and she pressed into that caress. His heated skin felt so good against hers, the electricity between them fueled by so much more than mere magic. Yes...she would give in. She would take what he offered and let herself revel in it.

But he pulled back abruptly, breaking the spell. She barely caught herself from falling as she startled back to reality. Kyne had moved away from her, the air feeling even colder and darker than before. She followed his gaze to a spot of light over the landscape behind her. It was growing brighter, approaching.

"Someone's coming."

His words rang judgment in the quiet night. Someone knew they were here; someone knew what they were doing. They'd been caught.

"Admit to nothing," he murmured. "We've done nothing wrong."

She cringed at the notion of lying to another of her kind. If Kyne had half an idea of the thoughts and intent that had circled through her with just that one simple caress, there was no way he could expect her to claim they'd done nothing wrong. They most certainly had, and she'd been well on her way to doing it again. If this intruder was here to accuse them, she could only confess guilt.

There was nothing to do but wait quietly. In a matter of seconds, the dim light became a dim form, which appeared clearer, and soon they could recognize their worst fear. And she did recognize him.

Another fairy. His name was Swift, and he worked in the

Department of Restraint and Obedience. Two things Raea had sadly been lacking these days.

"Raea and Kyne," he said as he grew closer. "Stay where you are."

"We're not going anywhere, Swift," Kyne called back. "We don't have any reason to leave."

"If you don't want to stand punishment, you might have good reason."

He was with them now, his green wings stroking the air in carefully measured tempo. Everything about Swift spoke of control. He was the epitome of fairy efficiency and clear-headedness. Since he'd come all the way here, there was no doubt he'd known what he would find.

"Punishment?" Kyne asked, matching Swift's wingstroke and control. "Is it a punishable offense to hover over the shore of the lake?"

"Don't play your games, Kyne. It's been barely three weeks since that little mermaid episode, so you've got no room for misbehavior."

Raea was nearly shaking too hard to keep herself airborne, but she remained silent. What could she say? What could she do? Swift seemed to know everything that they'd done. There was no way to protect herself or Kyne from the retribution they'd face.

But Kyne furrowed his brow. He seemed to be unsure what Swift had referred to.

"Mermaid episode? Refresh my memory on that, if you don't mind. I've been so busy doing my job lately I can't quite recall."

"You know perfectly well what I'm referring to! You and Raea had some sort of involvement with a mermaid and a human. The matter is under investigation and rest assured we will get to the truth. We've had more than enough reason to keep you under close watch, Kyne. Don't think we don't know what you've been up to."

"I've been doing my job!" he growled in response. "I'm a Summer Fairy and if you haven't noticed, it's summertime here. Flowers, bees, another growth ring on the trees…If you've been watching me you know what I've been doing."

"We know you two thought you could sneak off alone out here."

Now she could not stay silent. As if she had planned their encounter tonight!

"No! I came out here alone," she announced. "And so did he. Any interaction we've had has been purely professional."

"Professional?" Swift said. "Since when does a Wish Fairy have anything to do on a professional level with one of our Season Fairies?"

"We see each other in passing, just as I'm sure all of us see any number of fairies in passing. How dare you imply something more!"

"I imply nothing. I merely report what my investigation determines."

"Investigation? We've been under investigation?" she asked.

"If you have nothing to hide, it would hardly matter, would it?"

"I just didn't know fairies had such little privacy these days."

"And what do you need privacy for?"

Kyne stepped in before she had a chance to let anger press her into saying things she might later regret. She'd have to thank him for that.

"The Fairy Council has had something against me for a long time," Kyne said. "I know all about that and I know what's been expected of me. If you have a problem with me or any of the rumors about me, that's between us. You leave Raea out of this."

Swift shook his head. "You have no idea how I wish I could do that. Raea has always been an exemplary worker, a good fairy and valuable to our cause. We have reason to believe she's been corrupted and I think the council will agree that finding you together like this tonight only further proves that."

"We did nothing wrong!" Kyne insisted.

"Then perhaps you can explain that to the council. They are reasonable. If you truly have nothing to hide, then you truly have nothing to fear."

Unfortunately, that was true. The Fairy Council was known throughout the Forbidden Realm for being reasonable and fair. If Raea and Kyne had nothing to hide, then of course they'd have nothing to fear. Trouble was, they *did* have something to hide, and it sounded as if Swift had enough evidence to lay it all out in the open.

"Are you bringing charges?" Kyne asked. "If not, then we don't have to go with you to see the council."

"Yes, that's the law. But it's going to look so much better for you if I can tell them you came willingly."

"Well, I won't. If you want me to see the council, then let's do this right. You come up with some legitimate charges, and I want to see an advocate. Now."

Was he serious? Raea tried to get Kyne's attention, to let him see the warning look she was glaring at him, but he stared only at Swift. It was not a pleasant stare, either. Swift seemed unimpressed, though. He merely rolled his eyes, let out a frustrated sigh, and pulled up a pinch of whatever dust he carried in his pouch.

"Are you sure you want me to do this?" he asked Kyne.

"Yes. Do it."

Instantly, Swift released the dust. It evaporated with a green puff. There was only a moment of silence, then another light was seen in the distance, coming from the direction Swift had appeared. Apparently his dust had been the kind used for long-distance contact. He must have known this would happen, so he had someone waiting for his summons. By the Skies, she doubted Kyne had expected that. He likely thought he was calling Swift's bluff, that he could gain a reprieve or at least stall Swift's plans for the night.

Raea watched as another fairy appeared. A female this time, prim and dainty and blue. She seemed just as efficient and official as Swift.

"Kyne has requested an advocate," Swift said to her when she arrived.

The blue fairy nodded. "I'm Pimma, Advocate for the Accused."

"So I *am* being accused," Kyne said, barely acknowledging her. "Of what?"

Swift cleared his throat and pulled himself up tall and straight. His wings beat faster and he rose higher, enough so that he was looking down on Kyne, and the rest of them had to strain to look up at him. He smiled, and Raea waited for the charges to be leveled. It would be bad. They would be accused of an unpardonable crime. She waited for him to say the word: "passion."

But he didn't. He ignored her completely and kept his crystalline green eyes directly on his detainee.

"It pains me to do this, but I must charge you with the worst sort of crimes. Kyne, Summer Fairy, I accuse you of Co-Mingling."

Please turn the page for a preview of the next book in the
Forbidden Realm series,

Licked by the Flame

Available Winter 2014

Chapter One

Nicolai Stefanya Vladik paced the length of the boardroom and wished in his very core there was a window in this damn place. It was not in his nature to be cooped up in these constructions, human boxes made of plastic and wood, substances that would wither and melt into a wisp of smoke at the very least hint of fire. It was a tenuous way to exist. No wonder humans were so short lived—they spent so much of their time in these fragile spaces.

Not that Nicolai had been back in his own timeless lair any time recently. He'd given that up to go on this quest. It was for the good of his kind, yet so many things in this new life still felt unnatural to him. Clothing, machines, shallow entertainments…all of them were so frail, so meaningless. This meeting today with a dozen so-called experts in their fields was a waste. None of these learned humans knew anything. Of course, he ought to be glad for that, but he was tired of the isolation and boredom this situation offered.

He would never be a human despite the years and years his duty had kept him here, walking among them. There were times his nature burned to come out, to take him over once again and let him rid himself of this human foolishness. Today was one of those days. It was all he could do to maintain his appearance.

But he had to maintain. For the sake of his mission, he would keep it together. He would act like a human, live like a human. He would *be* a human. For just a while longer, he could keep up this charade.

He knew what he needed. It was always this way if he let himself go too long without. This human body must be given what it craved or Nic would lose control over it. He would have to do what must be done if he wanted to continue in his role.

The question, of course, was how. Even as the meeting droned on, as the men around him talked about projects and statistics and governmental regulations, he could only wonder how he would tend to his needs. This site inspection, after all, was scheduled to go on for another two weeks. In the middle of nowhere. Nic didn't dare leave at this critical time, but he also couldn't figure how to manage his problem.

He needed a woman. Badly. By the fires of below, he thought he could almost smell one, though he knew only men had been assigned to this remote project site. Pity his cravings didn't lean that way; it would make things infinitely easier. But no. Nic liked women. *Human* women. And there was a definite shortage of those around here.

Still, his need was growing and his senses were overheating with awareness. Just beyond his carefully calm exterior, he could feel the very real presence of a woman. His nostrils flared. His skin tingled on alert. It was as if the air in the building crackled with the hot essence of woman. Damn, but his situation must be worse than he'd thought.

If he didn't sink himself into warm female flesh soon, he was likely to explode. And this was not just the wishful thinking of the usual frustrated human male. No, this was serious. If Nic thought he might be about to explode, everyone here had good reason to worry. He'd likely take this whole damn mountain with him. He wasn't just any sex-crazed mortal man, after all.

Nicolai Vladik was a full-fledged dragon.

* * *

She was a woman and there was no way to hide it. Lianne McGowan didn't generally notice that she was often the only female on a given project, or in a department, or perhaps even the only one assigned to any particular building. She was oddly aware, however, that as of her arrival at this jobsite today, she was the only female for a good hundred miles. Or more, maybe.

Iceland, as it turned out, was overflowing with volcanoes and geothermal hot spots. Not so much civilization, however. Not that this concerned her.

She was used to making her way in a man's world. It meant she had to get the point across right away that she was confident in her role here and wasn't going to let any good ol' boys—there were always a couple of those in the group—push her around. Also she wasn't going to let any of them think she wasn't just as tough and as determined as they were. Geo-Diagnostics had sent her here with one goal: the project had been lagging and she was supposed to get these guys back on the ball. The higher-ups needed to see some results if they were going to keep the investors happy.

Lianne was here to get those results. It was as simple as that. She knew her job and she knew how to do it. Twelve men or a hundred men weren't going to distract her. She was ready for whatever attitude problems or temper tantrums they were going to throw at her.

She didn't bother to knock, but pushed the boardroom door open and stood there for a minute, letting the group inside figure out that something in their little world had just changed. It gave her a minute to look them over, too. First impressions were important on both sides.

A few of the guys she recognized, having worked with them at other sites before. Mr. Casper she knew from way back, and Mr. Blanchard sitting at the head of the table with his usual smug expression made her want to roll her eyes. The other men looked about like every geologist, engineer, and technical geek she usually worked with. No surprises here. Except…one guy was pacing at the back of the room.

Wow. He was not like the other ones. He paused in his pacing to stare at her, silver-blue eyes practically throwing sparks against exotic bronze skin. His gaze stalked her, wild and ferocious as a caged animal. No, he wasn't like the other ones. Not at all.

The smile he gave her wasn't very much like the usual patronizing smiles she got, either. His lips curled like he'd been starved for a week and was just handed a plate of lasagna. She'd never really wanted to be lasagna before, but for half a second she was ready to slather on some Parmesan cheese and tell the man dinner was served.

The insanity lasted only a heartbeat, though. After a quick draw of breath and some rapid internal scolding, she grabbed control of herself and managed to take her eyes off him. It wasn't easy, but she knew better than to get carried away by a pretty face and a pair of ungodly wide shoulders. Any man who looked like that most likely knew he looked like that. That meant he was probably an asshole.

She'd had enough assholes for a lifetime.

"Hello, gentlemen," she said, enjoying her moment of authority before they all started trying to assert their male dominance. "I'm not sure what you're up to right now, but I'm here to tell you vacation time is over."

She heard one of the computer techs mutter her name under his breath. Good. Her reputation had preceded her so maybe she wasn't going to have to be a total bitch to get these guys to work with her. She hated playing that role, even though she'd learned it well enough over the years.

"For those of you who don't know me," *like the steaming-hot asshole with the silver eyes*, "I'm Lianne McGowan. Yes, that's McGowan, as in Crandall McGowan is my father and he's the one who all of you work for and he's not been too happy with the way things are being done here. Or rather, the way things *aren't* being done, so he sent me to hold your little hands and kick you in the balls until he starts seeing some improvement. Any questions?"

The men glanced back and forth at one another. She noted a couple of raised eyebrows. One of the computer geeks leaned in to his buddy and whispered something. They both snorted and tried to hide idiotic schoolgirl giggles. This was where she either gained them or lost them, right here when these pubescent juveniles tested her. It happened at least once on every site. Sooner or later, they always wanted to see what she was made of.

So she'd have to show them. They'd better not let her damn freckles or the fact that she wore a bra confuse them into thinking they could push her around. She knew exactly what she was doing, and whether it threatened their collective manhood or not, she was in charge. She nailed the giggling techs with a malicious glare.

"You two have a question?"

They shook their heads frantically. She was not about to let them off so easily.

"It sounded to me like you had a question. Did anyone else happen to hear what these two boys were mumbling about?"

Peer pressure was a wonderful thing. She loved to use it to evoke cooperation whenever possible. The men would band together, united in submissive silence, as no one wanted to be the rat who threw the pimple-faced kids under the bus. It would establish her role as leader instantly. Men were so wonderfully predictable at times.

The asshole, however, surprised her. He cleared his throat and stepped forward.

"I believe the first young man wondered if you left your leather whip in your suitcase," he said. "And the other asked if we ought to call you Lianne, or if you prefer something more formal, like Mistress."

The horror on the faces of the young techs proved that the asshole had, indeed, heard their whispered conversation. They probably thought they were being clever to insinuate she was some kind of dominatrix. They didn't look so clever now. One looked like he was almost going to cry, in fact. Poor idiot kid. They'd be more respectful toward her after this.

The asshole, though…now he concerned her.

She shifted her glare to him. "And who are you? I don't recall running across you in the personnel files."

"I'm a consultant," he said, and she detected the dark tones of a slight Russian accent. "Nicolai Stefanya Vladik. You can call me Nic."

"All right, Nic. And since you're so eager to help us answer the young tech's question, what do you suppose I like to be called?"

He narrowed his silver eyes and contemplated her. "Here on the job no doubt you expect to be called Ms. McGowan. In your private time, though, I suspect you prefer something else."

Yep, asshole. His eyes were already undressing her; she could feel it. Hopefully he had a good imagination, since that was the closest he was *ever* getting to the goods.

"Well, nobody here is going to find out about that," she said sweetly. "From this point on, there is no private time, gentlemen. When you're not in the lunchroom or in your beds, you're on the job, twenty-four-seven. Got it?"

The men who had worked with her before rolled their eyes and nodded. The others grumbled. The asshole smiled.

"I'm always on the job," he said. "In the office, in the lunchroom, or…wherever I happen to be applying myself."

An uninvited little thrill coursed up then down her spine. Damn, but those silver eyes of his…they did things to her she really did not need right now. At all. And was that the jagged hint of a dagger-shaped tattoo she saw peeking out from the man's collar at the broad, bronze nape of his neck? What kind of consultant was this, anyway?

Hell. She flew halfway across the world to this frigid, rocky wasteland to play Queen of the Bitches for the sake of dear Dad and *this* is what she was stuck with. It would figure.

Assholes with tattoos just happened to be her weakness. This was going to be a long, miserable assignment.

Chapter Two

The sky was a dramatic wash of wispy blue clouds and the cold yellow glow of early morning. Raea fluttered her wings, Fairy Dust glittering around her as she stretched out the stiffness in her limbs. Not that they hadn't been getting a workout.

For the past three days, she and Kyne had been hiding here in this cabin high on a densely forested hilltop, hidden by special magic she still did not quite understand. They'd been safe from anyone who might happen to be out hunting them, and no doubt someone was, considering she'd helped break Kyne out of his interrogation cell at the Fairy Council meeting hall. It had been too easy to forget about all of that, though, and make the best of their time together here.

By the Skies, they certainly had made the best of it. Passion had ruled them night and day, and Raea's body still hummed from the pleasure she found over and over again in Kyne's arms. A lifetime of giving in to these forbidden wonders could never fully satisfy her. Still, she knew they couldn't hide here forever. Kyne would wake soon and they'd have to discuss their future.

And perhaps elements of his past he'd not yet been willing to talk about.

A sound in the doorway behind her alerted her to the fact that this time had come. Kyne was up, strolling out onto the wraparound porch of the cabin to join her in the dewy morning air. She smiled at him and his wings unfurled, barely clearing the door frame.

The Sizing Dust they had used still lingered over him, his fairy body holding to this human size longer than Raea's did when she was influenced by the powder. She was tiny in comparison to him now. Her toes wriggled as she swung her legs, sitting on the porch rail in her usual fairy form.

"I can never get over what a giant you are," she said. "Too bad the powder wears off on me so quickly."

"It's all right," he said, breathing deeply and yawning. "We've still got a week's worth in that little pouch."

A week. They could continue this way for a week, avoiding their lives and loving each other. But then what? Without the precious powder, their activities would be cut short. Literally. Kyne's fairy body was unique; when he reached his climax in the heat of their passion, he grew to human proportions. Huge, massive proportions that still took her breath away every time. Without their supply of the Sizing Dust, Raea would no longer be able to be with him that way.

"We can't wait that long to go back," she said. "This has been wonderful, staying here with you this way, pretending we don't have a care in the world, but you know it can't go on like this, Kyne. We have to go back."

"No, I have to go back. You need to stay here, where it's safe."

"Forever?"

"No, of course not. Just until…"

"Until what? We don't even know what we're really hiding from."

He was silent at that. What could he say? So she continued.

"Besides, the powder will run out. Whatever we do and wherever we go, we need to find more."

Now he smiled. "You mean you're not done with me yet?"

"Not by any means."

He leaned against the railing beside her, and she realized his body was changing. He was reverting back to his usual form. She smiled, watching him shudder as if with a chill and then shrink with a puff of golden mist. He plopped down to sit beside her.

"And now we are equals again. Are you certain you still have no regrets, Raea? I should have never involved you in this."

"I'm not involved in anything I didn't run into willingly," she assured him. "But don't you think it's time we try to find out just exactly what it is that we did run into?"

He sighed. She knew he would not welcome this discussion, but it couldn't be avoided. Strange things were happening and the only way to get to the bottom of them would involve dredging up the history Kyne would much rather ignore.

"You want me to go find my father again, don't you?"

"I think we're going to have to. I don't know what the Fairy Council has been plotting, or what that strange machine we found at the base of the mountain is for, but it seems that your father is involved in all of it. I'm afraid if we want to learn anything, we have to start there."

"You keep saying 'we.'"

"That's because we're in this together, Kyne."

"No. *I'm* in this. It has nothing to do with you."

"Nothing to do with me? I'm sorry, did I miss something? Who were you with when the council sent Swift to take you into custody? And then who came sneaking into the hall to seduce you out of confinement? And who has been climbing all over you like a raging wild animal ever since? Me, Kyne. It's me. You're not alone anymore, and neither am I."

His amber eyes searched hers, and she could see the concern that filled him. She loved that he worried for her, but she worried for him, too. Someone back at their Fairyrealm had been plotting against him and she wanted to know why. Fairies and humans were in league and that could only spell trouble. Somehow she and Kyne had to uncover the truth.

"Please, Raea," he said, laying his hand over hers. "Don't make me drag you into more danger. Let me keep you safe. I don't know what I'd do if something happened to you. I need you to be safe."

"You think I'd feel the least bit safe if you went off and left me here, alone?"

"I'd rather have you alone than dead," he declared.

The words rattled inside her. Did he really think things were quite that serious? Of course, certain members of the Fairy Council had been behaving mysteriously, and those two fairies they'd seen in the forest three days ago had clearly been up to no good…but was this truly a matter of life and death?

"You think it might come to that?" she asked softly, stroking his cheek and letting the warmth of his skin seep into her fingertips.

"I won't take any chances, Raea. I have to go look into this alone. I just couldn't live if I let something happen to you."

"Then you know exactly how I feel, Kyne. I can't let you go, not now. Whatever you do, I'm doing it with you."

"I can see we're going to have an argument over this," he said, clutching her hand to his lips and kissing it gently.

"I'll win it, of course. You know I have my ways."

"Don't be so sure of yourself. I've got a few persuasive tricks of my own, if you recall."

"Then I guess I'll have to be especially convincing, won't I?"

"I'm not going down without a fight," he said with a crooked little smile that assured her they weren't talking about investigating the council right now.

"You're not going down?" she asked, flashing him her own wicked grin and letting the glittery aura emanating from her speak for itself. "Then you know I will."

She fluttered up off the railing and hovered before him, raking her fingertips over his solid form and slowly sinking lower, lower, until her lips were perfectly positioned. Oh yes, he was going down, all right. And she was going to take him there.

Their argument might be on hold for right now, but one thing was certain. They were going to need more Sizing Dust again very soon.

About the Author

Serena Gilley grew up reading fantasy and fairy tales, and believing there was a distinct possibility that both were real. Somewhere. Even all these years later, Serena's belief in magic and mystery hasn't diminished. In fact, she is living out her own happily-ever-after with a handsome prince in a beautiful castle, taming dragons and granting wishes every day. Okay, so the prince is a regular guy, the dragons are really just teenagers, and the wishes she grants are as spectacular as frozen pizza on Friday night, but it's a fantasy world just the same.

Learn more at:
SerenaGilley.com
Facebook.com/SerenaGilleyAuthor